M000230166

FOOL ME TWICE

HIDDEN NORFOLK - BOOK 10

J M DALGLIESH

HP

First published by Hamilton Press in 2022

ISBN (Trade Paperback) 978-1-80080-429-6
ISBN (Hardback) 978-1-80080-320-6
ISBN (Large Print) 978-1-80080-275-9

EXCLUSIVE OFFER

Look out for the link at the end of this book or visit my website at **www.jmdalgliesh.com** to sign up to my no-spam VIP Club and receive a FREE Hidden Norfolk novella plus news and previews of forthcoming works.

Never miss a new release.

No spam, ever, guaranteed. You can unsubscribe at any time.

FOOL ME TWICE

PROLOGUE

TIME HAS VERY LITTLE MEANING these days. The enforced routine, stable and consistent from one point of view, coercive and inflexible from the other, makes a clock, a schedule or personal plans utterly pointless. It was far easier at night, a time when many found it harder… almost unbearable for some. And it was those simple life experiences that he so often took for granted, no, not took for granted, but, in reality, never thought of at all; the choice of when to go to bed, what time to put the light out, when to close his eyes.

Some nights were calmer than others. Sound carried. The neighbours were prone to arguments; debating how many bricks they could see and heatedly discussing whose guess was closest to winning the bet, being the most recent. Then there were the others, the ones who should never be in a place like this in the first place. That stood for half the people on his wing, if not more. They should be elsewhere, undoubtedly held securely in another facility for their own sake as much as for that of others, but not here. Never here.

As for himself, where did he belong? He wasn't offhand or cavalier regarding his fate. He accepted it. And it was terrifying. Every day was terrifying. And when that door opened, the noise grew louder. The pull onto the landing felt like a whirlpool dragging him down into the abyss or walking into what he imagined quicksand to be like – if it was the same as it had been portrayed in the films of his youth, anyway – but either way, no one was there to rescue him. He was alone and everyone knew it.

His pad mate was okay; unstable and prone to outbursts, certainly, but most of the time he was all right. At least the aggression had never been directed towards him thus far and for that he was grateful. *Spiral*, as he liked to be called, not his real name – he wouldn't share his real name – could easily be described as a character. *Weren't they all in this place?* He was in for a minimum of fifteen years for aggravated burglary. What the *aggravated* part was related to was anyone's guess. Lying on the top bunk waiting to hear the reassuring drone of snoring coming from below lent itself to growing anxiety after lights out. Only then could he close his own eyes and hope to dream of a place beyond these four walls and the cracked window leaking chilly air across his face every night. On a quiet night, he could imagine this was his choice, keeping the room cool with fresh air for a comfortable night's sleep.

That didn't happen often.

Spiral, or Dave as he'd been named by everyone else on the landing, not to his face for obvious reasons of self-preservation, was already comfortably settled into the new regimen. He had done so within a few days. This wasn't his first stay at Her Majesty's pleasure. *Fifteen years.* That was some sentence, one that he could never hope to manage himself. The thought of it would be too much. The looming thought of what he might receive was enough to spark the fear of dread into him. Those moments of peace, night time, was when those thoughts would come to him, when he had the safety of a locked door between himself and those out there.

Spiral was sanguine about his time. Was it bravado, false or otherwise? For his own part, he kept his head down, stayed out of the way. If Spiral would let him then the door to their cell would remain closed, a personal choice to isolate, to put a physical barrier between him and them. If he could lock it, then that would be all the better. Pushing it closed was the best he could do and even then, only if Spiral was at work or circulating during association. Was it better to be completely alone? Every step heard on the grates outside the door made him focus on the threat, and there was always a threat, even if it was only in his head. It didn't mean it wasn't real.

Footsteps. They stopped on the landing outside. He heard voices and then the door creaked open. A face peered in at him, sitting quietly at the little table he shared with Spiral. It was Liam, at least he thought that was his name. They'd never spoken before. Although that wasn't rare.

"You all right, mate?"

He nodded, glancing past Liam to another man standing on the landing behind him looking both left and right. He glanced into the cell and their eyes met.

"What are you staring at?"

"Me?" he averted his eyes from the man at the door, looking at Liam and then the floor. "Nothing. I wasn't staring at—"

"What were you staring at?"

He didn't answer, hoping he would go away if he said nothing, sensing Liam take a half-step into the cell.

"Spiral around, is he?"

"No... no, he isn't. A–At work... in the machine shop, I think."

He was all but whispering.

"Ah… right. Of course."

He looked up. Liam locked eyes with him briefly. There was something unsaid in his expression, and then he glanced behind him towards his friend at the door, nodded and retreated. He felt relief. Once they left, he would close the door again. Be safe. Liam stepped out onto the landing and he got up, quickly closing the distance between himself and the door, happy to see the two men move out of sight. Putting a hand on the cast-iron cell door, he gently made to close it only to find a figure step into view and force it back open. Hurriedly, he stepped away from the newcomer. There was something in his hand. What was it, a kettle?

"This is for you!"

The arm came up in a flash, snapping out at him, and the liquid contents of the kettle flew out at him. Instinctively, he brought his hands up to protect his face, but it was a fraction of a second too late and he heard screaming – he was screaming – the sound reverberating off the walls around him and he knew then that he was in trouble. He was burning. Boiling water mixed with sugar, what inmates called napalm because the mixture turned to paste, sticking to the skin and intensifying the heat. He didn't hear the alarm sound on the wing outside the cell. He didn't hear the instructions shouted at his fellow inmates to stand back.

He was still screaming.

He was alone. And everyone knew it.

CHAPTER ONE

THE SPORTS FIELD was well maintained, the sweet smell of recently cut grass hung in the air along with the freshness of the overnight dew, rapidly burning off where the sun had already crested the trees flanking the field. The children were lined up in their respective house groups, sitting neatly in rows in the morning sunshine, the youngest at the front and their older peers behind.

"Where's Saffy?" Alice asked.

Tom Janssen pointed the little girl out to her mother, sitting in the third row and barely visible as she playfully wrestled with one of her friends, both children grinning until being asked to stop by their teacher. The smiles dimmed ever so slightly, but Saffy's broadened as she looked over at them. Alice waved excitedly – ignoring the possibility that other parents might think her quite mad – keen to show her daughter she'd arrived. There was a good turnout. There must be almost one hundred adults present, a mix of parents and grandparents by the look of it.

Tom thrust his hands into his pockets. Once the sun gained some height it would feel much warmer, but at the moment the wind was whipping in off the sea a few hundred metres away from them and driving straight across the open field. His jacket was back in the car, a five-minute walk to the car park, and he decided he was more likely to miss Saffy's first race if he went for it.

"How's your mum?"

Alice's smile faded. "She didn't have a good night. I spoke to the hospital this morning and they're thinking of putting the chemo back a day or two to see if she's any better. You know how it knocks her for six."

Tom nodded.

"When is Saffy's first race?" she asked.

Tom took the race schedule from his pocket, helpfully handed to him by a prefect as he arrived. Unfolding it, he scanned the list of events and located Saffy's name.

"Forty-metre dash." He glanced at his watch. "She should be running soon, I think."

As if taking her cue from him, Saffy's teacher announced who was up next and Saffy stood up along with two others from her group. The little girl looked over at them once more, waving as she stepped through her peers and hurried to join the others at the starting line. Fortuitously, Tom had picked a spot that was just shy of the finish line for this age group, so they'd have a great view of the children running at them.

Alice frowned as she looked on while the children were lining up. "Oh no."

"What is it?"

"She's the smallest of all six... and she's not the quickest."

Tom nudged her in the ribs with an elbow. "It's not the winning that counts—"

"Yes, yes, yes," Alice said, waving his comment away without breaking her gaze on Saffy's opponents. "But if she comes last in front of all these people, she'll be devastated."

"She won't come last."

Tom scanned the other runners. To be fair, all but two of them were adopting a stance that indicated they were keen to do well. The other two were Saffy and a little boy who he didn't know. He was taller than Saffy by at least a head. Silently, he rethought his predicted outcome. There was every chance she would come last.

The starter's arm dropped and a cacophony of encouragement erupted from those watching on, both fellow pupils and family alike. Tom found himself shouting for Saffy as well, although Alice was making a decent fist of drowning him out. The line of parents edged forward to get a better look, many filming the occasion on mobile phones and for a second Tom lost sight of most of the runners. Rising on tiptoes, he used his superior height to see over as well as through the throng as the children came back into view, charging past him with determination etched into their expressions. Saffy wasn't last. In fact, she had a decent chance of stealing second as she flew past them.

It wasn't to be and Saffy ended the race third but a good few strides ahead of the next competitor behind her. She stopped as she crossed the line, unsure of how or if she should celebrate. A teacher stepped forward, handing out slips of paper, and directed the first three across the line to a nearby table where their names would be recorded for the points tally before returning to their seating positions to be mobbed by their peers. Saffy's house appeared to take first and third in that particular race.

Alice was almost bouncing on the spot with excitement, waving at her daughter as Saffy sat down and looked across seeking approval. Tom found himself smiling. He had no idea an eight-year old's flat race could be so entertaining, but it was more than that. He hadn't seen such natural happiness exhibited by Alice in some time. It had been a rough few months since her mother's diagnosis. Treatment was underway and everyone was confident, but it had taken its toll on all of them, especially Alice.

"When's her next race?"

Tom looked at the schedule again, struggling to find Saffy's name among the others and tracing the lists with his forefinger.

"Tom, isn't it?"

He lifted his head, looking to his right having not realised someone was alongside him. The man hadn't been there moments before, he was almost sure. The throng that had gathered around him during the race had dissipated now as the track was clear, parents returning to their social groups until the next race lined up. Saffy hadn't been at this school very long and, aside from a handful of parents of children sharing classes, neither Tom nor Alice had made great strides in meeting people.

Tom smiled, accepting the hand offered to him. The man was in his late fifties, Tom guessed. He was tall, slim, with a well-lined complexion that gave away his age beneath a shock of almost white hair, styled and swept away from the face. Could he be a grandparent? It was difficult to judge.

"Henry Crowe."

Tom wondered if this was a name he should know, searching his memory of Saffy's classmates to consider whether he should be aware of this one.

"Olivia's father."

Tom nodded, as if this explained everything. It didn't, but at least he knew Henry was a parent which would help avoid the potential for an embarrassing gaff on his part.

"Nice to meet you," Tom said, gesturing to gain Alice's

attention and bringing her forward to introduce them. "This is Saffy's mum, Alice."

Henry offered her his hand as well, matching Alice's warm smile at the introduction. Tom could read her expression; she had no idea who Olivia was either. Tom felt buoyed by that.

"It's nice to be out in the fresh air for a change, isn't it?" Henry said.

"Yes, it is." He wasn't great with small talk in social settings where he wasn't familiar with those present. It had never been something he excelled at, preferring to allow Alice to take the lead and he would chip in when he had something sensible to say.

"Olivia isn't much of an athlete, I have to say. The poor thing has been a little nervous about today."

Tom felt sympathetic, casting an eye over the children as if he could pick her out which, of course, he couldn't.

"Winning isn't important though, is it?" Tom said. "As long as she enjoys herself, that's the main thing."

"Spoken as a true father," Henry said smiling.

Tom politely returned the smile, choosing not to correct the man's assumption. Saffy was not Tom's child. Following the sudden death of her father, he was the closest thing she had to a father but, nonetheless, he wasn't. He caught Alice glance in his direction but look away when she realised he'd clocked it; an unreadable expression on her face.

The next race finished, Tom and Alice applauding the participants as they passed but having no skin in this particular race, so to speak.

"Ah… shame," Henry said. Tom looked at him quizzically. He pointed to the little girl just trotting over the line as he gestured. "I feared this would happen." He shook his head. "I told you, not cut out for sports."

Tom found himself mildly irritated as realisation dawned. The emotion switching to disappointment soon after. The man hadn't raised his voice to cheer on his daughter as she ran her race. Her effort was lacklustre, giving up after the first fifteen metres as she was clearly way off the pace. Several of the other parents along with the teaching staff encouraged her onwards and she picked up the pace to finally trot across the line, head down and disconsolate. Tom found Henry to be standing just close enough to put him into his personal space, sensing the need to engage when he didn't feel he had much to say. The urge was impossible to ignore.

"Is Olivia's mother with you today?"

"Oh yes. Have you not met Natasha?" Henry asked. Tom shook his head and Henry angled his head from left to right, peering through and around people, eventually settling on a small group near to the starting line. He casually flicked a hand in their direction. "The one on the right; in the red dress."

Tom looked, noticing Alice following his gaze as well despite appearing not to be involved in this particular conversation. He masked his surprise when he took in Natasha Crowe, not that it was necessary as Henry was already looking towards the children making their way to the start line for the next race.

"How long is this due to go on for, do you know?"

Tom shrugged. "The headmaster said it would be an hour and a half, but," he glanced at the schedule, "they started almost half an hour late and I don't think we are even a quarter of the way through."

"Ah, right you are. Well, I have a meeting, so I must be off. At least I saw the little one compete in at least one event. Good show. Are you working today, Tom? Policeman, aren't you?"

"Yes, that's right. No doubt I'll be ducking into the office in a bit, yes."

Henry smiled. "The beauty of public service... hey, Tom? Come and go, and no one will take your job away."

Tom smiled again, raising his eyebrows at the comment and internally refusing to be drawn on the cuts to police numbers they'd faced in the previous decade. Alice looped her arm through his, no doubt a gesture of support as well as tacit encouragement for him to keep his mouth shut.

"Anyway, I must be off. It's been a pleasure meeting you," Henry said, extending his hand once more. Tom accepted it. Almost as an afterthought, Henry paused, hesitating before releasing Tom from his grasp. "Tell me, are the two of you free tomorrow?"

"Tomorrow... Saturday? No... I don't think we have any plans." Tom glanced at Alice, who shrugged. She had no idea where this was going either.

"Ah... well, we are having a bit of a do at our place along the coast. It's for the children really, an aperitif prior to the full onset of the summer season. It would be wonderful if you could come along, bring—"

"Saffy."

"Yes, bring little Saffy for a bit of fun and games. What do you think?"

He met Tom's eye, holding it, and Tom was certain he wasn't going to be able to kick this one into the long grass. He would have to answer, convincingly.

"Well... um... yes, I guess we could swing by for a little while," he said, nervously looking at Alice who remained impassive.

"Wonderful!" Henry said, genuinely pleased. "I'll send the details across to you later."

He turned to leave and Tom and Alice exchanged glances. Tom called after him. "Henry, don't... you want to take a telephone number?"

Henry waved away the question, answering without looking back. "No need. I have it already."

Tom watched the man striding away in the direction of the car park. He hadn't even said goodbye to his wife who was still deep in conversation with her friends. Turning back to watch the next race, he felt Alice tighten her grip on his arm. He leaned in to her, ensuring no one else could hear him.

"That was odd," he whispered.

"Yes, he was. How old do you think his daughter is?"

Tom looked for Olivia.

"No, I meant her," Alice said, inclining her head in Natasha Crowe's direction. She was evidently much younger than her husband. Tom squeezed her arm with his in a gentle telling off.

"Maybe he just looks a bit older than his years."

"In which case, he must have had one hell of a paper round," Alice said dryly.

Tom laughed.

"Do you get the impression he sought you out?" she asked.

"Now that you mention it, yes. At first, I thought it was copper's instinct, but—"

Tom glanced over his shoulder at the departing figure disappearing from view among the cars in the distance. He shrugged and pushed it from his mind. Saffy was getting ready to run a relay. Judging by her capacity to drop bowls of food as she carried them to the sofa during their weekly movie night, he had a feeling the success of this event wasn't looking too promising.

CHAPTER TWO

THE CROWE RESIDENCE lay roughly equidistant between the villages of North and South Creake, a little over six miles inland from Burnham Market, nestling into the surrounding farmland. Although Tom and Alice hadn't visited before, it was impossible to miss the house. The grounds were hemmed in from the passing highway by a substantial brick and flint wall running the entire frontage. Moss grew atop the crafted stone pier caps flanking the entrance to the driveway and Tom passed through them carefully. The gap wasn't particularly wide. Evidently, this entrance was original and crafted before the onset of the motor car.

The gravel driveway wound through the manicured grounds to either side, passing a large pond to their left. A jetty stepped out into the water and a small row-boat was tied up, reeds swaying in the breeze against it. Approaching the main house, they came upon a dozen or so cars parked in front of the main entrance. There was plenty of room. The property was also of brick and flint construction, an old manor house Tom guessed judging by the size and period style. The frontage was impressive, spanning three storeys and possibly an extensive cellar below, with an imposing front door that looked as old as the house itself.

They were met upon their approach by a young man dressed in a crisp white shirt, black waistcoat and matching trousers. He endeavoured to open Alice's door for her before she was able, catching her off guard.

"Can he open mine?" Saffy called from the back seat. Tom smiled as he got out. The valet did as requested, opening Saffy's door and bowing slightly as she got out, playing up to the little girl's wishes. He smiled at Tom and gestured to an open door beneath a brick arch.

"Mr and Mrs Crowe are to be found in the walled garden, sir."

Tom thanked him, unsure if he was supposed to hand the man his car keys. Seeing as he wasn't asked for them, he slipped them into his pocket and joined Alice who looped her arm through his and they walked towards the arch. Saffy ran a few steps ahead and a little girl appeared in front of them. She was dressed in a floral-print dress, her hair neatly plaited and she ran to intercept Saffy. The two girls greeted one another with big smiles, the newcomer almost dragging Saffy back the way she'd come. Saffy looked over her shoulder and called back to them.

"I'm going to play with Olivia!"

Alice waved her off, leaning into Tom as the children vanished from sight. "Well, at least someone knows Olivia."

They passed through the arch into a showpiece garden worthy of any flower show entry. If the grounds to either side of the approach road were well maintained, then this was a completely different level. The garden was encompassed on all sides by a high wall, presumably offering shelter from the driving North Sea winds that could rattle across the low-lying farmland at all times of the year; particularly brutal during winter. Borders were clearly marked and the mix of flowers, shrubs and trees were obviously far from random in their presentation. There must be a small army of people taking care of this area.

No doubt whoever did the bulk of this maintenance wouldn't be overjoyed to see several bouncy castles staked out at one end of the garden, including one with a slide, offering children a choice of five chutes to pick from for their descent. To the right of these was a swimming pool. This alone must have been at least fifteen metres long and set before a large pool house formed from a rectangular outbuilding. Most likely from the building's traditional roots at the heart of a far larger estate, unless the Crowes still ran an agricultural estate, but Tom figured it unlikely due to the number of nearby barns and houses that were modern conversions into domestic residences.

The party was in full swing, children shrieking with excitement while the parents mingled with wine and snacks in hand. Music, playing from a set of speakers taller than most of the children present, added to the atmosphere. The smell of barbecued pork drifted over to them, emanating from a hog turning on a spit in the nearest corner of the garden to the house. Alice chewed on her lower lip, looking anxious.

"Do you ever feel under-dressed?"

"On occasion, yes."

"How about now?"

He smiled at her. "Very much so."

She returned his smile. He took his arm and put it around her shoulder, pulling her into him.

"It's going to be fine," he said, encouraging her. "Who isn't called *sir* on the weekend by some random guy, sweating in a waistcoat?"

"People call you sir every day," she countered.

"They're paid to. That's different," he said, raising a pointed finger as they walked.

Henry Crowe saw them approaching, excused himself from those he was chatting to and strolled across the grass to greet them, smiling warmly.

"Somehow I doubt that little fella at the cars is doing so through altruism," Alice whispered quickly before Henry came within earshot.

"Lovely to see you both," Henry said, taking their hands in turn. "So pleased you could make it."

Tom cast an eye around the garden and the main house, noting that it was set in an L-shape with the rear extending much further than could be seen from the front. "Lovely place you have here."

"Well, it keeps the rain off as one might say."

"It would keep a lot of rain off," Alice said, nodding.

"Yes, indeed. It certainly beats the noise, grime and sheer volume of people we were used to down in London."

"Oh, are you recently moved?" Tom asked, internally wondering if this was why he wasn't familiar with the Crowes.

"We've always had a home up on the coast, but it's only now that we are settled here. I used to split my time between Norwich and London depending on what we had going on at the time. These days, I'm much happier to have a sea view when I rise in the morning."

He saw both Alice and Tom look at the house quizzically. He read their minds.

"No, not here." He gestured as if he was pushing the house away behind him. "We don't live here. This is our holiday home… a commercial home, so to speak. We lease it out for much of the year but we like to have a gathering here before the season gets underway."

"Oh, so you don't actually live here?"

Henry smiled. "Perhaps one day, but—" looking over his shoulder at the house "—it is a little large for our present needs, wouldn't you say?"

"I don't know," Alice said with a smile, "I think I'd give it a go, try to manage the best I could."

"Come and join us. Let me get you both a drink," Henry said, taking Tom by the elbow and drawing them towards the assembled group. "Does your little one enjoy the water? I'm amazed the children aren't already in the pool."

"We didn't bring her costume," Alice said, disheartened. "We didn't realise—"

"No matter. I'm sure we will have one of Olivia's here that will do the trick."

They were quickly introduced to a number of unfamiliar faces in passing, and Tom recognised one or two that he'd shared a brief chat with or the occasional nod in greeting over the past few months. A tennis ball bounced alongside them, dropping in from the court set on the other side of the nearby garden wall. A distant shout of *sorry* came from an invisible child and someone ducked, retrieved the ball and launched it back in the direction from where it came.

"What would you like to drink?"

"Anything soft for me," Tom said, glancing at Alice.

"A glass of dry white would be perfect," she said.

"Right you are," Henry smiled. "Off duty, but never off duty, right Tom?"

Tom smiled. "Yes, something like that. I'm also driving—"

"Of course, set a good example. I'll be right back."

They found themselves momentarily alone among the sea of people laughing and joking. Tom lowered his voice. "Feel free to shoot me now. Anytime… anytime at all."

Alice slapped his arm. "Behave. We've only been here five minutes."

Saffy appeared at their feet, tugging on her mother's dress.

"Mum, can I go in the pool, pleeeease!"

"Yes, of course, darling." Saffy turned and ran off in the direction of the pool, a handful of children were waiting for her. Alice panicked, shouting, "Make sure you—" people turned to her and she stopped short of what she was saying, instead seeing Saffy pull off her shoes and drag her dress over her head and hurl herself into the water head first "—take your clothes off first," Alice said under her breath, smiling at those around her who were still paying her attention. "Never mind."

Tom chuckled. A lady came over to them, Tom recognised her but couldn't place the name. Seemingly, Alice knew her well and the two embraced just as Henry returned with their drinks. He passed them their respective glasses and steered Tom away from Alice, who noticed but was already in conversation and didn't seem perturbed by his leaving.

"Young Sapphire is a credit to you, Tom," Henry said. "A lovely little girl. You must be immensely proud of her."

"We both are, yes."

"She has your eye colour, I think."

Tom smiled, nodding. He still didn't feel the need to enlighten Henry on their domestic arrangements. He did find himself considering how well Henry knew Saffy, bearing in mind he wasn't aware of the death of her father and the series of events that brought them to this particular school.

"Come and see the house, Tom." Henry took Tom by the elbow, guiding him towards a set of French doors at the rear of the house. Tom glanced over his shoulder, seeing Alice had been joined by two other women and the conversation was flowing. Despite her reservations, Alice really was good at the socialising. Maybe it was a talent honed by the bedside manner she'd developed as a nurse. Mind you, she'd always been good with people, even at high school. Tom was yet to see Natasha Crowe, however.

They entered through the open doors, Henry pushing aside the net drapes wafting gently in the breeze.

"It's Grade II listed, you know. Once owned by the Hammond family, I am led to believe."

Tom nodded appreciatively. The Hammonds were a highly connected family in north Norfolk, particularly during the eighteenth century.

"Not that I believe they lived here themselves, but they purchased the titles of the estate. Much smaller now, of course."

Henry took them through several rooms commenting on various features as well as artefacts positioned in alcoves or safely locked away within glass cases. It was a descriptive tour that Tom felt had likely been delivered many times in the past, his host speaking in a monotone, punctuated by frequent bursts of enthusiasm designed to elicit a prescribed response. Finally, they arrived at a heavy wooden door, one that was probably as old as the house itself. Henry produced a large iron key, sliding it into the lock and opening the door.

"The one room the guests don't have access to," he said, smiling and beckoning Tom to join him inside.

It was a study, incredibly grand and well cared for. The walls were lined with wood panelling, possibly oak, heavily stained with a dark colour that made what was a rather large room feel enclosed and confined. There was one double-casement window facing out over the rear garden and Tom could see people mingling. He wondered why they were here. He hadn't professed any great interest in the property. He sensed Henry had an ulterior motive to all of this but, for the life of him, he had no idea what it might be.

"Drink?"

Tom declined. Henry smiled.

"Of course. Driving," he said, nodding before crossing the room and opening a glass cabinet and taking out a glass and a small decanter, a third full of what looked like scotch. Henry removed the stopper and met Tom's eye. "Are you sure? It is a Talisker; forty-year-old Bodega. Lovely drop. And I don't share it with just anyone, you know?"

Tom smiled politely. "All the same, I'd better not. At any rate, I rarely drink. I imagine it would put me down."

Henry laughed. "A man of your size? I doubt it. Still, your loss."

He poured himself a good two-finger measure, returning to the chair behind his desk, he gestured for Tom to sit down. The day was warm and the sun must have been on this room for much of the day. With the windows and door closed, it was stuffy and felt oppressive.

"Do you like what you do, Tom?"

"Yes. Most of the time at any rate. Not so much when I'm wading through some of what I deal with at times."

"Quite right," Henry said, sipping at his scotch. "Ever thought about doing something else?"

Tom turned the corners of his mouth down, shaking his head. "No, can't say I ever have, to be honest. I fell into being a policeman, and I've never considered doing anything else. And, let's face it, the world is always going to need the police."

Is this what all of this is about, a job offer? He had no idea what Henry Crowe did for a living. The nagging feeling came to him that he probably ought to.

"You make a good point. Without crime, what would we all do?"

"What is it you do, Henry?"

Henry swivelled his chair around to face the window and cast his eye over the garden and the gathered guests chatting in the sunshine, either ignoring the question or choosing not to answer it. Tom was unsure which.

"Careers can be strange beasts, Tom. Just when you think you have tamed them, they turn on you and you have to find a new approach. Sometimes fresh ideas come to us and then, at other times," Henry angled his head to one side, "they are thrust upon us, don't you find?"

Tom didn't, but he agreed anyway. Henry appeared to drift off in thought, his expression taking on a faraway look as he absently turned the tumbler in his right hand. The silence carried, almost to the point of awkwardness. Tom sat forward in his seat.

"Henry?"

Henry Crowe snapped out of it, shaking his head and lifting his gaze to Tom, his expression shuttered.

"Indeed, Tom. Best if we get back to the party, wouldn't you say?" His face split a broad grin and Tom nodded, levering himself out of his chair.

The two made their way back to the garden, Henry excusing himself and moving to speak with the caterers who were readying the carving of the hog. Alice smiled as Tom came to her, slipping her arm around his waist and asking a searching question with her eyes. He leaned in and kissed her on the cheek, taking the opportunity to whisper in her ear.

"I have absolutely no idea."

The answer was unsatisfactory, but nothing if not honest. Alice smiled, shaking her head.

CHAPTER THREE

TOM PICKED his way along the narrow roads of Burnham Thorpe, a small, picturesque village a mile or so inland from Burnham Market, consisting of traditional brick and flint buildings both agricultural and residential. The sun was above the horizon but this early on a Sunday morning only the enthusiastic dog walker or twitcher was up and about.

Turning onto Walsingham Road, Tom drove past *The Lord Nelson* pub sitting directly opposite the village bowling green, separated from the road by a drainage ditch and accessed by way of a small wooden footbridge. Several cars were parked in the pub car park. He was pleased to see that. No one would be in work already and he judged these belonged to Saturday night's patrons who'd overindulged and either walked or got a lift home rather than do what many who live in lesser-populated rural areas often do: take the back roads and chance it.

Somewhere in the back of his mind, he remembered the pub used to be called something else – maybe *The Plough* or similar – but was renamed to celebrate Horatio Nelson's victory at the *Battle of the Nile*. After all, with his father being the rector of the local church, Nelson was born in the village and Tom heard of locals describing the admiral holding a dinner at the pub for the men of the village before leaving for his next ship. Whether that was true, he didn't know, but it was local folklore and eminently plausible.

A liveried police car, positioned at a gated entrance between two pillars, came into view on the outskirts of the village and Tom slowed, acknowledging the constable with a brief wave whilst driving into the courtyard, stifling a yawn as he came to a stop. The house was an imposing barn conversion, possibly the largest agricultural barn he'd come across in the area and seemingly laid out in a U shape, the central structure being easily double storey, potentially three due to its height, with single-storey wings to the east and west and a cart lodge being used as a garage. Two cars were parked inside, a large Mercedes alongside a Range Rover Sport. Neither stood out from the crowd in these parts.

Early mornings were still rather chilly, mist lingering over the nearby meadow, and Tom drew his coat around him as he made his way to the front door. Eric's car was parked alongside the FME's and a CSI van was parked nearby. Two forensic investigators were assembling their kit and readying themselves to enter the building once it was clear for them. Tom spotted a carved stone block recessed in the flint wall beside the entrance denoting the building's construction in 1797. That was a later addition, probably set into the wall during the conversion works.

Double doors opened into a grand dining hall with a galleried landing crossing overhead, vaulted ceiling exposed to the rafters. Tom's shoes echoed on the wooden floor as he admired the interior design, an impressive mix of space and contemporary grandeur. Eric appeared through a doorway on the other side of the room and waved a greeting. He didn't smile, which was unlike Eric, but more common recently. Tom rounded the dining table, roughly counting a dozen or more chairs. The settings still looked small for the room.

Tom eyed Eric as he approached. The detective constable's hair was longer than he tended to keep it, dark patches hung beneath his eyes.

"Morning, Eric."

Eric nodded. "Sorry to have you out so early, but I figured you'd want to see it first-hand. I hope I didn't wake the whole house when I called?"

"Just me and the dog, Eric. Saffy takes after her mum and could sleep through an air raid. What do we have on this bright and sunny Sunday morning?"

"Nothing cheerful, I'm afraid." Eric looked over his shoulder. "The homeowner has been… assaulted in his study."

Something in his tone, in conjunction with the moment of hesitation piqued Tom's curiosity.

"I don't think there's any ambiguity in this one," Eric said, sniffing and wiping his nose with the back of his hand. "You should come and see, and you'll know what I mean."

Tom gestured for Eric to take the lead. The forensics examiners entered the building, their coveralls rolled down to their waistlines, and Tom held up a hand to stop them.

"Give us a couple of minutes first, would you, fellas?"

They agreed, setting their bags down in the entrance. Tom caught up with Eric as he led them through another room. This room had no exterior windows and Tom clocked a projector mounted on the ceiling facing a blank wall with large, voluminous sofas set out facing it. Tom figured this must be a snug, although if it was then it was on a footprint larger than the entire ground floors of many homes. Perhaps it was a cinema room of sorts.

"How are you getting on with nights, Eric? Is George sleeping through yet?"

Tom thought he detected an audible sigh, but he wasn't sure. It was well known that Eric's infant child didn't much care for sleeping through the night. Instead, he would regularly wake and Eric was certainly a dedicated parent.

"Nope, he's still up every hour and a half to two hours most nights," Eric said, flatly. "Sometimes, even that gap could be considered long."

Tom supportively patted him on the shoulder, Eric smiling gratefully at the sentiment. Passing out into a narrow corridor, they came to another door. This one was open and Tom found Dr Williams, their local on-call medical examiner inside. She looked up and smiled at Tom as they entered the room, holding position at the threshold.

"Good morning, Fiona," Tom said.

"Hi, Tom. Not quite what I had in mind for a lazy Sunday morning, I have to say."

She rose from her crouching position, where she'd been examining the victim, and took a step back from the body, her coveralls rustling as she moved. Lowering the mask from her mouth, she frowned, casting a glance at Tom.

"Not a nice way to go, I must say."

Tom pursed his lips, looking at the figure sitting in a chair in the middle of the room, head slumped forward over his chest so Tom could only see the crown of the man's head. He had been stripped to his underwear, a pair of blue briefs and a white vest all the clothing he wore. The vest was spattered with blood, crimson splashes alongside streaks where blood had run from above, dribbling onto the cotton from facial injuries, Tom guessed. His wrists and ankles were tightly bound to the arms and legs of the chair with duct tape. By the looks of it, the victim had struggled somewhat because the tape was creased and bunched up. Was that a result of trying to break free or movement caused by the beating he must have taken?

There was a strange smell lingering in the air and Tom's nose wrinkled as he looked around trying to understand what it might be.

"Turps."

Tom looked at Fiona. She indicated a large, empty transparent bottle cast aside on the floor against the far wall.

"Turpentine?"

"Yes. White spirit, to be exact but the same difference, let's be honest," she said. Then she pointed at the base of the chair and the victim's feet. Tom followed her indication and came a little closer, careful not to compromise the crime scene, dropping to his haunches. He felt a wave of revulsion. "I think someone doused his bare feet and then set him on fire."

Tom looked up at her, failing to mask both the surprise and the horror at the suggestion. She confirmed her thought with a curt nod. He looked back at the man's feet and then the carpeted floor beneath them. The carpet was a short pile but was definitely scorched, most likely when the liquid soaked into the fibres and caught light at the same time as the feet.

"Your forensics chaps will no doubt confirm it, but I reckon whoever lit him also put him out too," Fiona said, raising her eyebrows. She pointed to a fire extinguisher a few feet away. Tom looked across, nodding. It was not fixed to the wall with a bracket but was set down in an odd position and appeared out of place.

"Is there any detective work left for me to do?" he asked, his lips forming a slight smile.

"Wait until you get my bill," she said.

Tom turned his gaze back to the victim, looking up from below to see the man's features.

"Henry," he whispered, surprised.

"You know him?" Eric asked.

Tom tried to examine the man's face, but it was savagely beaten, covered in blood and sweat and swollen to the point of being almost unrecognisable. He shook his head.

"Not really. A little. I only met him for the first time this week… and visited his place yesterday."

"You were here—"

"No, no, not here," Tom said, waving away Eric's question. "He has a daughter at Saffy's school and he hosted a bit of a do for the children and some parents at his holiday home."

"Ah, right," Eric said, nodding. "Classmates?"

"No, different age, but they know each other. It's a small school. It was odd though."

"What was?"

"He took me aside, briefly, and I had the feeling he wanted to speak to me about something."

"About what?" Eric asked.

"I've no idea… he never actually broached the subject, whatever it was." He looked at Eric. "Like I say, it was odd."

"I guess you'll never know, now."

Tom nodded, taking in the scene. Henry Crowe had indeed taken a proper thrashing. "Any idea of cause of death, Fiona?"

"I could hazard a guess, but that's all it would be. No sign of any penetrative wounds as far as I can see, so I think you can rule out guns, knives or other sharp implements. The eyes are far too swollen to see any tell-tale signs of asphyxiation, but there's no trauma to the skin around the neck or throat to suggest he was strangled either by hand or ligature. My guess, blunt force trauma as a result of the beating or there's always the possibility of a heart attack, brought on by the shock of being set on fire."

"Nasty," Tom said, shaking his head.

"Kind enough to put him out again though," Eric said.

"Yeah, very decent of them," Tom said glumly, glancing up at Eric standing by the door. "Can you give me a time of death?"

Dr Williams sucked air through her teeth as she thought it over. "Rigor has fully set in. As you know, it starts in the muscles of the face and then progresses to the limbs... usually starting within a couple of hours after death and, in these conditions, is most likely complete six to eight hours later." Her expression was fixed in concentration, her brow furrowed. "I'd expect sometime between ten o'clock and midnight, last night. If you work on that for now, then you'll not be far wrong."

Tom thanked her, turning to Eric. "Who found him?"

"His wife... um..." Eric said, reaching for his notebook.

"Natasha?"

Eric dispensed with the search of his pockets. "Yes, Natasha. She came home early this morning and found him."

"Came home?"

Eric nodded. "Around seven this morning."

"Up and about early on a Sunday wasn't she? Where had she been?"

"Oh... sorry, I haven't asked her yet." Eric pointed to his left as if they could all see through the wall. "She's with Dave Marshall in the kitchen."

Dave was a constable Tom knew well.

"Is..." he struggled to remember the child's name from the day before, picturing her and Saffy running off towards the pool. His heart sank as the image of Saffy came to mind and how the loss of her father the previous year almost broke her. "The daughter – Olivia – is she also with them?"

"No, I don't think so," Eric said, frowning. "Actually, no, I'm pretty sure Mrs Crowe was alone."

Tom bobbed his head but didn't comment. Instead, he

turned his attention to the room. It was laid out as a study, but nowhere near as grand or imposing as the one he'd been shown to the previous day by Henry Crowe. There was a large desk and chair beside a window overlooking the courtyard, but the furnishings were minimal with what little shelving there was holding the odd ornament or book. It looked like a style choice. The walls were exposed brick and flint in places with white painted plaster or render elsewhere. He saw the spray of blood spatter on one wall and, looking up, he spotted it on the ceiling as well. There were no filing cabinets, files or folders to speak of and Tom couldn't imagine anyone working for lengthy periods in this space. Perhaps it was a quiet space to retire to of an evening.

"What could they have been after?" Tom asked, all but whispering.

"Sorry, Tom. Say that again?" Fiona asked.

He absently waved the question away. "I was just thinking aloud, that's all." He turned to Eric. "Do you know what Henry did for a living?"

Eric shook his head. The crime scene investigators appeared at the door, fully suited and ready to process the scene. Tom took another glance around the room and then the victim before rising and signalling for them to begin their work.

"Let's go and speak to the wife."

CHAPTER FOUR

Tom entered the kitchen, the room itself equally as grand and impressive as the other parts of the residence he'd seen. Eric was a half-step behind. The exterior wall of the kitchen overlooking an enclosed courtyard was a curtain wall of glass. Presumably much of it could be opened up, weather permitting. Tom saw a swimming pool on the far side of the yard with a covered seating area beyond it.

Tom caught Eric stifling a yawn as PC Marshall came across to meet them. Natasha Crowe was sitting at a large wooden table, fashioned from reconditioned scaffold boards by the look of it with cast iron legs, adding to the contemporary urban chic of the room's styling. The kitchen units, extensive island, and porcelain flooring were all white and Tom lowered his voice as the constable greeted them, fearful that it would carry in the space. Natasha hadn't reacted to their entrance, remaining in her seat, elbows on the table in front of her and nursing a cup of tea whilst staring out over the courtyard.

"Morning, Sheriff," Tom said, referencing PC Marshall's nickname. "How is she doing?"

The constable mock grimaced. "Okay, I think given the circumstances. She's quiet, not said a lot. I reckon she's in shock. I asked her if I could have someone give her the once over but she declined. I still think it'd be a good idea."

"Maybe we'll give it another try later," Tom said.

He fell into step alongside the constable and walked over to the table. Natasha looked up at them, eyes wide but her expression vacant. Despite her fastidiously applied make-up, Tom could see the haunted expression around her eyes. She had been crying, although clearly having done her best to stop her mascara from streaking. She looked younger than he'd thought when he'd first come across her two days previously. She was dressed in an elegant red dress with a cream jacket over the top. Her black hair hung past her shoulders, straightened and well presented. He didn't know anyone who looked this good so early on a Sunday morning.

"Mrs Crowe," PC Marshall said, "this is Detective Inspector Tom Janssen."

Her gaze drifted to Tom and she smiled a half-hearted greeting. Tom was fairly sure they hadn't spoken much the previous day at their holiday home, unsurprising seeing as they shared only a couple of mutual acquaintances and there must have been thirty or more guests milling around. If she recognised him, she didn't show it.

"May I?" Tom indicated towards the chairs around her. The table could seat up to a dozen people with six individual seats on this side and a full-length bench on the opposing side. She nodded, turning away from him and looking out of the window again. The sun was higher in the sky now and the courtyard must be broadly southerly facing as the sunlight extended across to them. "I don't know if you recall, but we met briefly?"

She trained her gaze back on him, searching his face. If she remembered then she didn't show it.

"I attended you and your husband's party yesterday with my…" he almost said daughter then, which surprised him, "with Saffy. She is at school with Olivia."

Natasha nodded, her somewhat stoic expression softening as she dipped her head towards him, smiling briefly. "Of course. Sapphire is a lovely little girl. Olivia speaks very highly of her."

"Thank you. As does Saffy of her," Tom said. That wasn't true, at least, if it was then she had never mentioned it to him. However, anything that might help put the woman at ease would be helpful at this point. Tom glanced around. "Is Olivia here with you?"

Natasha shook her head. "No, she spent last night at my mother's in Sheringham." She looked worried. "I should call my mother, let her know I'll be late."

"We can arrange that for you, if you like?" Tom said. "Have someone drop by—"

Natasha forcibly shook her head. "No, no, poor Olivia will be distraught if the police show up at the door."

"I can send someone in plain clothes, it need not be frightening. I'm sure the two of you will want to be together as soon as possible."

She hesitated and then nodded, averting her eyes from his. "Thank you," she said quietly.

"That's okay. We can arrange that for you. Would it be okay for me to have a chat with you, ask a few questions? I appreciate this is… not the best—"

"It's fine, Inspector… anything I can do to help."

Tom smiled appreciatively. Usually, he chose not to speak to relatives of the deceased so soon after their loss, often finding them far too distracted and emotional to be particularly helpful, however in this case, a few basic questions would be useful before he arranged for her to see her daughter.

"Can you talk me through your arrival home this morning?"

Natasha lifted herself upright, taking a deep breath and setting her cup of tea down on the table. Tom could see there was no steam rising from the liquid and that she'd barely touched it, probably holding the cup more for comfort than anything else, the comfort provided by a moment of everyday normality. A layer had formed on the surface where the tea cooled and the milk had begun to separate. She exhaled, visibly steadying herself.

"I got home shortly after seven this morning. I don't remember the exact time. The lights were on in the entrance hall which was surprising." She looked at Tom, her tone inexpressive and flat. "Henry was always championing the environment, heralding his green credentials." She shook her head. "We have three houses, two of which have oil-fired central heating and Henry loves his Range Rover, but," she splayed her hands wide, "he does care about setting a good example."

"Hence switching off the lights?" Tom asked. She nodded, smiling whimsically. "Every little bit helps."

She met Tom's eye and the smile widened, her eyes tearing a little. She dabbed at the corner of one eye with the back of her hand, sniffing and then looking down.

"I swear he would follow Olivia and me around the house switching things off as we left each room." The smile dissipated and Natasha pursed her lips. Tom could see something reflected in her expression that she was visualising in her head. "It was odd... and I called out to him, but he didn't answer. The front door was ajar and Henry is, and has been recently in particular, very careful about security, almost obsessive at times."

"Why is that?"

Natasha took a deep breath, raising her eyebrows as she answered. "He's been quite stressed lately, which I'm sure has been a factor, but he's made comments... referred to things that I found more than a little strange."

"For example?"

She shook her head. "To do with his work, I think. He never talks about his work, or not these days, I should say. He used to talk about little else."

"And what does Henry do for a living?"

"He's a barrister."

Tom realised that explained how he knew of Tom's profession, they no doubt knew mutual acquaintances if not friends, but not his interest in Tom. He put that aside for now.

"Where does he work?"

Natasha snorted. It caught Tom off guard. It was an odd reaction.

"He works from here now," she said, looking around. "He was a partner at Quercus in Norwich until last year..." she stared into space and Tom waited for her to elaborate, but she merely shook her head. "Seems a long time ago now."

"So he doesn't work with them anymore?"

"No. He is in private practice now. Semi-retired, he likes to call it."

The use of present tense told Tom she was still processing her husband's passing, talking about him as if he was likely to enter the room at any moment. That was quite normal.

"Take me back a little, if you can. You said you called to him?" She nodded. "Around seven this morning, is your husband usually an early riser?"

"Yes, absolutely. He gets himself up at five o'clock every

day, regardless of what day it is. He is a creature of habit, follows the same routine with little deviation. Unless he has a day in court or something. On those days he might travel into London the night before or drive into Norwich, dependent on where the court is sitting."

"His routine, can you tell me what it is?"

"Yes, of course. He will either go for a run before breakfast or, if the weather is appalling, he'll work out in the gym." She pointed across to the opposite side of the courtyard. Tom could see an extensive range of gym equipment laid out through yet another wall of glass. "He'd round off with a swim in the pool. Although he was quite keen on wild swimming nearby, so he would often do that. He knew several locations where he would meet up with like-minded people."

"He must be quite a fit man," Tom said, smiling. "I don't think I could manage half of that before work, let alone getting up at five each day."

"Henry is... was... very driven," Natasha said. "He had an ability to focus in on the detail and... I imagine that was one reason he was so successful at what he did." She sighed. "Anyway, I couldn't find him in the gym... or anywhere else. I don't know why I went through to the quiet room, but..."

"The *quiet room*?"

She nodded. "Yes, that's what Henry calls it. It's where he goes when he needs some space from me, Olivia... work, house, whatever. I guess you could call it a man cave. You know what I mean?"

"I have a boat for that."

She shrugged. "He spends a lot of time in there."

Tom wondered what he could be doing as there was no television, computer or anything else of note for stimulation.

"And you found him."

Natasha sat very still, eyes wide and lips parted. She

dipped her eyes to the table in front of her and bobbed her head. "Who would do such a thing?" she whispered. "Who would do such a thing to my Henry?" She looked up at Tom, imploring him with her eyes to make sense of it all. He couldn't.

"You said Henry was security conscious?" She nodded. "And this was a recent change in his behaviour?"

"Yes, these past few months he has been increasingly..." she looked at Tom almost apologetically, "I want to say *paranoid*, but I guess I can't call it paranoia now, can I?"

"Did he ever say what he was concerned about?"

"Not really. Things have been really... all over the place this past year, what with the change of work, setting up and adapting to a new kind of normal. I thought we were getting there at the turn of the year but then," she paused, her brow furrowing in concentration, "Henry started to get nervous, act strangely."

"How do you mean?"

She sighed, shaking her head. "He *claimed* someone was watching the house, intercepting his mail... following him around. That sort of thing."

"You didn't believe him?" Tom made sure not to sound at all judgemental.

"It's not that I didn't believe him, Henry is a very serious man, he doesn't do drama, it's just..."

"Just what?"

She sounded exasperated. "It's just so *out there* that that sort of thing would happen to us, to him! You know?"

"Did you ever see any evidence, or did Henry point it out to you?"

She shook her head. "I assumed it was a delayed reaction to the events of last year, that's all."

"What happened last year?"

"Henry's work, his..." She sat forward, speaking pointedly. "Henry didn't want to leave. He loved his place within Quercus. He loved the work they did. Not that he ever went into great detail with me, but when he left there he lost that spring in his step. I saw it come back a few months ago, and that's what I mean when I said I thought we'd moved past it all. But then he started with all the..."

"The what?"

"The nonsense," she said. "All the cloak and dagger stuff. I swear to you, he was checking all the windows every night. He'd even contacted a local company to discuss having a guard dog at the house. I flatly refused to entertain the idea; I had Olivia running around and I don't care how well trained those dogs are, it only takes a second. You hear about children being savaged by attack dogs all of the time."

"But Henry never suggested who he thought might be behind this or why?"

She shook her head. "Like I said, I figured it was in his head and... that he might be suffering some kind of breakdown or something."

"Does your husband employ anyone else, anyone he may have confided in if this was related to his work?"

"Yes, you should probably speak to Alex. Alex Tilson. He worked with Henry at Quercus and came with him when he set up on his own. If anyone knows about Henry's case load, then it will be him. I can get you his number."

"Thank you, that would be helpful. Now, thinking about it, is there anything you can remember, anything at all no matter how insignificant you thought it might be, that you find out of the ordinary, the last few days in particular? A stranger calling at the door? Someone loitering nearby? Angry confrontations? Anything you can think of."

Natasha chewed on her bottom lip, thinking hard. Shaking her head, she looked at him despondently.

"I'm so sorry, I–I really can't think of anything." She looked on the verge of tears, as if her failure to offer up a lead for them to investigate was a personal failure. "I'm so sorry."

Tom reached out and gently touched the back of her hand, drawing her eyes to his.

"Don't worry. Something may come to you later once the initial shock subsides and if it does, you can tell us then."

He wanted to tell her it would be okay, that from here on it would get better. It wouldn't. She was at the foot of a very steep hill and she would also have to pull her daughter up it.

"The letters!"

Tom withdrew his hand. "Letters?"

"Yes," Natasha said excitedly. "Henry received letters, threatening letters. He told me about them."

"Do you know who they came from or the content?"

She shook her head. "No, Henry didn't show them to me. They were anonymous, but he was shaken by them, of that I'm absolutely certain. He was proper upset."

"And when did he start receiving them?"

She thought hard. "New year, I reckon. Around then was the first one. We came back from our holiday –we spent Christmas in the Caribbean – and one was waiting for us when we got home."

"Here at the house?"

"Yes," she said, nodding vigorously. "We hadn't long moved here after we left our house, so Henry was terribly surprised to find it waiting for us. We hadn't even told all of our relatives the new address yet. They were still sending cards and such to our old address and it was redirected here. But this one was addressed to this place," she said scanning the room around them.

"Do you still have a copy of it?"

"No. Henry took it. More arrived over the next few weeks, almost like clockwork. I opened one – I recognised the handwriting – and Henry hit the roof... started yelling at me. I'd never seen him react like that before. He has always been such a gentle man."

"What was in the letter? Do you remember?"

"I'm sorry. I never got the chance to read it. After that, Henry spoke to the postman and had him deliver all our mail to his office."

"Which is where?" Tom asked, looking around.

She pointed across to the far side of the courtyard. "Henry converted the end of the east wing into his office. That's where he and Alex work from when he's not in court."

"Do you have access to it, the office, I mean?"

"I don't have keys, no." She shook her head. "Henry said I had no business going in there. He's right. I'm not interested. That's always been his world, not mine. We can call Alex—"

Tom held up his hand. "We will. Did Henry speak of the letters again?"

She turned the corners of her mouth down, shaking her head. "I can't say he did. I assumed it all stopped. It was months ago now."

"But Henry was concerned about security," Tom said. "Do you think that could be related?"

"But that was only recent. I reckon we had a good few months in between where Henry seemed all right, you know? So... maybe, I guess. Henry had a bloke come round to look at security. I saw him come in but I was on my way out. Henry said he was a specialist."

"Did he install cameras?" Tom asked, looking around for indications of a security system; sensors, cameras or panic alarms. He didn't see any.

"No, I don't know what he did. He came back the other week though."

"Did you happen to catch his name or the company he worked for?"

She shook her head.

"What did he look like?"

"White...brown hair... forty-odd. Just a normal guy really. Sorry."

"That's okay," Tom said, glancing at Eric who was making copious notes in his book. "I think we can leave it there for now. Do you have anyone you can stay with for a couple of days, you and Olivia. Your mother perhaps?"

"I'll need to speak to her... but do you think whoever d–did this will come back—"

Tom sought to allay her fears immediately. "No, I highly doubt that. It is more the fact of having us around," he indicated Eric and PC Marshall, "and everything that entails. It might be better for you, and indeed Olivia, to not be here to see it."

"I see. Of course."

"If you want to step out with PC Marshall, he will take the details of your mother and we'll get in touch."

Natasha Crowe rose on unsteady feet and went with the constable to make the arrangements.

Tom called after her as she was walking past him. She turned.

"Where were you last night, Mrs Crowe?"

"Excuse me?"

"You said you arrived home this morning, just after seven." She confirmed with a brief nod. "And you said Olivia stayed at your mother's last night. Where were you?"

"Oh, I had a night out with friends in Sheringham. After the get-together yesterday I went out with some old school friends. A bit of an old high-school gang reunion, you know? I stayed out until nine-ish and then headed back to my mum's."

"And was that the plan, to stay away from the house all night?"

Natasha looked surprised. "Why do you ask?"

"We need to know where everyone was and who might be aware of Henry being home alone last night. That's all."

"I see," Natasha said, biting her lower lip. "Yes, I expected to be back at Mum's. Olivia struggles to sleep unless I put her down. My mum can do it on occasion, but I don't like to impose. It was easier to drop her off earlier and stay there, rather than leave her with Henry because he had work to do. I'd always planned to stay overnight."

"Working, on a Saturday night?"

"Henry was always available for work, Inspector. No exceptions."

"Okay," Tom said, smiling. "Thank you. That's really helpful. Does anyone else have access to the house besides the two of you and presumably Henry's assistant."

She looked confused.

"Housekeeper, cleaner… a gardener perhaps?"

"We have a gardener who comes by a couple of times a month, but I really don't see him being capable of anything like this. And we have had a couple of cleaners working for us. We had Estelle – she was from Spain – but she went home. Afterwards we struggled, but we hired a local lady. That didn't work out."

"Why not?"

"Oh… it's how it goes. In the beginning they are lovely, enthusiastic and hardworking but after a while they can get a little comfortable and complacency creeps in." Natasha frowned. "Henry thought she was stealing, so he was quite pleased to let her go."

"What did she take, do you know?"

She shook her head. "It was more a feeling he had when he was around her. Personally, I thought it was all in his head. He really liked Estelle. This one, not so much."

"And when did she leave your employ? Was it recent?"

"Oh no, it was six or seven months ago now. And she was old... well, old to me. She must have been coming up to retirement if not past it. I think the job was getting too much for her anyway."

Tom thought about it. He couldn't see a woman in her mid to late sixties managing to do this to Henry Crowe.

Natasha left with PC Marshall and Eric came over to sit down in Natasha's vacated seat. He drew breath, exhaling heavily.

"This is really bad. The poor woman."

Tom agreed. "What did you make of her?"

Eric frowned, pursing his lips. "Credible. Shell-shocked, and rightly so. You?"

"I don't disagree."

"But?" Eric asked.

"There's something there..." Tom said, momentarily drumming his fingers on the table. "We'll see. Come on, let's go and have a look at the office."

"Didn't Mrs Crowe say it would be all locked up?"

"Yes, but unless the killer was looking to fulfil some sadistic fetish on a random stranger, then he, or they, were after something and I wouldn't rule out torture as a method to get it."

CHAPTER FIVE

AT THE LEFTMOST point of the wall of glass, they found a locked door leading out onto the courtyard. The key was in the lock but they found it open and stepped out. The sun felt warm on his face and Tom led them the short distance across the open space, presented with a mix of carefully positioned plants, white stone chips in decorative borders and contemporary stone slabs. It struck Tom as being more akin to an LA-style residence than a barn conversion in rural Norfolk.

The office section of this wing of the property occupied the end of the building with dual-aspect windows. Looking through them, Tom could see a wonderful view across the neighbouring farmland and a wild meadow. Peering through the first window, he could see the layout was open plan with two desks set out at opposing ends of the room with an open, modular set of bookcases positioned centrally as a separator.

"I don't think we'll need a key to get in," Tom said, pointing to the far end of the office. The glazed window set into the door was smashed, the glass now strewn across the floor. The door was open, sweeping the glass that lay in its path aside.

"I'd better nip to the van and get us some boot covers," Eric said.

"I think we should have it processed by the techs before we look around," Tom said, stopping Eric in his tracks. "It will be a while before the body can be transported anyway. Have a word with Natasha and get a number for Alex Tilson, Henry's assistant." He peered through the window, observing the carnage inside. Someone had been through the office like a whirlwind. "With a bit of luck he might be able to guide us on what is and isn't missing here. And you never know your luck, maybe he'll have a bead on who might be behind all of this."

Eric hesitated. Tom raised his eyebrows in query.

"Should we wait? I mean, what if there's something in there that can tell us what brought all of this on?"

Tom admired Eric's willingness to question him. He'd come a long way in a short time, becoming every bit the confident detective Tom had fostered in him.

"By the sounds of it, Tilson is the only person who will understand Henry's caseload and we have no idea what we're looking for. Besides, who often knows what you think about things better than Becca?"

Eric thought about it. "Cassie, Kerry... you!"

Tom smiled. "Exactly. We spend more time in conversation with our colleagues than we often do with our partners. It's the way of things when you spend that much time side by side. Tilson could shed light on this."

"I'll find him," Eric said, turning and striding purposefully away.

They were tentatively picking their way through the office an hour or so later. A full forensic sweep for trace evidence; fingerprints, blood stains, would have to wait until the body was removed from the main house and everything there catalogued and boxed up. However, the crime scene photographer had been able to document anything of note in the office once the technicians had carried out an initial sweep. As long as the detectives were careful to avoid touching any door handles, frames or objects that may contaminate the evidence then they were able to proceed.

"Strange," Tom said. Eric lifted his eye to him, standing a few feet away. "There's no blood. I find it unlikely whoever broke into the office did so to get to Henry Crowe. If there had been an altercation in here, then it stands to reason there would be some."

"Agreed," Eric said, looking around. "Particularly bearing in mind the state they left Henry in. Maybe he didn't put up a fight and stayed locked inside in the mistaken belief that in doing so he would be safe?"

"If that's the case, he could have made a telephone call for help." Tom pointed to the entrance door and the frame in particular. "The manner of the damage to the door frame suggests it was a bit of a struggle to get in. That would have given Henry enough time to make the call to us."

He hadn't. Tom checked with the control room while waiting for the techs to complete their initial pass of the office and no emergency calls were logged from this address the previous night.

The two desks were clear, whatever had been positioned on them was now lying on the floor amongst all the other debris. Tom knelt and inspected a picture frame, the glass cracked, containing an image of Henry and his daughter, Olivia. He had his arms around her and she was grinning at the camera with that carefree expression children often have, enjoying one of those beautiful moments between parent and child. Henry was smiling too. Olivia looked a little younger than she was now, perhaps by a year or maybe more.

The pedestals to either side of both desks had been forced

open, Tom directing Eric to what he assumed was Alex Tilson's desk while he moved to examine Henry's more closely. The three drawers were still open, the contents removed, seemingly without care and tossed aside. If someone was looking for something then they either had a keen eye for what it was they were after or their frustration got the better of them. Perhaps that was what prompted the apparent torture of the victim.

Tom caught sight of a greenish tinge to a piece of paper lying on the floor, and he carefully lifted the sheets on top of it with the end of a pen he took from his pocket. It was the right side of a prescription, the half torn away to be kept for submission to your GP for a repeat. Angling his head to see better, he read the medication names and their dosage regimen.

"Eric, have you ever heard of *Coumadin?*"

"No, I haven't. What is it?"

Tom shook his head. "No idea, but Henry Crowe was taking it along with *Lipitor*, which I think is one of the statin family."

"You take statins for stress, right?"

Tom smiled, realising Eric was perhaps young enough never to have come across them. Tom knew of several colleagues taking any number of the same family of drugs.

"Used to prevent cardiovascular disease in those at risk, I think. High cholesterol, I should imagine, but we can check it out."

"Ah… right… but the victim doesn't look fat."

Tom made a mental note of the GP surgery before glancing over at Eric. "You can have fatty arteries that are only visible on the inside, Eric. Think about that next time you're tucking into your bacon, egg and fried mushrooms at morning refs."

Eric frowned, returning to his inspection of Tilson's desk, replying absently. "I do like a good fry-up. Becca's been on at me to eat better, says I'm putting on weight. She wants me to eat muesli – which I'm not totally adverse to – but with *water* instead of milk. I mean… what's that about? There's healthy and then there's not living."

Tom smiled. "You'll thank her in fifteen to twenty years."

Eric snorted a laugh. "Yeah, if I haven't died of boredom by then."

"Sorry to interrupt, sir."

Tom glanced over at the door. PC Kerry Palmer was there, a nervous looking stick of a man standing just behind her.

"Good morning, Kerry," Tom said, smiling. The young constable had impressed on a brief secondment with CID a little while back and he'd been keen to have her join the team permanently. The paperwork was done, but somehow the internal move hadn't happened yet and he thought the slow progress was more on her part than the system's.

"Hi, Kerry," Eric said, warmly smiling. She smiled back at him but their eyes didn't meet.

"Sir, I have Alex Tilson here to see you."

Tom made his way to the door, Kerry stepping back to allow him room to pass. He noted her eyes drifted from him to Eric who'd already resumed his examination. Tom introduced himself to Tilson, nodding appreciative thanks to the constable. She smiled and lingered at the entrance catching Eric's eye.

"Everything all right with you?" Eric asked.

"Y–Yes, of course," she replied. "You? How's little George?"

"Oh, he's grand," Eric said, dropping to his haunches to inspect some paperwork on the floor.

"Right, I'll be off," she said to no one in particular, looking briefly to Tom who silently dipped his head to say goodbye.

Tom noticed Eric look up at her, watching her leave, before coming outside to join him.

"Thank you for coming down so early, Mr Tilson," Tom said. Kerry Palmer looked back at them momentarily before disappearing inside the main house.

"N–No problem at all," Tilson said.

Tom took the man's measure. He was in his early thirties, slightly built with wavy blond hair that flopped to one side. It was possibly a result of the shock but his demeanour was awkward and since Tom clapped eyes on him, he hadn't been able to stand still; repeated hand and arm movements, shifting his weight between his feet and touching his facial features. He was on edge.

"It must be quite a shock for you."

He nodded vigorously. "I can't believe it... I really can't. He's really gone? Henry... is..." He looked about to cry.

"Yes, I'm sorry."

"I can't believe it." Tilson shook his head, blinking away the water from his eyes.

"When did you last see Henry?"

Tilson composed himself, raising his eyebrows as he looked skyward, thinking hard. "Friday... no, Saturday morning. Yes, I saw him here yesterday," he said, confirming by making pointed eye contact with Tom.

"Working the weekend? You're dedicated."

Tilson smiled, awkwardly. "Henry is – was – very demanding."

"You are in the middle of a case?"

He scoffed. "We are always in the middle of something. Henry is open to adding to his caseload when he probably shouldn't."

"Why would you say that?"

"Oh... Henry has always been one for grand statements.

Maybe it comes with the profession, the ability to project yourself, but I don't think he knew his limitations." He smiled again, as if recalling a fond memory. "I think that's a positive character trait, to be honest. Henry was a *can-do* kind of man."

"It sounds to me as if you and he go back a way?"

"We do, yes. I came with him from his time with Quercus, in Norwich."

"And Quercus are?"

"The law practice, Inspector. Henry was a senior advocate with them up until late last year when he… well…" he frowned, searching for the right words, "left them, and went out on his own."

"Why did he make that decision?"

Tilson hesitated. It was momentary, but Tom spotted it nonetheless.

"Henry… wanted to make a real difference, and not many of the senior partners agreed with him."

Tom found that to be an odd statement. With very few exceptions, all of the barristers he'd interacted with over the years, despite their individual specialisations, had one thing in common and that was their unwavering respect for the judicial system. It was the cornerstone of their profession. Every advocate made a difference, and much like the police service, it was far too consuming a profession, emotionally and mentally, to be working in if you felt differently.

"Make a difference, how?"

"The cases he wanted to take, or *to bring* would be more apt."

Tom looked at him quizzically. Tilson looked a little exasperated at the need to offer clarity.

"Inspector, Henry was very vocal in his belief that the system was being, and to a large extent has already been, hollowed out for the benefit of the few but at the expense of the many."

"I see," Tom said, nodding. "Could you be a little clearer on what you mean by that in regard to how he went about his work?"

"All we have seen for years now is an assault on the criminal justice system; funding cuts for pay, access to legal aid, court closures... on and on it goes. Do you know the victim of a sexual assault may have to wait for anything up to four years to have their day in court? Imagine that, living with all of the incumbent stress of the case hanging over you. Where's the justice there? Then, all too often, the CPS will dismiss the case because the wait has been too long and is considered *no longer in the public interest*. It's a disgrace."

Tom inclined his head. "You don't need to explain that to us, Mr Tilson."

Eric was scribbling in his notebook but he managed a nod of agreement without looking up.

"No, of course not. I should have thought," Tilson said. "I'm sorry for preaching to the choir."

"And you think Henry Crowe was on, what, some sort of mission to fix the system?"

Tom was careful not to appear scornful of such a task. It would be admirable, unforgiving and a forlorn hope, but certainly worthy of praise.

"Something like that. Obviously, he had to maintain a working practice. You can't live on a diet of morality alone, can you?"

"No, certainly not."

"But he also brought cases on behalf of other like-minded organisations or people if they approached him and he felt their cause had credence."

"For example?"

"Um… he has advocated on behalf of several activist groups looking to cast light on corruption cases, bribery and the like."

"Cases against whom?" Tom asked, curious.

"Most recently, we were approached for representation by two companies whose public sector contracts were not renewed and were reissued to new bidders without the opportunity for them to tender. They were looking for a judicial review."

Tom thought about it. "And the implication being that something untoward took place?"

Tilson nodded. "Absolutely. In this world it is often who you know rather than what you know, isn't it? Quercus didn't agree. The partners wanted to maintain what they were already doing and saw such cases as ideologically driven and potentially damaging to their core business rather than being the matters of public interest well worth pursuing."

"By the way you speak of it, it sounds as if these cases weren't particularly lucrative. Is that fair to say?" Tilson agreed with a slow nod. "So, what were the cases that Henry took on that put food on the table, so to speak?"

Tilson shook his head. "Whatever came his way, within reason. Henry has built quite a reputation across his career and he didn't struggle for work. Recently, he's been taking on more of the *ideological* work ahead of that which was more lucrative. I know that has caused…"

"Caused what, Mr Tilson?"

He shook his head. "I probably shouldn't say."

"In that case, I think you definitely should."

Reluctantly, Tilson agreed. "It has caused some friction for Henry… at home."

"Between husband and wife?"

"Yes. A significant amount from what I understand.

Natasha has... expectations of a certain standard of living and any threat to that does not go down well, I can assure you."

"I see. And you think Henry wasn't able to meet them?" Tom found that an odd thought bearing in mind where he found himself the previous day, in company with the Crowes.

Tilson sucked air through his teeth. "Please don't misunderstand. They are hardly on the breadline, but... words have been exchanged on occasion these past few months." He lowered his voice as if fearful of being overheard. By whom, Tom didn't know. "Henry has seen his income slashed by more than eighty percent and he has been in no mind to adjust the course he has set upon. I believe Natasha hasn't been as supportive as he might have liked."

"Right, that's useful for us to bear in mind. Now, Mrs Crowe mentioned that her husband had been in receipt of threatening letters recently. What can you tell us about those?"

"Oh yes." Tilson chewed on his lower lip, thinking hard. "They started last year, at the end of summer if I recall."

"Sent by whom?"

He shook his head. "All anonymous. We have no idea who was sending them."

"How many?"

Tilson's forehead creased as he thought, taking a deep breath and exhaling slowly. "Perhaps seven or eight over the course of four months or so."

Tom did a quick calculation. "So you haven't seen any recently?"

"No, no. I thought that all stopped around the turn of the year."

"What was said in them?"

"Nasty stuff. Really, very nasty! Threats, to hurt him, hurt his family... even to kill him." He shook his head. "Not great at all. Henry was very concerned and he had many sleepless nights around it all."

"Did he report this to anyone?"

"No," Tilson said, looking perplexed. "I said he should, in fact I actively encouraged him to do so, but he wouldn't."

"Why was that do you think?"

He shrugged. "I think he thought it might make matters worse, escalate things somewhat, and if he ignored it then it would eventually go away. I thought he was right when the letters stopped, just some bored troll who moved onto other targets. I suppose, with hindsight, maybe he was terribly wrong."

"Perhaps," Tom said, turning to look into the office. "Do you know if Henry kept the letters?"

"Oh. Yes. He definitely kept them, just in case." Tilson also looked through the window, frowning. "And yesterday I could have laid my hands on them quite easily, but now..." He looked at Tom, horrified. "D–Do you think that... those letters may have... led to what happened to Henry?"

Tom didn't wish to fuel the fires of speculation. "We are keeping an open mind, Mr Tilson. If you could give us a steer as to where these letters would have been kept, that would be helpful. Along with that, if you could provide Detective Constable Collet with a list of your current clients and the nature of their cases, we would also be grateful." Tom looked around the office. "Once our forensic teams have processed the office, we will need someone to help steer us towards anything that has gone missing. Is that something you can help us with, Mr Tilson?"

Tilson nodded. "Yes, yes, of course I can. Anything I can do to help." He followed Tom's eye around the office. "They made a real mess... it might take me some time to figure it all out."

CHAPTER SIX

TAMARA GREAVE UNLOCKED the front door and immediately caught a whiff of the tell-tale smells of grease and burnt food; it appeared to have permeated the downstairs. She knew what it was: bacon and fried eggs. In her student days, she was quite partial to that particular aroma which was good because the kitchen in the dormitories of a weekend reeked of it.

She entered the kitchen. Both her parents were sitting at the breakfast table overlooking the garden, where she saw one solitary window open to the right of the hob. Her mum and dad didn't look up, so engrossed were they in their Sunday papers. The cat sprang up onto the worktop next to the hob, a scraggy-looking tortoiseshell creature her mum brought with them from Bristol, assertively making her way to the frying pan still sitting on the hob. The animal dipped its nose into the pan and licked at the grease just as Tamara crossed the short distance between them and shooed it off the worktop.

It was her pet hate; animals prowling the food preparation areas. At least they only had one cat and not the four which they had when Tamara was growing up. Those cats ate better than she did as a child, received more attention – at least from her mother – and weren't held to the same levels of personal responsibility that Tamara and her siblings were. To be fair, the last could be forgiven.

"No need to be so aggressive with her, Tammy dear."

"Good morning, Mum. Nice to see you up so—" she glanced at her watch "—*early* in the morning."

"Sarcasm is not befitting of a young woman."

Tamara rolled her eyes.

"And must you harass Buttons in that way? She's skittish at the best of times and you're not helping her mental state acting like that."

"Good morning, dear," Jonathan, her father, said, rising from his seat, folding the paper before setting it down next to his empty plate. "There's tea in the pot. Shall I pour you one?"

"No thanks, Dad." She kissed him good morning and he smiled, sitting back down and reaching for his paper. She loved her father. Not only did he have that familiar smell, the one he'd always had that she still couldn't determine where it came from, but he also had that beautiful innocence of a man who very much lived in the moment. He was kind and thoughtful. Her parents were polar opposites. "I've asked you to keep the cat off the worktops, Mum."

"Well, what can I do?" her mum said, setting the literary supplement down on the table and looking across at her over the rim of her glasses. "I've had a heart to heart with her and she disagrees."

Tamara opened the fridge, taking out a carton of fresh orange juice. "Now who's being sarcastic?"

"Well," her mother scoffed, "cats have a mind of their own. Once they've settled in they like to make a place their home, don't they?"

"Speaking of which, did you have any luck with the property paper I left out for you?"

Francesca Greave looked back at her article, raising her eyebrows and running her tongue along her top lip. "Nothing suitable this week."

"Really?" Tamara said, pouring a glass of juice and putting the carton back in the fridge.

The property paper, a free publication Tamara picked up for them every week in the months they'd been living with her, lay on the kitchen island. She spun it to face her, flicking through to the listings she'd spotted the previous day and indeed circled for them.

"What about this one: chalet style, three bedrooms, manageable south-facing garden? It's well in your price range."

Her parents had eventually managed to secure the sale of their house in Bristol. Finding a buyer took longer than anticipated, however they hit their target in the end. It was over the odds, but they got lucky with there being little else available in the area at the time. Tamara picked up the paper, crossing to the kitchen table and placing it between her parents. Her father inclined his head, raising one eyebrow as he looked at it.

"Look, this one. I've highlighted it for you."

Her mum tutted, only briefly glancing over.

"What's wrong with it?" Tamara asked, genuinely surprised as it ticked every box of their requirements. Well, almost.

"It only has the three bedrooms, Tammy. We need four."

"Since when?"

"Well," her mum said, sounding exasperated, "since your eldest sister had another baby."

Tamara's eyes narrowed. "And that means... what exactly when it comes to where you live?"

"Oh, Tammy, don't be so obtuse. You know very well that Sophia has a boy and a girl."

"That isn't new information, Mum. They are five and eight years old."

"Exactly. So when they come to visit they will need to have separate rooms. That's one for us, one for your sister – and her husband, if he can be bothered – and one each for the children. Boys and girls are not expected to share once they reach a certain age. It's not fitting."

Tamara knew why her brother-in-law was less likely to make the visit along with his wife and family, and it certainly wasn't down to whether or not he could be *bothered*.

"Right. And how often do they visit?"

Her father lowered the paper that he'd returned to reading, looking over at her. "I don't think we've seen them for... must be coming up eleven months now."

"Closer to twelve, I think, Jonny."

"Yes, twelve. I think you might be right." He lifted his elbow off the table and jabbed it towards Tamara, indicating the paper with his head. "Come and see this, Tamara. A new road and rail bridge is being proposed to link Scotland to Northern Ireland. That'd be fantastic, wouldn't it? Driving across rather than taking the ferry."

Tamara made a show of looking over at the article, nodding approvingly. "Wonderful, Dad. I'm sure with the Atlantic winds it wouldn't be closed *all the time*, if it was even possible engineering-wise."

"A *can-do* attitude will overcome anything, Tamara. You of all people should appreciate that."

Tamara wasn't sure if he was serious. With regard to her father, it was growing increasingly difficult to tell these days. "Absolutely, Pops. You're right," she said gently patting his forearm. He smiled at her. "So... houses—"

"Oh, Tammy. You'll just have to keep us for another week," Francesca said. "There really isn't anything suitable in there."

Tamara repeated the phrase silently in her head, *another week*.

"Besides, I think we'd like to live a little closer to the coast than we'd previously thought. Perhaps within walking distance of the beach. That's right, isn't it, Jonny?"

"Yes, absolutely." He smiled at Tamara. "I've always loved the beach. Do you remember when we used to take all of you down to Clevedon? Building sandcastles and paddling in the sea. Lovely afternoons, they were."

"How could I forget it, Pops. We used to go in the middle of winter. It was often raining and always freezing—"

Her mum reached over and laid a hand on the back of Tamara's, smiling. "But it was much quieter. Fewer people around."

"Yes, there would be fewer people on the beach in the middle of winter."

"Your father and I were terribly busy, Tammy. We had to steal time to make those memories. You used to love it, even if you did feel the cold a little too much."

"In my defence, I couldn't have been much more than six years old."

"Fun though," her father said, head down, still reading his article. "Character building as well."

"It was fun," Tamara said, sighing as she closed the property paper. "Maybe next week, huh?"

Her mum smiled and winked at her. "So, how did it go last night?"

Tamara was walking back to the kitchen to put the kettle on, grateful her mum couldn't see the grimace she'd made upon hearing the question.

"Last night?"

"Yes, you were out on a date, weren't you?"

Tamara took a deep breath, bracing herself. "Not exactly a date, Mum. We just went out for a drink."

"Oh dear. I'm so sorry, love."

Nibbling her lower lip, Tamara put water in the kettle. "Why are you sorry? It was a lovely evening."

"Well, it can't have gone well if you're denying it was even a date."

"I'm not denying anything—" her mobile rang. She was grateful. It was Tom. "Excuse me. I have to take this." Scooping up the phone off the island, she headed for the living room. "Hi, Tom."

"Now there's a nice young man she could settle down with." Tamara heard her mother telling her father as she closed the door behind her.

"I'm sorry to trouble you on a Sunday."

"No trouble, Tom. Probably a good save, if I'm honest."

"Why, what's going on?"

She absently waved the comment away. "Don't worry. Just Mum being… well…"

"Your mum?"

Tamara laughed. "Yes, something like that. What's up?"

"I'm over in Burnham Thorpe with Eric."

"Eric dropped me a text earlier. He said it was a suspicious death. How suspicious?"

"Murdered. Particularly brutal," Tom said. "I think this one is going to attract a lot of attention."

"They usually do—"

"This time will be worse. The victim is a local barrister. Well connected."

"You've come across him?"

"No, not professionally. But I have met him. His daughter is at the same school as Saffy. Not that I know him, but I attended a garden party at his place yesterday. Not where the body was found, but at a holiday home he lets out."

Tamara gave herself a moment to take in the information. "Early thoughts?"

She heard a sharp intake of breath. "I don't see it as a burglary that went wrong, escalating into something more. The house hasn't been turned over, just his office."

"Professionals?"

"Not necessarily. The office looks like it's been searched by a crack head with a bulldozer. This is different."

"In what way?"

"I'm not sure, but I have the sense they were looking for something and it's likely the victim was tortured in order to get it. When the word gets out, this is going to be big news."

"Then we should move early to dampen it."

"Agreed."

"I'll speak to the chief super and put out a preliminary statement to try to head off the more salacious rumours that will probably emerge. If we can get a Home Office pathologist assigned for the post-mortem today, then all the better. Then we can look to arrange a press conference for Monday."

"In this case I think reality may well trump fiction."

"That bad?"

"Either someone wanted to get something out of him or they enjoyed the prospect of tormenting him. I've not seen the like of this before. Not in Norfolk at any rate."

"Okay, leave it with me. Arrange a briefing for this afternoon, please."

They said goodbye and Tamara touched the mobile to her lips. Any prospect of peace for the remainder of the weekend already forgotten. She returned to the kitchen, her mother looking up as she entered.

"Are you all right, Tammy? You look serious all of a sudden. Is Tom okay?"

"Yes, I think he is. I didn't ask."

Francesca shook her head. "It wouldn't hurt to show some care for your team, Tammy. You need to show you care about people. That's how you pull people along with you, rather than having to drag them."

Tamara bridled slightly but she thought better of joining in this particular debate. "He's well, Mum. It's just a case has broken."

"Ah, I see. Good job you won't have time for that second date, seeing as it didn't work out—"

"It wasn't a date, Mum. We just had a drink, that's all."

"What did you say he did for a living?"

She was fishing now.

"I don't think I said, Mum. It's not important. I don't think we'll be going out again anytime soon anyway, so no matter."

Her father lifted his gaze from the paper, smiling warmly. "Never mind, love. He obviously wasn't right for you."

Tamara closed her eyes. *It was just a drink.*

"Maybe if you made a little more effort, Tammy," Francesca said, drawing a stern look from Tamara. "I just mean put a little bit more make-up on and get your hair done. A wardrobe update wouldn't be a bad idea either. You're not quite dressing your age at the moment."

Tamara looked down at herself, frowning. "I like how I dress."

"Comfort isn't necessarily attractive though, is it?"

"I'm not dressing to please some random bloke, Mother!"

Francesca shrugged, purposefully turning the page. "Well, you don't want to be alone all your life, do you?"

"Chance would be a fine thing," she said pointedly, glancing between them both and picking up their empty tea mugs. Her father smiled at her. "Besides, I had my hair done yesterday." She walked back to the kettle, touching the side. It was still hot. "You never said what you thought of it."

"Of what, dear?"

"My hair."

Francesca looked up, pursing her lips as she studied her. "Mmm… looks good from the back."

Tamara stood with her back to them, feeling her shoulders tighten. Her father cleared his throat.

"Ignore your mum, Tamara. Your hair looks lovely," he leaned towards his wife, "from *all* angles!"

Tamara emptied the old leaves from the teapot, rinsed it under the tap and made to add fresh leaves from the caddy.

"You are going to warm that first, aren't you, dear?"

Tamara let out an exasperated sigh. Putting the teapot down, she turned to her mum and glanced at the clock on the wall behind her. "Look at the time. I don't have time for tea. I have to head into the office."

Her father put his paper down, stood up and crossed the room to her. "I'll do it, love." He put his hands on her upper arms and squeezed them gently. He was about to say something that would make her feel very awkward, she knew it. It was in his eyes. She acted pre-emptively, leaning forward and kissing his forehead. Her dad was a short man. He released her from his gentle grip and smiled.

"Thanks, Pops. I love you too."

She hurried out of the kitchen before another word could be said.

"I'll be back late," she called over her shoulder. "Don't wait up. And keep that mangy cat off my work surfaces, please!"

CHAPTER SEVEN

Tom pressed the doorbell and waited. A dog barked from inside and a calm voice could be heard encouraging it to come away from the door. The door opened and a man glanced up at him, smiling in greeting. He had a hand on the dog's collar and despite the owner's instruction, the dog was desperately trying to greet Tom, straining at the man's grip, tongue lolling out as it stood on its hind legs trying to force itself forward.

"It's okay, I'm good with dogs."

"Easy to say but she'll not stop at you and she'll be off down the road," the man said. Giving up, he looped an arm under the creature's stomach and scooped her up in his arms. She decided he was more interesting and turned her attentions to licking his face. That went down as well as trying to introduce herself to him.

Tom opened the wallet and presented his warrant card. "DI Janssen. Doctor Jenkins?"

The doctor smiled, offering his hand with some awkwardness bearing in mind he had a struggling border terrier under the other arm. "Thank you for seeing me on a Sunday."

"Not at all, Inspector. Please come in."

Dr Jenkins escorted Tom to the rear of the house, putting the dog in the kitchen and quickly closing the door so that she couldn't turn tail and leap on him. He then gestured towards a door further along the hallway.

"We can talk in my study. Sue will be back with the children soon and it will be pandemonium. I recall my parents telling me that parenthood will be the best time of my life, however they failed to mention weekend sports clubs being the focal point of our existence for a decade."

Tom smiled politely. He could relate. Saffy had several after-school clubs along with a weekend ballet class and was also agitating to play rugby. Tom wasn't sure if there was even a girls' rugby team locally, not that this fact bothered Saffy as she confidently stated she'd *just play with the boys*. He was certain she would hold her own if she did. They wouldn't know what'd hit them if he managed to find a team for her.

Dr Jenkins held the door, allowing Tom to pass through, and then he closed it ushering Tom towards one of the club chairs set to left and right of the window overlooking the garden. The study was most likely the original drawing room, the period details of cornicing, picture rails and open fireplace remained, tastefully modernised through decoration.

"You were a little cryptic on the telephone, Inspector. What is it I can do for you?"

"Yes, apologies for that. I wanted to ask you a few questions regarding one of your patients: Henry Crowe."

"Henry! I see. Of course, we go back a long way do Henry and I." Dr Jenkins brought his hands together before him, forming a tent with his fingers. His forehead creased. "Slightly unusual, Inspector. Obviously, it goes without saying that patient, doctor—"

"I'm afraid I have some bad news, Dr Jenkins. Henry was found at his property this morning, deceased."

Dr Jenkins sank back in the chair, placing his hands on the padded arms, his lips parting ever so slightly. "Dear Lord. Henry? Are you sure?"

Tom nodded. "His identity was confirmed at the scene. He was found by his wife."

"Poor Natasha... and little Olivia... are they both okay?"

"Yes, neither of them were at home at the time."

"Dear Lord," Jenkins repeated, raising a balled fist to his mouth, staring straight ahead.

"You say the two of you go back a way? Are you friends?"

Jenkins was momentarily lost but shook himself out of it, dropping his hand to his lap and meeting Tom's eye. He nodded. "Yes, yes, we were. Good friends. We met at school, you see."

"Are the two of you still friends?"

"Do you mean are we close?" Tom nodded. "Not particularly. We'd play a round of golf every now and again, share family drinks at Christmas. That sort of thing, but we weren't in regular contact on a personal level, no."

"We found a repeat prescription at his home with your name on it. Henry was under your care?"

"Yes, of course." Jenkins took a deep breath, sitting forward and resting his elbows on his knees. "Henry had an ongoing condition that needed managing. Nothing serious as long as we kept on top of it, but I didn't see much of him. The practice nurses are more than capable of taking the regular bloods and so forth."

"Yes, the prescription listed," Tom took out his notebook and read from it, "Lipitor and Coumadin." He looked up at the doctor. "I recognise one as a statin, my mother used to take it but I've never come across Coumadin. I was going to Google it but seeing as I was coming here. What was the nature of his condition?"

"Coumadin is an anti-coagulant, a branded name for Warfarin, Inspector."

"Blood thinner."

"That's right. As opposed to the rat poison most people think of when they hear the name, yes. I'm afraid Henry's earlier self was catching up with him as he progressed through middle age. Who would have thought dining on French cheese, red wine and clotted cream could have such an impact a few years down the line?"

"He liked his food?"

"Fine dining was Henry's greatest vice, as far as I know. However, as many of us would do so only on a special occasion, Henry would partake on a weekly basis. He was a man who enjoyed the finer things in life."

"High cholesterol?"

Jenkins' expression shifted to a sideways smile as he tilted his head to one side. "Unfortunately, that was only part of the issue." He cleared his throat, concentrating hard. "Now, when was it, last November if I remember correctly. Henry suffered a *transient ischaemic attack.*" Tom looked at him quizzically. "TIA. A mini stroke, Inspector. A temporary blockage in the blood vessels supplying oxygen to the brain."

"Sounds bad," Tom said.

"It certainly isn't good, no. As opposed to a full stroke, these blockages can clear themselves and on occasion they may even pass unnoticed, if mild enough – which was the case with Henry; a little nausea or dizziness and a moment of slurred speech – but he was wise enough to come and see me. His blood pressure and cholesterol were both higher than I would have liked and we also detected atrial fibrillation – an abnormal, irregular heart rhythm – which we needed to manage. The heart condition on its own was not too much of a concern but alongside the other factors, it moved him towards the higher end of the risk scale when it comes to a future stroke. As I said to him at the time, I'm surprised he was still with us! I was joking of course."

Dr Jenkins smiled at the memory. The smile faded quickly.

"Anyway," he continued, scratching absently at the side of his head, "we managed the abnormal heart rhythm with the Coumadin and treated the high cholesterol with the statin, Lipitor. The two work well together with fewer, if any, side effects in comparison with the other options in the family. Speaking of which, Henry's father was diabetic and his death came about through cardiovascular disease. It would appear to run in the Crowe family, so prescribing statins was highly likely at some point in the future, I should imagine. I'm a big believer in proactive medication. A pre-emptive strike on the enemy, so to speak."

"And how often did you see him?"

"In the surgery? Every month. Not me personally, as I said. The practice nurses would administer the blood tests to monitor how he was getting on. His condition required a constant balance, so we kept on top of it. Should there be anything adverse in the results then I would give Henry a call but, as I said, his condition was manageable." He fixed Tom with a beady eye. "Is there a concern as to the nature of Henry's passing?"

Tom was curious. "Why do you ask?"

"It is not uncommon for me to receive a call from the family in search of a death certificate. However, rarely do I have a home visit before lunchtime on a Sunday from a senior detective. Am I right to think this is in some way suspicious?"

"You missed your calling, Dr Jenkins. You would make quite a decent detective yourself."

He smiled. "I read the Hardy Boys books when I was a child."

"I was more of a Tolkien child myself."

"You surprise me, Inspector. I would imagine Sir Arthur Conan Doyle would prepare you better for your line of work."

"Or put me off it…"

Jenkins nodded slowly. "You didn't say what happened to Henry."

"Inquiries are underway, Dr Jenkins. It is probably best if I don't say anymore at this time."

"Of course, Inspector." Jenkins splayed his hands wide apologetically. "Forgive me."

"No need."

The doctor looked pensive, concerned. It piqued Tom's curiosity.

"Is there anything else you would like to add, Dr Jenkins?"

The doctor hesitated, making to speak and then changing his mind. He shook his head but the gesture was unconvincing.

"Whatever it is, it might be relevant. No matter how unrelated you think it might be, I'd sooner hear it than not."

"The last time I spoke with him – with Henry – he said something that I found rather odd."

"Which was?"

"He was asking about blood groups and how we get them."

"Why?"

Jenkins shook his head. "I've no idea. He didn't elaborate. It was rather strange though. I remember he was a bit of a duffer back at prep school when it came to all things biological. His skills lay elsewhere, as he has proven repeatedly over the years. Anyway, I did my best to explain how it all works, but I saw his eyes glazing over as I spoke. He said he understood… but I'm not so sure."

"Could it have been related to the condition you were

treating him for?"

"I highly doubt it." He shrugged. "Who knows? Maybe I'm just making too much out of it."

"No, not at all," Tom said, making a note. "Aside from treating his condition, what would you say are your perceptions of Henry himself?" Jenkins eyed Tom expectantly. "Have you seen any change in him over the past year? Has he confided in you over any concerns he might be having? That sort of thing."

Jenkins took a deep breath, looking out of the window. He turned the corners of his mouth down and gently shook his head. "I can't say that he did. Not explicitly at any rate."

"How about implicitly?"

The doctor's mouth formed an oval and he appeared reticent.

"However small, Dr Jenkins. Believe me, this could help."

He shook his head, as if resigned to revealing something he was reluctant to. "Er… I suppose it doesn't matter now anyway. Henry spoke to me on a delicate matter, regarding his sexual stamina."

"Stamina?" Tom repeated in a dead-pan tone, writing it down before fixing the GP with his gaze.

"Yes, he is… was… a great deal older than his current partner. Henry left me with the impression he was struggling to maintain his performance in the bedroom. He asked if there was anything I could prescribe to help?"

Tom waited.

"There was nothing I could do. I mean, I could have prescribed him something but there was no medical need. Henry didn't have erectile dysfunction or anything akin to it that would affect his performance. I did suggest that if he really felt he was having trouble, then the first port of call might be a therapist."

"Why would you suggest that?"

"Henry was a worrier. He certainly suffered with anxiety, which came on later in life. Many of these issues can be tied into psychological issues rather than physical ones. As a child, I don't recall Henry being particularly anxious, but then perhaps he was better at masking it back then or perhaps it didn't manifest as frequently." He waved away the thought. "Anyway, that's by the by. I felt he was over thinking the situation and that could arguably lead to a dip in performance. After all, he was trying to keep up with someone almost half his age. I dare say I'd be worn out as well."

The sounds of voices beyond the door carried. Dr Jenkins looked at the closed door.

"It would seem the terrors have returned."

"I won't keep you, Dr Jenkins." Tom made to stand, closing his notebook and putting his pen back into his pocket. "Can I ask, did Henry take you up on the suggestion of therapy?"

Jenkins emphatically shook his head. "He immediately shot the idea down. I have always held Henry in high regard, but…"

"But?"

"He was always very shuttered. It is hard to know what he thought about anything. Don't get me wrong, he was proficient at saying the right things, but you only ever learned anything about Henry if he chose to let you." He shrugged. "At least, that's what I think anyway."

"How did he feel about his profession?"

Jenkins sighed. "Barristers are not much different to any other professional, Inspector. We can all claim lofty ideals but, when all is said and done, many of us are seeking the trappings of success; status, material goods… power and influence. And Henry was no different."

CHAPTER EIGHT

TAMARA STOOD by the window looking out over the car park. The statement released to the press on Sunday evening appeared only to stem the tide of media interest for twenty-four hours. The calls fielded the previous day by Norfolk Constabulary's press team were largely from local journalists although a regional BBC crew did arrive in the village and set up an outside broadcast unit near to the Crowe residence. They'd packed up and left by eight o'clock in the evening. What was gathering outside demonstrated a shift in perception. Seemingly, the murder of an experienced barrister had garnered more interest as the working week really got underway.

Tom came to stand alongside her, observing the media vans parked outside the station.

"Looks like you'll be on the telly later," he said quietly.

"With you alongside me, Tom. I hope you brushed your hair?"

He smiled. "I've even cleaned my teeth again, just in case. The team's ready."

She turned to face the room. The operations room was set

up for them. What information they'd accumulated since the discovery of Henry Crowe's body the previous morning was documented on the white boards mounted on the far wall. This largely consisted of workplaces, family connections and crime scene photographs. Other than that, the boards were sparse. Tamara wanted that to change quickly.

Tom sat down on the edge of a desk to her right, crossing his arms and waiting for the briefing to begin. This was the unspoken signal to the others to quieten down. DS Cassie Knight hurried to take her seat. Eric was at his desk, PC Kerry Palmer alongside him.

"Right," Tamara said, stepping in front of them, "thank you for all the groundwork you've already undertaken. I want to take a moment to understand where everyone is and set an expectation for the rest of the day. Eric, where are you with Henry Crowe?"

Eric scanned his notes, his brow creasing. He looked tired.

"Still waiting for scenes of crime to provide us with the inventory taken from the victim's office. It was quite a mess," he pointed to the corresponding photographs on the board, "and it's too early to know what, if anything, was taken from the filing cabinets."

"The letters?" Tamara asked, referring to the threatening correspondence Alex Tilson and Natasha Crowe spoke of.

Eric shook his head. "Tilson was able to tell us where the copies were kept but they didn't turn up in our processing of the scene. It is possible that Crowe moved them somewhere else without telling his assistant. We'll keep looking."

"Great. And what of his former employers?"

Eric glanced at Tom, who answered. "We have an appointment with the lead partner tomorrow. He's in court at The Old Bailey today and won't be back in Norwich until tomorrow. It's not a conversation I want to have over the telephone."

"How was the news received?" Tamara asked, curious after hearing of Crowe's rather sudden departure from the practice he was a partner in.

Tom shrugged. "Hard to tell. Lawyers are good with words."

"Healthy scepticism," Tamara said, "as one might expect, Tom."

"Always," he said with a smile. "We'll know more tomorrow morning. I'll be interested to see how open they are with us."

"You think they'll withhold?"

"By all accounts, Henry Crowe worked with Quercus for years. He was a senior advocate, and a quick Google search this morning has his face and name all across their literature until very recently." He appeared thoughtful. "A divorce like that can't have been entirely amicable, particularly bearing in mind what Alex Tilson told us about Henry's departure."

"You'll go along armed with his prior caseload, yes?" she asked. Tom indicated Eric.

The detective constable tapped his finger on the desk. "Already on it."

"Good. What about the wife... Natasha, isn't it?"

Eric referred to his notes again. "She is staying with her mother in Sheringham at the moment along with their daughter, Olivia. I took her statement yesterday at their home, but I intend to speak to her again. Hopefully, she'll have more for us now that the initial shock has subsided."

"Okay," Tamara pointed to Kerry alongside him. "Take Kerry with you, please. Tread lightly." Eric nodded and Kerry smiled. "Have you checked out the wife's background?"

"Yes, she's interesting," Eric said, frowning. "A Norfolk girl, born and raised in Sheringham. She doesn't work, at least not as far as I can tell anyway. They've been married for seven years, and she only appears on our files in a fleeting moment."

"What for?"

"She was arrested for shoplifting in her teens," Eric said, glancing at his notebook again. "She worked in the local *Boots* – a part-time Saturday job – and she was caught stealing. That was the allegation at least."

"Prosecuted?"

Eric shook his head. "The company were happy with a caution and summary dismissal."

Cassie rolled her eyes. "As usual. They don't want the bad publicity or the bureaucracy of a court case and so they let them get away with it."

Tom smiled, catching Cassie's eye.

"Well, it's true," she argued. "What message does it send out? That you can rob your employer blind and all that'll happen is you get a slap on the wrists and a note on your file. Nonsense."

"What would you prefer?" Tom asked playfully.

Cassie didn't need time to think. "A public branding... a month's litter picking... something like that but on a sliding scale."

Eric glanced at her. "How about a chain gang? Little orange overalls and all that."

"Be a start," Cassie said, doodling a circle on her notepad and smiling apologetically at Tamara for going off on a tangent.

"Eric," Tamara said, "you found Natasha Crowe interesting. Why?"

His frown returned, only deeper this time. "It's not so much her. It's more the unlikely pairing of them. Natasha is only a year or two older than me—"

"Practically still a schoolboy," Cassie said quietly, smiling sideways at him.

"—putting her in her late twenties and pushing thirty years between her and her husband. I mean, age aside, because these days that isn't considered an issue for many people but looking at their backgrounds... they just make such an odd pairing." He shook his head. "Henry was public-school educated, studied law at Cambridge and moved in social circles that Natasha would never have access to. At least, not from what I can see." He met Tamara's eye. "It's not necessarily relevant to the case, but I do find it interesting."

Cassie cleared her throat. "Henry was shopping in the junior department. He wouldn't be the first."

Kerry Palmer agreed. "Nor would she be the first to accept the trade off."

"That's right," Cassie said. "Marry an older guy for the safety of the financial security, the trappings of wealth and elevated social lifestyle. You've got to service an old bloke for a while, but when he pops his clogs – well ahead of you – you land all the assets and are young enough to still live it up. It certainly helps to knock out a child as well; ties them to you no matter what."

Tamara sighed. "I see you are still prophesising, Cassandra."

"And destined never to be believed," Cassie said dryly.

"I'm not saying you're wrong," Tamara said, "so let's keep the wife in mind until we can rule her out. We should check out who benefits financially from his death."

"She doesn't strike me as the type to do what was done to her husband though," Tom said. "Although, she could have put someone up to it."

"Speaking of what was done to the victim," Tamara said, "any word from the pathologist?"

Tom nodded. "I've just had a preliminary chat over the phone. Cause of death is still not clear. Toxicology test results haven't come back yet and that may well put a different light on it. Dr Paxton is of the opinion Henry was tortured and severely beaten, but whether this was the cause of his death is another matter."

Tamara was intrigued. "He must have something in mind."

"He does. Apparently, Henry Crowe's heart was enlarged, weighing in at 580 grams, which is quite unusual by all accounts. Coupled with the enlarged blood vessels in the eyes at the time of death, with no indication of asphyxiation, Dr Paxton thinks there could be another factor in play. He wants to hold off until the lab samples come back. We know from speaking to his GP that Henry had a condition managed through blood thinners and statins. With high blood pressure, the stress of this particular episode... who knows how his body may have reacted?"

"Reading between those lines," Tamara said, "he's not sure Crowe was murdered, is he?"

"He didn't go that far. It is possible what was done to him resulted in his death, but you're right, it doesn't mean there was the intent to kill him. After we're done with the media briefing, I'll be heading over to speak with Dr Paxton directly. Hopefully, he'll have more for us by then."

Tamara thought about it.

Cassie sucked air through her teeth. "It's the wife. I'll put a tenner down, if anyone's up for it?"

Tamara shot Cassie a withering look and she averted her eyes from the DCI's scrutiny.

"Just saying," she whispered.

Tamara turned her attention to the white boards. Kerry Palmer leaned back in her chair and whispered to Cassie. "You're on."

"Who do you think it is then?" Cassie asked conspiratorially.

"It doesn't matter, does it? As long as it's not the wife then I win, right?"

Further discussion ceased as Tamara turned back to face the room.

"Okay, initially I want to run with three lines of inquiry," Tamara said. "Cassie, I want you digging into our victim's current case load. His assistant is the one person who can fill us in but look into everything he was working on, who was involved, who has something to lose from his success as well as anyone who gains from his failure or demise."

"On it," Cassie said, scribbling in her notepad.

"Eric, dig around in Crowe's relationships; spouse, friends, associates, golf partners, tennis ladder… anything and anywhere he spent time. Has he fallen out with anyone, is the rumour mill in overdrive about extramarital activities? Anything you can find out that might point towards someone with an axe to grind."

Eric nodded. Tamara looked at Kerry.

"There's every chance this isn't related to his friends, family or current cases, but we can be sure a man as experienced as Henry Crowe will have come up against, or worked for, people of dubious character over the years. I want you to go through the records Eric passes to Tom for his trip to visit Quercus tomorrow and see if anything jumps out at us. Someone was sending him threats and that someone may well have gone through with them. If the letters have been coming for a while, then it stands to reason this is something from his past. It may be recent past or from way back. Check it out, please."

Tamara looked around the room. "I also want you to get the word out among our colleagues to keep their ear to the ground about burglaries gone wrong. This could be a simple robbery that got out of hand. Let's not ignore the obvious for the sake of the complicated. Any questions?"

No one had any, so they all set about their tasks. Tom hopped off the desk and came to stand beside her. He must have read the look of concern on her face.

"It leaves us a little light for the press conference, doesn't it?" he said.

"Yes, it does. As it stands, we don't know if Crowe was intentionally murdered or if this was just a gigantic cock up."

"Do we bring up the letters?" Tom said. "If someone was festering a great deal of animosity towards him, they would be unlikely to keep it to themselves."

Tamara thought about it. The standard play book in appealing for information was to ask those who may know the perpetrator to come forward rather than keeping quiet. On the other hand, this was a detail likely known only to the victim, his immediate colleagues and now the investigation team. Tipping their hand and thereby alerting the killer, if that was who the culprit was, to that particular line of inquiry might cause more harm than good.

"No, I want to sit on that for a while," she said. "If that's our guy, then I want him to feel comfortable."

"Let him relax, think he's likely got away with it—"

"And then he'll make a mistake," Tamara said. Tom nodded. "Exactly. This is a small place and you seldom get away with much without *someone* noticing."

"Unless this guy is all alone."

Tamara had to admit that would present them with a problem. "In which case, what's his beef with Henry Crowe?"

"I'll push pretty hard when I visit Quercus tomorrow. The letters started around the time he parted company with them and, if related to his work, then we may get a bit of joy there."

Tamara checked the time on her watch. It was ten-thirty-five. The press conference was due to begin in less than half an hour and she still had to brief the chief superintendent before the cameras started rolling. She took a deep breath and exhaled hard.

"Press conference?" Tom asked.

"Yes. We're not going to announce it as a murder inquiry yet, and that leaves us with one of the vaguest – and let's face it, dullest – press announcements ever."

"Taking questions?"

"I'd rather not, but if we don't then there's not a great deal of point in holding the bloody thing, is there? We might as well put out another press release on the back of one of Cassie's betting slips."

Tom smiled. "If we don't give the press something, they'll just go and make it up."

She waved the comment away. "Least of my concerns right now. They are always going to make it up unless we give them all the details, and I'm not prepared to do that. Not yet anyway."

"I've just got to check in with Alice before we get underway downstairs."

"Everything all right?" she asked.

"Ah, yes. I left early and Alice had to drop Saffy off with one of her friends, who she'd go to school with, and then take her mother down to King's Lynn for her chemo."

Tamara felt for them. It was a grim time. "How is Alice's mum getting on?"

Tom raised his eyebrows. "Okay, I think. Her consultant is positive about her response to treatment, but... you just keep on keeping on, don't you?"

She reached out and touched his forearm. He smiled and

left her side, heading for his office. "I'll see you downstairs for the press conference."

Tom acknowledged the gesture with a little thumbs up as he walked away, just as Cassie appeared next to her, gently elbowing her in the ribs.

"So how did date night go?"

"Don't you start! It wasn't a—" she looked at Cassie, reading her grin. "Who told you anyway?" She held up her hand before Cassie could answer. "No, don't tell me, I'll just get annoyed and I already have enough on my plate as it is."

Shaking her head, she set off to see the chief superintendent who would no doubt be brushing down his suit to appear pristine before the cameras. Not that she minded if he wanted the exposure. She didn't.

"I love the hair, by the way," Cassie casually called after her.

"Mother!" Tamara muttered under her breath, inaudible to anyone but herself.

CHAPTER NINE

DR PAXTON LIFTED his gaze from the report in his hands, peering over the rims of his glasses as Tom entered his office. The pathologist placed the paperwork down in front of him, looking past Tom and into the corridor beyond as the detective inspector closed the door behind him. Tom glanced over his shoulder, curious as to what the doctor was looking for.

Paxton took a breath, removing his glasses. "Travelling alone today, Tom?"

Tom nodded. "Yes, I'm afraid you will have to make do with just me. I hope that's not a disappointment?"

"Of course," Paxton said, rising from his chair. "I thought you'd bring one of your many trusty sidekicks."

"No, sorry. Any particular preference for next time?"

"Young Derek is a likable character—"

"Eric Collet?"

"Yes, yes, yes… Eric, of course." Paxton waved away the correction, retrieving his white lab coat from a stand beside the door. "To be honest, anyone apart from that spiky one from the north." He sighed, grasping the door handle, looking at Tom and shaking his head. "I feel like prescribing myself Valium after every time I see her."

"I'm sure she doesn't mean it."

They stepped out into the corridor and Paxton gestured for them to walk to their right. Tom knew the way but allowed himself to be led.

"She has a nickname for me, does DS Cassandra Knight. Did you know that?"

Tom shrugged.

"*Doctor Death.*"

Tom made an approving sound to acknowledge him but wouldn't be drawn to commenting directly. "Well, as I said, I'm sure she doesn't mean—"

"I'm quite sure she does, Tom. However," he paused as someone passed by them, "I rather like it."

"You do?" Tom asked, unable to mask his surprise.

"Yes! That's the most interesting description I've ever had," he said, smiling to himself. "It gives me a measure of gravitas, wouldn't you say?"

Tom laughed. "I suppose so, yes. I'll tell her. She will be pleased—"

"Oh no, whatever you do, don't do that! She says it to wind me up. If you let on I like it, then she'll come up with something far nastier. Something I might not care for. No, no. Doctor Death it is."

"Fair enough."

They reached the morgue moments later. Entering, Tom felt the chill in the room, a result of the chillers and a need to maintain an ambient temperature. Dr Paxton raised a pointed finger as he selected the fridge containing Henry Crowe's body and opened it, dragging the tray out with ease. The sound of the mechanism echoed in the room, reverberating off the tiled wall and flooring.

"I must say," Dr Paxton said as he left Tom's side, heading to a desk set against the far wall and gathering a folder before returning to stand alongside him again, "I do appreciate you providing me with such interesting offerings with which to test my knowledge and ingenuity."

Tom looked at him, narrowing his eyes. "Okay, call my curiosity piqued. What is so interesting in this case?"

Paxton began leafing through pages in his file. "I won't read out my entire analysis to you, Tom. You can do that in your own time, but I have to say this Henry Crowe chap had quite an eventful last day, by all accounts." He slipped his glasses back on, clearing his throat as he scanned his own notes.

"Please do go on," Tom said, drawing his gaze over Crowe's body. The man appeared so different to the one he'd met only a couple of days previously. Crowe had been red-faced, and a larger-than-life character. He seemed thinner now, almost gaunt and his skin held a greyish-green hue to it. That which wasn't deformed or discoloured from the beating in his final hours, at least.

"I don't think I need to explain to you that he took a significant beating prior to death, so I won't insult your intelligence, Tom." Tom inclined his head at the comment. "However, he suffered multiple fractures to both cheekbones and jaw. Broken nose, four broken fingers, three to one hand and, curiously, only one to the other. Cuts and abrasions to the upper torso, front and back, seemingly systematic and controlled incisions rather than the frenzy of a blood-lust attack." Paxton looked up from his notes, meeting Tom's eye. "One can tell from the length of the cuts, angle of the blade," he said, demonstrating the type of swipes he was describing with his right hand whilst balancing his file in his left, "and depth of the incision. I think these were controlled."

"To what end? Torture?"

Paxton sighed, returning his eye to his paperwork. "The speculation I'll leave to you, Tom, if you don't mind. I went round and round in circles on this one, and in the end I realised it was your conundrum and not mine."

"The conundrum being?"

"I'll get there soon enough, don't worry." Paxton smiled without lifting his eyes from the notes. "Onwards with more torture, I'm afraid. I've not come across this before," he said wearily. "His feet were exposed to an accelerant and then set alight." He frowned. "It must have been terribly painful for the poor fellow."

"We had an idea at the scene, but can you confirm the substance used?"

"Oh yes, it had soaked into the carpet fibres at his feet. I took the liberty of speaking with your forensic chaps and they confirmed it to me. Nothing exotic, I'm afraid. Good, old-fashioned white spirit. Turpentine."

Tom pursed his lips. "The choice of which is…"

"Curious. Yes, I agree. An interesting choice. Sadly, from your point of view, available in every DIY superstore, hardware shop, petrol station and, probably, supermarket. That won't help track the culprit down, but it certainly makes you think about who they might be. You'd think petrol, lighter fluid… if you were looking to do such a thing, but white spirit? It is a little old school, wouldn't you say?"

"I have some on my boat," Tom said.

"Of course, you do. And DCI Greave will have bottles of it lying around her workshop, not marked in the appropriate containers, I should add. Please mention that to her, would you? I imagine she's not taken care of it."

Tom could picture Tamara's workshop, her Austin Healey and all the tools, bits and bobs she had on shelves in jars, tubs and assorted random containers. He was surprised to learn Dr Paxton had been to the house though. He wouldn't have seen the two of them having much in common. However, he didn't mention it.

"You said on the phone this morning that you weren't sure about assigning a cause of death."

"Oh, I can certainly give you that now, Tom." He looked sorrowfully at the body. "Mr Crowe died as a result of a cardiac arrest."

"Brought on by the beating?"

Paxton looked thoughtful. "Contributory factor, certainly. However, I mentioned to you about the enlarged heart, did I not?"

"Yes. What is the significance of that?"

"Are you aware of the deceased having any problems with drug addiction?"

Tom shook his head. "Not that we are aware of, no."

"Hmm... thought not. There is no sign of cardiomyocyte necrosis or any areas of older fibrosis indicating lack of, or presence of, cardiovascular disease within the heart. As I told you over the phone this morning, the heart was enlarged with concentric left ventricular hypertrophy."

Tom glanced across at him with a blank expression. "In layman's terms, if you don't mind, Doctor."

Paxton smiled. "Of course, I'm sorry. His heart was enlarged. You're a big chap, Tom, no stranger to the gym I should imagine. Picture your upper body after an extensive spell lifting weights. Your muscles expand, increasing in size and definition. This man's heart looked as it would if it had been bench-pressing multiple sets at the top end of his ability, really pushing it."

"What would cause that, drugs?"

"Oh yes. I suspected as much and that's why I wanted to

wait for the toxicology results to come back before voicing it to you. Needless to say, I was correct." He turned the page in his file. "Henry Crowe suffered a cardiac arrest with the contributing factor of acute methamphetamine intoxication."

"Methamphetamine?"

"Yes, speed, whizz, base, crystal… whatever you want to call it, it's pretty much the same thing, a psychomotor stimulant that ignites the central nervous system causing a person's mental and physical processes to speed up. The more a person uses, the faster the nervous system operates."

"Crowe wasn't a habitual drug user as far as we know."

Paxton shook his head. "I wouldn't be surprised to hear that was the case. He showed no signs to me of being a regular purveyor of such recreational pastimes. In a regular user we would often expect to see damage to the body, such as the heart. Prolonged use of these drugs will undoubtedly leave a trace. Often methamphetamine is combined with heroin use or, in other cases, cannabis. A user will often go several days taking it where they don't eat or sleep, seeing them use a relaxant, like heroin, to both ease a come down as well as aid sleep." He shook his head. "There was no other substance in the blood other than those we are aware of on prescription along with a 0.02% alcohol concentration."

"Methamphetamine is a strange choice of drug if you are already taking statins, isn't it?"

Dr Paxton nodded emphatically. "An absolutely lethal decision if it was one he took of his own free will. Although I would say Mr Crowe's heart was in fairly good condition for a man of his age, and certainly one with a higher than advisable cholesterol level. It is no wonder he was taking statins along with a blood thinner—"

"That's the Coumadin, right?"

"You have been paying attention, Tom. Excellent."

"It is my job, after all." Tom smiled wryly. "Besides, I've already spoken with his GP, Dr Jenkins."

"Ah, yes. William Jenkins. Good chap. I was at medical school with him. A long time ago now, mind you."

"Could he have been forced to take it, the amphetamine?"

"Without a doubt that is possible. However, it strays into speculation once again. What I would add, though, is that the levels of intoxication Mr Crowe here was experiencing was highly likely to lead to a cardiac event of some sort. I dare say an experienced user would have been at grave risk of a cardiac arrest or a stroke with so much in their system, let alone a man who seemingly was not experienced in such matters and definitely not someone who was already having to manage a condition that would be gravely exacerbated by this particular recreational activity. It would be akin to playing Russian Roulette with a fully-loaded revolver."

Tom frowned, drawing a deep breath. "What would the effects on him have been do you think?"

Paxton thought about it. "There would have been any number of reactions from agitation, restlessness, chest pains and hallucinations right the way through to bouts of panic and paranoia before the threat of breathing difficulties, seizures and, in this case, cardiac arrest. I dare say, at the point of overdose, he would have experienced convulsions and slipped into unconsciousness and coma before death. I doubt he would have known much about his passing." The pathologist sighed. "Not that it would have given him any comfort to know that, I'm sure."

"We will have to speak to his partner and friends to see if he was a user."

"Ask them if he was prone to bouts of anxiety, bursts of physical activity, insomnia, irritability or paranoia... they are some of the tell-tale signs of a user."

Tom raised his eyebrows. "That covers the majority of my colleagues back at the station!"

Paxton laughed. "Mandatory drug screening is the way forward."

Tom half-smiled at the thought. "Any chance he could have been taking it for a medical condition? It is used as a treatment for some conditions, isn't it? I know it's a long shot but I have to consider it."

"It has been known to be used in treatment of ADHD, narcolepsy and even obesity in certain cases, however not with this man." Paxton shook his head, glancing at the body. "It would be insane to combine these treatments and there is no record of it in his medical history."

"You have his file?"

Dr Paxton flicked through to the back of his file, stopping once he'd found it. "Yes, like I said, I was at med school with him. I recognised the name signing off the prescriptions. Knowing him so well certainly expedited things. It is so much easier to speak to a doctor than it is to just read the facts in a file, wouldn't you say?"

"In person is always best, I agree."

"Well, he confirmed to me that Crowe's condition was considered eminently manageable, and the prescribing of both Coumadin and Lipitor were on very low doses. The suggestion of a recreational drug habit was swiftly dismissed. Henry wasn't the type."

Tom mock grimaced. "They always say that."

"Well, that's true." Paxton sighed. "Oh, there was one more thing that may be of interest to you, Tom. Our victim had sex on the day of his death, most likely on the *night* of his death to be more precise, although I'm basing that on the fact he hadn't yet showered. He could have been walking around grubby for much of the day, I suppose, but I can't really speculate on the standards of his personal hygiene."

"That is interesting. You're sure?"

"Oh, yes. I found traces of semen on his genitals along with a substance that turned out to be spermicidal jelly; what you find lining the inside of a condom. I thought you'd be keen to know and therefore I pushed to have samples tested as soon as possible. Apparently, this man's death is a high priority because I didn't get any push back from the lab on hurrying them along. I doubt they'd pull out all the stops for a homeless man, found dead on a park bench—"

"The results, Dr Paxton?"

"The sample was matched to him, Tom. Did the scenes of crime team find evidence of his last moments of carnal pleasure?"

Tom frowned, shaking his head. "No, that didn't come up. I'll have them double check. No sign of any other DNA we could match a suspect to if we can find one?"

"I'm afraid not, Tom, sorry. Perhaps if you could locate the sheath itself, then I'm sure you'll have more joy." He looked at the body and then up at Tom. "Not as much as this man had at the time, no doubt. They say the line between pleasure and pain is a thin one, don't they? I wonder if he knew what was coming his way later that day. The poor man: not a good way to go, is it?"

"Is there a *good* way to go?"

Paxton shook his head. "I suppose not, no."

"So, in your opinion…" Tom eyed the body, "murder or torture that went too far?"

Paxton shrugged, following Tom's eyeline. "In my professional opinion… I'd say both! Not that I can prove it, mind you."

CHAPTER TEN

ENTERING THE POLICE STATION, Tom did a double-take on the figure sitting in the lobby. He stopped, genuinely surprised. The glass screen of the counter slid open and the civilian desk clerk gestured towards the man, sitting patiently in the corner reading a newspaper.

"There's a gentleman waiting to see you, Tom."

Tom casually acknowledged the clerk with a wave just as the man lowered his paper and his face split into a wide grin. He looked older, which stood to reason because they both were, but Tom was momentarily lost for words. The man stood up and strode confidently across the gap between them, tossing the paper onto an empty chair to Tom's left.

"It's not often you're so quiet, Tom. Surely, it hasn't been that long?"

"No, no, of course not," Tom said, reaching out a hand.

"A handshake? Is that all I'm worth?" The man grinned and threw his arms around Tom and the two men embraced. They parted and Tom found himself at arm's length, his old friend eyeing him. "How are you, Tom?"

"I'm well. Really well." Tom shook his head, his friend smiling warmly at him. "Pete... what are you doing here?"

"That's a fine way to greet your old friend after... what... three years?"

"Closer to four, I reckon."

Peter Chard, former colleague and long-term friend of Tom's, raised his eyebrows as he released his grip on Tom's arms and blew out his cheeks.

"Four years! Is it really?" He cast an eye over Tom from head to toe, inclining his head. "I'm afraid to say, Tom, that I can't believe how you're faring."

"What? I'm in good shape," Tom said, suddenly feeling self-conscious.

"Yeah," Pete nodded. "That's my point. You always did look a million dollars. Nothing's changed."

Tom smiled. "That'll be the fresh air. You should get yourself out of London more often."

Pete stepped back, lifting his arms wide from his sides. "What do you think I'm doing?"

Tom's eyes narrowed as practicality and suspicion came to mind. "You're not here working, are you?"

Pete laughed. "Do you think a Met team would be operating on another patch without the courtesy of at least a telephone call?"

"You're damn right I do." He cast a glance towards the office where the screen was now firmly closed once again. He angled his head towards it. "If that lot find out you're a Met officer, they'll be all over you."

Pete smiled. "I was subtle. I know how you hillbillies get when the big guns ride into town."

Tom shook his head. "Attitudes like that are exactly why Met officers get so much grief when they transfer out here."

Pete waved the comment away, lowering his voice so as not

to be overheard. "I'm sorry, it's just... so... backward around here—"

"We prefer to call it peaceful, if you don't mind? After all, that's how it is most of the time."

He held his hands up by way of apology. "Point taken. But that's not true right now, is it? Imagine my surprise, when I'm tucking into a surprisingly good stuffed pepper lunch at a pleasant restaurant overlooking Cromer's pier, to see a police press conference come on the TV with none other than my old mate, Tom Janssen, sitting in the background, looking all suave and awkwardly too large for his chair as usual. Are you still struggling to find clothes that fit?"

Tom laughed. "You have no idea! Listen, what are you doing here? A holiday?"

"Cara's mum retired up this way, remember?"

Tom frowned. "No, sorry. I can't say I do."

Pete smiled. "She has a place out at Overstrand, pretty much right on the beach. It gives her the opportunity to walk those ratty little terriers of hers on the sand every morning and night. The rate the sea's coming at them, I'll bet her house will be in it before much longer."

Pete Chard had a unique way with words, always did, and Tom shook his head. "How long are you up for?"

"Another couple of days... probably."

Tom pursed his lips. "Probably? That doesn't sound very organised for you. You're always right on the detail. It was your strength."

"One of many, Tom. One of many." He grinned. "Ah, truth is the old girl hasn't been well of late, so we've come up for a spell just to help out. She's doing better but it's just about easing Cara away from her now. You know how she worries."

"How is Cara, and the kids?"

Pete rocked his head from side to side. "Cara's doing okay.

A few ups and downs. You know how it is in life." Tom nodded knowingly. "The children are growing up fast." He raised his eyebrows. "And police kids... they know how to act up, don't they?" He fixed Tom with his gaze. "Do you... have—"

Tom decided to put him out of his misery and answered quickly. "My partner has a daughter, Saffy. She's pretty great. And no, she doesn't act up."

Pete exhaled. "Lucky for you. I think it's in the genes—"

The security door opened and Eric stepped out into the lobby. He looked at Tom and then quickly glanced at Pete, unsure of whether to interrupt. Tom smiled and bobbed his head to indicate it was okay.

"Sorry, Tom, but the DCI is looking for you..." he glanced at Pete again, "... for an update."

"Of course," Tom said. "I'll be right there." Eric smiled, nodded to Pete and retreated back into the station. Tom turned back to Pete, shrugging apologetically.

"That's okay, Tom. Like I said, I could see you were busy when I caught the press conference. I just didn't want to be in the area and not drop in. It's been too long since... well, you know?"

Tom sucked air through his teeth. He didn't want to revisit that time in his life, but his friends were something different.

"Hey," Tom said, raising a pointed finger, "why don't you come across to ours for dinner tonight?"

Pete screwed up his nose in response, shaking his head. "I wouldn't want to cause a fuss, not when you're in the middle of all of this. I know how it goes. Your family will barely see you in the—"

"Nonsense! Come on. I'd love it if you met Alice and Saffy. Even if it's only for a couple of hours. Nothing fancy."

"Well if you're cooking, it won't be anything fancy, will it?"

Tom angled his head. "Come on. What do you reckon?"

Pete hesitated. "All right, yeah. Sounds good. As long as I won't be causing you any trouble. But I doubt Cara will leave her mother alone, so it'll just be me. The children stayed in London. They're old enough to look after themselves now." His forehead creased. "At least, old enough not to burn the house down while we're away."

"You hope."

"Yes, I do!"

Tom grinned, taking out one of his contact cards and scribbling his address on the rear before handing it over to him. Pete Chard accepted it and read the reverse.

"What time? Seven-thirty, eight-ish?"

"Sounds good," Tom said, clapping his friend on the arm. "I'll look forward to it."

The two men said their goodbyes and Tom hurried into the depths of the station, making his way up to ops.

TOM WALKED into the ops room, Tamara beckoning him over before he had even taken his jacket off.

"How did you get on with Dr Paxton?"

There was no hint of aggression or frustration in her tone, but she had a steely determination about her.

"In his opinion, Henry Crowe was both tortured and then murdered by way of an amphetamine overdose."

Tamara took the information in for a moment, turning her gaze onto the information boards and the headshot of a smiling Henry Crowe provided to them by his wife, Natasha.

"That's a curious method to kill someone," she said after a moment. "I mean, deliberately overdosing someone is one thing but torturing them first? One or the other, but both?"

Tom had to agree. "It is possible the overdose was accidental. If the killer was unaware of the effects for example, then it may have been given to Crowe in error, but if he's right – Paxton I mean – then this is far more than just a robbery. It has to be."

Tamara fixed her gaze on him. "Torture for information or for hidden money?"

Tom bit his lower lip. "Could be either... or both. However, it could be something else entirely, something altogether more personal."

Tamara looked curious. "Personal? What makes you say that?"

"It's something about the manner of it all; the house, the office, the wounds inflicted on him." Tom shook his head. "For instance, his feet," Tom said, pointing at the corresponding picture of Crowe's burned extremities; the reddened skin akin to severe sunburn. "Paxton says they were doused in turpentine and set alight before being extinguished. Forensics have confirmed that as the liquid soaked into the carpet at his feet."

"That's torture, though, isn't it?" Tamara countered. "If they were left burning then he'd pass out which is no good if you're interrogating someone, and possibly on the clock."

"True. But it strikes me as odd. Why not just batter his toes with a hammer? Why set him on fire in that way?" He shook his head. "It seems... elaborate, wouldn't you say?"

Tamara frowned. "I suppose if we ask the question why he would store turpentine in his house, then it stands to reason the attacker either brought it with them or searched the house for it."

"Exactly. If you were breaking into someone's house looking for anything of value, would you go in search of turpentine to try and draw information from the homeowner? Of course not. Burglars are in and out, less than five minutes to minimise the chances of being caught. This guy was in that house for quite some time. The trashing of the office, the torture, the methods..." Tom shook his head. "He was going at it for a while."

"Forensics have found a number of fingerprints in the house and office."

"Anyone interesting?"

"The wife, Natasha, and Crowe himself obviously. Alex Tilson agreed to let us take his prints for comparison and they are in the house and the office as one might expect. The daughter's prints are easily distinguishable from the size, but we'll take hers at some point just to dot the i's and cross the t's. There are two other sets that were found in the house. One of which only cropped up in the less-used parts of the house but, crucially, neither was found in the office, kitchen or indeed where Henry's body was found."

"Who do they belong to, do we know?"

Tamara stepped to her left and tapped a photograph pinned on the first white board. Tom cast his eye over him. It was a photograph taken during custody procedure. This man, more of a boy really, had form. He was red-haired, looking dishevelled and carried that haunted look of many who are arrested and processed, a curious mixture of irritation and terror.

"We got a hit on this kid," Tamara said, looking back at Tom. "Richard Carver. He has several convictions, although they date back quite a while. The most egregious was a burglary conviction from 2005; he was only fifteen at the time and served six months in a youth offenders' institution."

"Seems harsh for a fifteen-year-old," Tom said.

"He was disturbed by the owner, an elderly chap in his eighties. I read the account and the homeowner was a war veteran who didn't stand down and tried to tackle him. Carver gave the resident a bit of a kicking before leaving the house with a handful of cash and some old medals."

"The old man's?"

"Yes. Carver didn't get away with more than fifty pounds in cash and the medals weren't particularly valuable. Sentimentally priceless, mind you. He was caught trying to flog them at a pawn broker in the town."

"Not a great haul to exchange for six months of your life. What else has he done?"

"A bit of shoplifting," she read from the notes recently added to the board, "arrested for drunk and disorderly, again in his mid-teens, street-fighting when the pubs chucked out. Not that he should have been in them at that age… but it never stopped us, did it?"

"No, it didn't."

"Nothing major, not really."

Tom nodded. "Where is he now?"

Tamara shook her head. "We don't know, but Cassie is working on it. He served less than half his sentence, cut due to him having pleaded guilty before trial and therefore his sentence was greatly reduced. Add to that his behaviour was considered exemplary which brought it down further. Social services and the probation service followed up with him upon release, keeping an eye on his home life, and he never missed an appointment or a phone call. He finished high school and found work. Aside from the odd drunken fracas, and let's face it we've all been there, he didn't cause problems. Rehabilitation in action."

Tom smiled. "The system works after all then."

"He has subsequently disappeared though."

The smile left his face and Tom exhaled. "No one disappears unless they want to."

"And why would he want to?" Tamara asked.

"Has anyone asked Natasha Crowe if this man is connected to them in any way?"

She shook her head. "Not yet. But I'm curious to know how he came to be in the Crowe house. It doesn't fit well."

"Previous record for aggravated burglary, disappears like *The Scarlet Pimpernel* only to pop up at our crime scene? What's not to like?"

"That's just it; his prints are in the house but not the room where we found Crowe, or in his office for that matter."

"Gloves?"

"Which he took off in the kitchen whilst passing between the office and where he killed Crowe? That would make no sense."

Tom agreed. "Better find him and ask, I suppose. You said there was a second set. These definitely aren't Carver's?"

"No, and they were only found in areas of the house that appear less well used."

"Curious."

"That's what I thought. Perhaps they're historic. With only three of them living in the house, Tilson popping in occasionally and working in the office, maybe the previous owners left prints in rooms the Crowe's never entered."

"Natasha did say they had a couple of cleaners working for them. Maybe they belong to them. When we next speak to Natasha, we should ask her again for a list of people who have had access to the house in the last year or two. Now the dust has settled a bit, she may come up with some names that hadn't occurred to her before," Tom said, wondering if he could fit in a conversation with Natasha before the end of the day or whether he should leave it to Eric and Kerry when they follow up with her. "Where is Natasha now? Is she still staying with relatives?"

"As I understand it, yes. Their house is clear now, and they can go back, but the daughter doesn't want to... and who could blame her?"

Tom looked at the picture of Richard Carver, once more. The picture was taken around fifteen years ago when he was in his late teens. The young man looked thin in the face, youthful, in fact far younger than his years in Tom's eyes. He could have passed for someone several years younger than he was at the time. What would a spell in prison along with a decade and a half do to him? Tom was quite sure they could pass one another on the street this afternoon and he wouldn't recognise him.

"Carver," he said, gesturing to the picture, "is he local to us here?"

Tamara shook her head. "Grew up in Birmingham, Bournville to be exact."

"Nice part of the city, isn't it?"

Tamara smiled. "For those of us in the West Midlands, that place is a town within a town, if you know what I mean? Very middle class, large houses, good salaries."

"Strange place for a burglar to live—"

"Drug addict," she said. "Remember it's not just the lower income households that fuel the illegal drugs industry."

"Right," Tom said. "The only difference is you're more likely to have your collar felt if you're from a lower social set."

"Because you're more likely to need to rob to feed your habit. Rich kids don't have to steal." Tamara shrugged. "They just use their allowance."

CHAPTER ELEVEN

"TOM, DO YOU HAVE A MINUTE?" Eric asked. Tom had his phone in his hand and was about to call Alice. He figured she'd be home from taking her mother down to the Queen Elizabeth Hospital for her chemotherapy session and he wanted to give her time to prepare herself for accepting a guest for the evening; one of Tom's former colleagues. Although extending the invitation seemed a great idea at the time, and one he wanted to honour, he was experiencing a little anxiety around the forthcoming evening.

Pete Chard was a part of Tom's former life at a time when everything threatened to unravel around him; his marriage was disintegrating, and Pete had a ringside seat. Although incredibly supportive at the time, Pete hadn't wanted to choose a side between two serving officers, both friends, where one was sleeping with the other's wife. It was a stance Tom, with hindsight, could understand, even if he still felt distinctly let down at the time. For Pete, or any of the team to publicly admonish their colleague for overstepping the mark would have led to the fragmentation of the entire unit. Their roles were far too important at that moment; they were making a difference rather than merely wading through the dregs of society each day as many police officers often felt.

Following the unexpected arrival of his soon-to-be ex-wife the previous year, Tom had opened up to Alice about what had precipitated his return to his childhood home, but he never felt particularly comfortable reliving those days. He pushed the concerns aside. It was an evening with an old friend who would get to meet his new family and that was a positive event, or at least, it should be. He beckoned Eric into his office, putting the phone down.

"I'm sorry, were you in the middle of something?" Eric asked, entering. Tom noted a large brown envelope clutched in his hand.

Tom waved the apology away. "What's up?"

"This just arrived at the front desk," Eric said, holding the envelope aloft.

He handed it to Tom who looked at the front. It was handwritten and addressed simply to Norfolk Police with the station address beneath. It was sent first class and, according to the stamp, was franked in the Norwich sorting office, dated the previous day.

Eric gestured for him to look inside. It was lightweight and felt empty. Tom lifted the seal and inspected the contents. There was no letter, simply four loose photographs. By the look of it, they had been printed on an inkjet printer, the type most people would likely have at home. There were distinct lines where passes of the printer head had left colour distortions, likely caused by the cartridge running low on one particular element, cyan Tom guessed. The result was a set of grainy images whereas the original photos were probably taken with a half-decent mobile phone or a proper camera before scanning or uploading them to a computer.

"What have we got here then, Eric?" Tom asked, squinting to make out the figures in the pictures.

The holder of the camera was evidently some distance away from the target and were also taken through something, such as a window – car or building, Tom couldn't tell – thereby hampering the quality. The first was a shot of the rear end of a car, the number plate clearly visible. It was a convertible Audi, a few years old. Before Eric could answer his question, Tom's eyes drifted to the second photo where he recognised the woman centred in the shot. He'd only met her once, but he was certain it was Natasha Crowe. She was not as neatly presented as she had been the previous day. Despite her emotional state she was clearly someone who took great care in her appearance, however here her hair was dishevelled and, seemingly, she'd just run a hand through it before the picture was snapped. She was leaning against a door frame speaking to a man, who had his back to the camera, shielding her eyes from a low sun indicating it was either early or late in the day. The man had a heavy coat on whereas Natasha had drawn about her a light-fitting black lace robe, revealing what looked like matching lingerie beneath.

The third photo saw the man move closer and Natasha had thrown her arms around him, leaning in to a passionate embrace. The final picture was the only one to offer a frontal picture of the man as he opened the door to the Audi, Natasha Crowe watching on in the background. Tom put the photos down on his desk.

"Well, well, well," he said softly, looking up and meeting Eric's knowing gaze. "Any idea who this is or when they were taken?" Tom flipped one picture over looking for a date stamp on the reverse. There wasn't one.

Eric shook his head. "No, sorry on both counts. I was about

to run the plate and see what came up, but I figured you'd want a look first."

"Do it," Tom said, picking up the photos and shuffling them together before putting them back in the envelope. "And have these copied for the information boards and get them catalogued."

"Will do. Kerry is supposed to be coming with me to see Natasha today. What do you want to—"

"I think just give her a courtesy telephone call today," Tom said. "Nothing specific, make it a welfare conversation and see whether she is heading home or staying with family. Don't mention this." He indicated the envelope. "You and I can speak to her tomorrow. Hopefully by then we'll have an idea of who this man is as well as a little more background on Mrs Crowe. After all, these could have been taken any time and someone could be stirring the pot."

"Sent to us within days of Henry's murder, though. Odd, isn't it?"

"And sent by whom and for what purpose?"

Tom picked up his mobile, meaning to make that call to Alice. Eric lingered, hesitant.

"Something else, Eric?"

"Yes… no, I mean, I think so."

Tom gestured for him to carry on, putting the mobile down again.

"The DCI said to look at the obvious, listen out for any intel that comes our way that might seem out of the ordinary."

Tom nodded. "What have you got?"

"I know we're asking pawn brokers and the like to look out for anything surprising coming their way, but I thought it'd make sense to go back through the logs in the days running up to the weekend."

"Good thinking. How far back did you go?" Tom pictured

Eric sifting through pages of data churned out every morning from the Police National Computer, which cars were pulled over the previous day, local reports of suspicious activity, drunken brawls and any number of other day-to-day goings on that make the headlines each day.

"Two weeks." Eric frowned. "Much of it was the usual stuff, insignificant and not relevant to us…"

"But?"

"There was one report that uniform put in that caught my eye; a member of the public called in a suspicious camper van, all blacked out, parked up for the day and stayed overnight." Eric held up his hand. "I know, camper vans in lay-bys are not unusual around these parts, which was why I found it curious."

"Curious, why?"

"That it was deemed reportable by the member of the public and worth investigating by uniform."

"They checked it out?"

"Sort of. The camper had moved on by the time a unit stopped by. Initially, it wasn't deemed serious, but when they realised it had been parked up in front of a transmitter tower then protocols kicked in."

"Terrorism protocols," Tom said, knowingly. Eric agreed. In recent years any activity in and around sites of interest; critical infrastructure, power stations, substations or communications masts, was to be considered a high priority, reflecting the situation in the modern era post 9/11.

"Exactly. Although the van had gone, uniform took a description and the number plate from the person who phoned it in and put the details out. The van was spotted further around the coast by another patrol and the driver questioned."

"And you have that report?"

Eric nodded, taking out his pocket notebook. "The van was registered to *Prometheus*. That's a private detective agency. The driver identified himself as Sean Rogers. He was stopping to get some kip in the back of the van. He said he'd worked a night shift and had handed over to the day team."

"What were they working on? Did he say?"

Eric shook his head. "By all accounts he was reluctant to say, which I'm not surprised by, to be honest. You know how it is around here, everyone knows everyone else, and most of their business. You could blow an operation by talking to one of us. Anyway, uniform were content that he wasn't up to anything and so they moved on."

"And how does this tie into Henry Crowe's death?"

"It doesn't," Eric said, shrugging. "It just sounded unusual."

Tom thought about it. A private detective agency running an operation on their patch was not surprising. Where there were people, there would always be dodgy deals, estranged lovers and any number of other reasons that required someone to run an operation. He was perturbed at the thought of something serious going down that they were completely unaware of. One detective following a spouse or lover was one thing, immoral in many ways in his mind, but if a team was deployed then that elevated things a little. The costs of which would not be insignificant, far from it.

"Okay, when you get a moment have a dig into *Prometheus* and this Sean Rogers character. If there is any sniff of their being tied into anything Crowe was working on, past or present, or anyone he was affiliated with, then we'll go further."

"Will do."

"Eric!" Tom called to him as he made to leave whilst scooping up his mobile. The detective constable glanced over his shoulder. "Keep it within the team for now though, please? Not a word outside of ops, not even mates in uniform."

Eric nodded and walked out of the office. It wasn't a lack of trust in his team, but Tom knew how these private detectives worked. Many of them, the better ones, were ex police themselves. After all, they had the knowledge, skills and wherewithal to effectively do the investigative work of a police officer but in the private sector. They would also be savvy enough to have local connections, possibly even within Norfolk Constabulary itself. If he was running a private investigation himself, Tom was sure he would.

Beyond these, the lower skilled, and therefore cheaper, detectives were often sourced from the ex-military community. These guys were plentiful and useful for covert surveillance operations where a number of boots on the ground were needed, but they were far less effective when it came to the subtleties required in an investigation; potentially more of a liability than an asset.

He was curious to know which they were dealing with in this case. It was a good catch by Eric. Tom's interest was also piqued, and he couldn't shake the thought of there being more to such a coincidence.

"Tom, are you there?"

He heard Alice's distant voice then realised he'd dialled without noticing.

"Hi love… sorry, I was distracted there for a moment."

"Is everything all right?"

He heard anxiety in her voice.

"That was going to be my question," he said, and she laughed. "How did it go with your mum?"

"She's home, resting. The after effects of the chemo seemed to hit her faster and much harder this time around. I don't know why that is. Maybe they've done something different, but she's settled in at home; sent me packing as I was annoying her."

"Sounds like she's feeling better already," he said dryly.

"So, why are you calling? You never call me from work unless something's happened—"

"That's not true... most of the time. It's just..."

"Oh, here it is... go on, hit me with it."

"An old friend called by the station today. I've not seen him in years, an old friend from my Met days, and I sort of invited him for dinner."

"Is that all?"

"Well, yes," he said. "I thought dropping it on you at such short notice might be an issue, that's all."

"Is he a decent guy... or will I want to tear my arm off and beat him to death with the wet end?"

Tom laughed. "No, Pete's a great bloke. We used to be pretty tight back in the unit. He's married, has a couple of children in their teens. You'll like him... I think."

"Then it will be fine!" Alice went quiet. "Although, what with everything over the weekend, the party, you working, we haven't done the shopping yet. I've no idea what we'll eat."

"Don't worry. I'll be able to rustle something up."

"No way! Whenever you *rustle something up* the kitchen gets destroyed. I have an hour before the school run, so I'll sort something out."

"You don't mind?" he asked, hopeful.

"Don't be silly, of course not. Although..."

"Although what?"

"Well, even though it's okay, and I will probably like Paul—"

"Pete."

"*Pete*... you will still owe me... and you'd better believe I will collect."

He could picture the mischievous smile on her face.

"As long as it doesn't involve dancing—"

"It will definitely involve dancing, Detective Inspector Janssen, probably Latin... Oooh... salsa!"

"Geez..." Tom said with a sigh. "It's a good job my friends don't venture out to the coast very often."

"I think I should start encouraging them!"

"Right, I'm hanging up before you enrol me in ballroom classes, and I wind up on *Strictly*! See you soon. Love you."

He could hear her laughter as he ended the call, shaking his head and smiling as he did so.

CHAPTER TWELVE

IT WAS SHORTLY after seven o'clock when Tom pulled into the drive, later than he'd anticipated getting home but still time enough for him to grab a quick shower before Pete would arrive. He'd been surprised by the emotional reaction his old friend engendered in him that afternoon. When he left, both his job in the Met and his home in London, Tom had chosen to sever almost all ties with that life. The pain of his marriage break-up, as well as it straying into his professional life, was such that he felt the need to erect a barrier to protect himself. In doing so, he isolated himself from all of his friends; a decision that seemed excessive now with the benefit of hindsight.

He looked for Saffy at the front window, appearing to welcome him home as she did most days but not today. Slipping the key into the lock and opening the front door, the sound of laughter came to ear. He closed the door behind him and hung his coat over the newel post at the foot of the stairs and headed for the kitchen.

Alice was leaning against the breakfast bar, both hands cupping a mug of tea, laughing at a tale Pete was delivering in his customary, confident style. Saffy was perched on the bar itself, her feet swinging backwards and forwards, dangling below the lip of the surface, sitting on her hands and grinning at their guest. Even Russell, Saffy's terrier was at their feet, looking up at him.

"Hello!" Tom said loudly to ensure he was heard. All heads turned to him, Saffy waving and Alice putting her mug down and meeting him halfway. She slipped one arm around his waist as he kissed her hello. The dog angled his head in Tom's direction but clearly seeing little in it for him, otherwise ignored his arrival.

"I had a little spare time," Pete said, "and then I misjudged the journey time, so I got here a bit early. I hope you don't mind?"

Tom made to speak but Alice waved away the apology. "Don't be silly. It's absolutely fine, but," she said, separating herself from Tom, "I need to get on with making dinner or we'll be eating far too late."

"I don't mind staying up!" Saffy said, beaming.

"You, young lady," Alice said, "will be going up to bed at eight o'clock, as usual."

Saffy groaned, rolling her eyes like someone three times her age. "I never get to have any fun!"

Tom glanced at the wall clock, Alice following his gaze. She frowned, glancing at the hob and the saucepans. Dinner was under way but it was later than normal. She must have read his mind, because she smiled at Saffy.

"Maybe half past, but no later," she said.

"Great! That'll be nine at least," Saffy replied, swinging her legs with gusto, the smile returning.

Alice rolled her own eyes and Tom knew where the little girl got it from. Mother and daughter were so alike, it was frightening at times.

"What smells so good?" Tom asked. "What are we having?"

"Chef surprise," Alice said. Tom didn't press the question. It meant she was experimenting with whatever they had. Perhaps she hadn't made it to the shop after all. "Pete has just been telling us about what the two of you used to get up to back when you were carefree and far more adventurous than you are now," Alice said, winking at Tom.

He walked to the fridge in search of a glass of orange juice, glancing at Pete's near empty bottle of beer in his hand. He indicated it. "Don't believe everything he says. This isn't a man to be trusted. Same again?"

"Please," Pete said, raising the bottle to his lips and finishing it off.

"Oh, I don't know," Alice said, lifting the lids of the pans in turn and inspecting progress. "He seems on the level to me."

Tom laughed dryly, cracking the lid off a fresh bottle of beer and passing it across the breakfast bar via Saffy. "Yes, he was always good at that type of thing."

"What type of thing?" Pete asked with a mock grimace.

"Pulling a fast one and hoodwinking everyone around him," Tom said, matching Pete's expression with feigned horror of his own. "If you needed someone to convince the boss of the need for an operation, budget increase or over-time... send in Chard. He always gets the job done."

"Harsh," Pete said.

Tom poured a glass of fresh orange juice from the carton and tilted it in his friend's direction. "And that's just the good guys. You should see what he was like with the villains."

Pete grinned. "Ah... but they deserved it!" He pointed to Tom's choice of drink. "On the soft stuff because it's a school night?"

"I don't drink. At least, not often."

"Blimey, you have changed." Pete shook his head. "I can't imagine clocking off without a swift one after a shift or a cheeky G and T when I get home."

"And that, my old friend, is why I remain so youthful and you are showing your age."

Pete exhaled. "I'll drink to that!" He raised his bottle and tipped it towards Tom who replied in kind.

Alice touched Saffy on the arm, drawing her attention. "Did you come home with any schoolwork to do tonight?"

Saffy shook her head. The action was unconvincing.

"I could log into your class chat and take a look remember."

"Oh… yes, I might have some English to do," Saffy said, her sudden memory recall was as convincing as her denial of homework. "I have to research and write something about the history of Britain."

"What do you have to write about?" Alice asked.

Saffy shrugged. "Whatever I like, I think."

"Great, plenty of scope for you. If you get a move on, then you'll be done before dinner."

Saffy sighed. "Do I have to?"

Alice fixed her daughter with a stern look. It was enough to answer the question without saying a word.

Tom stepped towards her and Saffy reached out with both hands so he could lift her up, whisk her around in a swirl before putting her down on the ground. Russell climbed up against her, standing on his hind legs just in case she was bringing food for him. Disappointed, he dropped down and shuffled over to his bed in the corner of the room, sinking into his blankets and exhaling with a huff.

"Don't worry," Tom said. "You can do the research on Google with your laptop. What are you learning in history at the moment?"

"The Romans!" Saffy said. "They were *awesome*."

"In that case," Pete said, dropping to his haunches so that they could make eye contact at her level, "Julius Caesar's expedition to Britain would be a great place to start. The first, and arguably the most famous, of all the emperors of Rome, coming to Britain with his legions."

Saffy looked unconvinced, but Pete was undeterred.

"He didn't stay long, ran away in the face of the mighty Brits!"

"Is that true?" Saffy asked, staring into his eyes with a look of distrust.

Pete put his hand on his heart, his expression a picture of innocence.

Tom coughed. They both looked up at him. "Maybe Google it before you write that down, little one. Pete here is a policeman and not a historian for a reason."

"What's the reason?" Saffy asked, ensuring Tom regretted making the joke. "Well?" she persisted.

"He made a better policeman than a historian?" Alice suggested and Tom smiled.

"I can't argue with that," Pete said, grinning.

Saffy accepted the answer and hurried off in search of her school bag.

"How is Cara?" Tom asked. "I didn't really get a chance to ask earlier."

"Who's Cara?" Alice asked, rummaging through a cupboard for an ingredient.

"My wife, Cara," Pete said, looking back at Tom and turning the corners of his mouth down, exaggerating the action. "She's all right. Usual stuff, her mum's not well – dementia – but is refusing to go into residential care, so we have a private service dropping in daily to help, but that costs you know. Plus, she's at the stage in her career where she's questioning if it's what she wants to do."

"Clinical psychology, wasn't it?" Tom asked.

Pete nodded. "Yeah, sort of. She diagnoses people, helps them get the right treatment for their needs and so on. But, as is the way these days, cuts, cuts and cuts. She feels more like an accountant than..." he let the sentence drop, shaking his head.

"The children?"

"Teenagers! Enough said, I reckon."

"That bad?" Tom asked.

Pete smiled. "No, not really. It's more about me than them, if I'm honest. You just get used to them seeing you as the hero who never makes mistakes. It's kind of fun when they look up to you, back your arguments and hang on almost every word you say..." He gestured with his head in the direction of the living room where Saffy was crouched over the coffee table, tapping away at the keys of her laptop with a sheet of paper and a pen beside her. "Best days of your life right there, Tom."

Alice looked over her shoulder. "Does that mean it's down-hill in a few years' time?"

Pete sucked air through his teeth before inclining his head and breaking into a broad grin. "Yes... but it's one hell of a ride!"

Dinner was a comfortable affair. Alice worked wonders on scant resources and the conversation steadily flowed. It was comfortable because they skirted any subjects offering greater depth in favour of easy conversation and gentle humour. Tom's concerns were unfounded as Alice, and indeed Saffy, easily took to Pete. By the time Saffy was ushered upstairs to bed, a little after nine o'clock as she predicted, it felt as if the years apart had never happened.

"Can I get you another coffee?" Tom asked, readying himself to rise from his seat at the table only for their guest to wave the offer away.

"I'll be up all night as it is," Pete said. "You know I take six or seven coffees a day at the moment, more if I'm on a late shift. That can't be good for you, can it?"

Tom laughed, shaking his head. "If there was anyone who didn't need a stimulant, let's face it, it would be you."

Pete smiled, nodding. A thud came through the floor and both men looked up at the ceiling.

"Sounds like your little girl making her presence known."

Tom raised his eyebrows. "Over tired. We should be better at getting her into bed, but... you know how it is."

"Too right. The day fills up with so much stuff that, sometimes, you just want to let the rules go once in a while."

"Every night these days," Tom said. "We plan to stick to a schedule, but it doesn't take much to throw us off—"

"Especially ad hoc visits from exciting individuals like myself!"

Tom chuckled, absently turning the glass in front of him on the table.

"Go on, Tom. I know you're dying to ask."

Tom fixed his gaze on him. "I am?"

"Yeah, you want to know what's happening with the old gang. I can see it in your eyes."

"I guess so. Some of them at least."

"Well, not much to tell you, old chap." Pete drew in a deep breath, sitting back in his chair as he exhaled, cupping his hands in his lap. "Most of us have moved on... one way or another. Kim Streeting got a promotion to Inspector and then did a Janssen, leaving for some backwater in Wales—"

"Is that what you call it, *doing a Janssen*?"

"Only in jest, Thomas, only in jest. Come on, everyone gets sick of wading through London's rubbish soon enough and leaving the big smoke has a certain appeal to it. Professionally speaking, you must've been considered elite when you came out here, with your knowledge and experience?"

"It doesn't usually come across that way," Tom said. Pete cocked his head and Tom went on. "You're right, what we face in a couple of months in the Met, officers in Norfolk see across an entire career. They don't really like it when we stroll in with all the answers."

Pete sat forward again, wagging a finger at him. "But I'll bet you get promoted more quickly."

"That's true. A constable will usually make sergeant within six months or so of transferring out here. Unless they're not popular, which is also a risk when you come up from the city."

"Why?"

"They think you're arrogant," Tom said, scratching at his chin, "or they feel inferior. One or the other, perhaps both, but it doesn't make you popular. Especially if they perceive you as swanning in and taking their promotions."

"How about you? Is that what happened when you came home?"

He shook his head. "I came back as a DI—"

"And you've been back how long now?"

Tom grinned. "I know where you're going, but my situation's different." He thought of Tamara and how she'd come in at a time when he was considering taking up the DCI role himself. In the end it wasn't offered to him. "Right now, I'm happy as I am. I don't see the need to change things up. Besides, I have a pretty decent DCI that I like working with. She's great."

"*She?* Really, now I understand…"

Tom picked up a napkin and launched it at him. Pete deftly

caught it and tossed it aside, holding his free hand up by way of apology.

"I was just kidding, I swear."

Another thud upstairs, only this time it was less aggressive.

Pete looked up again. "Sounds like she's running out of steam." He lowered his eyes to meet Tom's. "You've got a good thing going here, you know. They're both lovely, Alice and Saffy. You've done well for yourself."

"I know."

"You deserve it, Tom. You really do. London never suited you, not really."

Tom raised his eyebrows. "Are you saying I couldn't cut it?"

He wasn't serious. Pete knew that too, batting the comment away with humour.

"Of course, you couldn't! You always spent far too much time walking around looking all chiselled and... Scandinavian..." He shook his head. "It was very distracting for the team, you know?"

"So, what about the others?"

"Sideways moves for most... nicer patches or assignments in the main. Gerry made DCI."

"Did he?" Tom said, failing to mask his surprise in his customary polite way. "I didn't even know he'd made inspector."

"Did so off the back of riding your coat tails, Tom." Pete shook his head. "You'd have been next in line if you hadn't... well... you know? If it hadn't all gone pear-shaped like it did."

"Yeah, well... life," Tom said regretfully.

He pursed his lips. It was going to come up eventually, it had to. It was the elephant in the room whenever his past in the Met was under scrutiny.

"You didn't deserve that, Tom. It was a really shitty thing for him to do."

Tom rubbed at his temples, nodding slowly. "Well, he always wanted the top job, and I was in it, so if you can't get the job—"

"It wasn't the job he wanted; it was your life! He admired you... loved you, I'd guess, in a twisted, stalker-esque and purely jealous kind of way."

Tom laughed without any real humour. "He went a funny way about showing it!"

"He wasn't trying to take your wife, Tom. He was trying to be you!"

Tom looked down at the table, tapping the surface with his index finger. Pete realised he was keen to change tack and obliged without prompting.

"I was overlooked successively for promotion myself. That was a bit tough to take after this many years' service and what I figured was a competent, if not sterling career."

"Not surprising," Tom said, drawing breath. "You're a God-awful DS, Pete."

"I'd be severely wounded by that if it wasn't true!" Pete said, lifting his coffee cup and frowning as he saw it was empty. "Thanks very much, by the way."

"You're welcome." Tom leaned forward, making eye contact. "You used the past tense. Does that mean you've given up on promotion?"

Pete grinned. "You always were a cracking detective, Tom." He shrugged. "I don't know about *given up* exactly... but motivations change over time, don't they? I mean," he looked around the room, "did you ever plan to move back this way? You were scathing about Norfolk not all that long ago."

Tom smiled. "Like you say, things change. There's no place else I'd rather be, that's for certain."

"So, how's this case you're working on panning out? It seems to have caught the media's imagination. Any juicy scandal for them to get stuck into?"

"This isn't London, Pete. Scandal isn't quite as salacious as you're used to in your neck of the woods."

"Nice deflection, Tom." Pete nodded approvingly. "I see you're as diplomatic as ever with your discretion."

"Have to be. It goes with the warrant card, remember?"

"True enough," Pete said, shaking his head. "I haven't worked a case like that for a while now. The last murder squad I was on had me trekking across half the country in search of family members taking part in an honour killing. Do you know how hard it is to crack the code of silence when it's a cultural thing?"

Tom shook his head. "Not really, no."

"Damn hard, that's how hard! The father, uncles and a couple of cousins did it, either killing her or helping dispose of the body – which they did badly, by the way – going off all half-cocked with it. Then they scattered to the four corners of the country. It was a year before we tracked them all down and that was eight months after we'd worked out what had gone on."

Tom frowned. "Yes, well, I don't think this is an honour killing."

"Not if it involves a barrister, no!" Pete said, chuckling at his own joke. He checked his watch. "Damn, I really should get going. By the time I get back everyone will be asleep as it is. I'd hate to wake the house up."

"Where did you park? I didn't see your car—"

"Cara dropped me off."

"Shame I wasn't here. It would have been great to say hello."

"Next time, Tom. I'll get a cab—"

"Rubbish. It will cost you a fortune. I'll run you back—"

Pete rose out of his seat, stretching his arms out at the side. "No, you won't. I've deprived you of enough family time already. I've already booked one anyway. Apps on your phone are so easy to use, aren't they? No more phoning around hoping someone picks up. Job done." Tom was about to protest just as Alice entered the kitchen. "Great timing. I'm just going."

"So soon?" Alice said, disappointed.

"Yes. You guys should get a little time together of an evening without an old bore like me playing gooseberry." He stood up, lifting his jacket off the back of his chair and putting it on. "It's been great catching up, Tom." He looked at Alice. "And lovely to meet you, Alice. Saffy is a credit to you."

Alice slipped her arm around Tom's waist, pulling him closer. "To both of us."

Pete stepped out of the house, giving Alice a warm hug and a kiss on the cheek. He shook Tom's hand, then held onto it for a moment afterwards as their eyes met.

"You're doing well for yourself, Tom. I'm pleased for you. Although, I miss you every day back home."

Tom smiled. "I wish I could say the same," he replied with a wink, earning a sharp dig in the ribs from Alice. He stepped out into the cool night air, and they embraced. "It's great to see you, it really is. Let's not leave it so long. I'd love to see Cara again as well. Please give her my love."

"Will do."

Tom looked up and down the street. "I don't see your taxi. Are you sure you've got the time right?"

"Of course. It'll be the same guy as earlier. He said I'll be his last fare of the day. I agreed to meet him up the road at the newsagent. I'll need some breath mints to mask the smell of beer anyway!"

He set off down the drive, waving an arm in the air as he went. Tom slipped an arm around Alice's waist as they watched him go.

"You were right," she said. "I did like him."

Tom smiled and they turned to go back inside. "Everyone does," he said, closing the door.

CHAPTER THIRTEEN

THE FRONT DOOR OPENED, and Natasha Crowe stood before them, dressed in a loose-fitting hoodie and sweatpants. Her hair was tied up and she wasn't wearing any make-up. Dark patches hung beneath her eyes. She couldn't have slept well these past few nights. Granted it was early, a little after eight o'clock in the morning, but for someone who evidently takes so much pride in her appearance, the toll her loss had taken on her was clear.

"Hello, Natasha," Tom said. "I'm sorry to call on you so early in the morning."

Both Eric and Kerry Palmer were standing beside Tom, and he was aware that to have three detectives calling round first thing could be intimidating and he wanted to put her at ease, for now at least. He needn't have worried, as she didn't seem remotely concerned. She smiled weakly, stepping back from the threshold, and left the door wide open as she turned away to head back into the house. Tom took it as an invitation. He glanced at the other two and followed.

Natasha led them through the house and into the kitchen, turning to face them and leaning against the kitchen island as they filed through before her. She crossed her arms, for convenience rather than to strike a defiant pose, in Tom's mind.

"How are things? You managed to coax Olivia home then?" Tom asked.

She shrugged. "Can't stay away forever. Mum came with us to help. Olivia is much calmer when she's around."

Tom looked past her into the dining area for signs of the little girl, the one who befriended Saffy the day of the party. He remembered her being so bright with a wide, genuine smile.

"Is she around?"

"Still asleep," Natasha said. "She's been having nightmares since... since all this happened." She shook her head. "I can relate."

"I appreciate it must be difficult—"

She scoffed, catching Tom by surprise. She must have registered his reaction because she averted her eyes from his and her body language softened.

"I'm sorry, Inspector. I don't mean to be... offhand. It's just... all so overwhelming. It's hard to imagine anyone really understanding. I mean, my mum tries, but I don't think she gets it. Not really."

Tom recalled how Alice reacted to the death of her ex-husband, Saffy's father, as well as the trauma the little girl went through in processing her loss. It took months before the real Saffy reappeared and, even now, she could still show signs of what she went through should the right triggers come up. Not that it was something he could bring up here and now. Instead, he nodded.

"I'm pleased that we have this opportunity to speak to you alone, Natasha," Tom said, looking over his shoulder at Eric who passed him an envelope. "We have a development in the case, and we need to discuss it with you."

"Do you know who did it, who attacked Henry?"

The question was asked with real hope in her voice, albeit tinged with fear.

"No, not yet, but we are working on it, I assure you. I'm afraid, what we need to speak to you about is a little delicate under any circumstances but more so in this case."

Natasha eyed him warily as he opened the envelope and took out copies of the photographs delivered to the station the previous day. He passed them to her. She stared at the first image without looking up. She shifted that one to the rear and examined the next. Aside from her lips parting, she made no response as she moved quickly through the remaining two images.

Tom noted her grip on the photos tightened, so much so that the colour beneath her fingernails turned white at the tips. She took a deep breath, turning away from them and gently placing the photos down on the granite surface of the island. After a few moments, she spoke, her words almost inaudible.

"Where did you get these?"

"I can't say at this time. Can you confirm that this is you in the photographs?"

She lowered her head, slowly bobbing it in confirmation.

"Do you know when they were taken?" he asked.

She turned on him then, her eyes burning with defiance. "What difference does it make?"

He cocked his head. "It makes a significant difference if you are still involved with this man," Tom said, casually pointing to the photographs lying on the surface to her left. She pursed her lips, crossing her arms tightly across her midriff. "Are you?"

"Am I what?"

"Still involved with this man?"

For a moment their eyes locked. Tom didn't flinch,

focussing his gaze on her and waiting patiently for an answer. In the end, it was Natasha who glanced away, the tension in her shoulders dissipating as she exhaled.

"Yes… no, sort of."

"Please explain."

She shot him a dark look, but it was fleeting. Running her left hand through her hair, she looked at the ceiling. Tom guessed she was formulating a response, one that would put her in the best light possible.

"Look, I'm not here to judge. None of us are," he said, indicating Eric and Kerry. "We just need to understand where this man fits into your life and, more importantly, Henry's."

She shook her head. "You don't understand… what it's like to live with a man such as Henry. He's so driven, so wedded to his determination that he doesn't leave a lot of energy in the tank for anything else in his life; not me, Olivia… or anything that he hasn't decided is a priority."

"That sounds like a lonely life," Kerry said, "both for him and for you."

Natasha fixed Kerry with a stern look. It was very difficult to read what she might be thinking. She inclined her head by way of agreement, but didn't comment, turning her attention back to Tom.

"I know it will sound shallow… but after a few years you get tired of going to bed alone… of being alone." Her eyes watered and she delicately touched the inner corner of her eyes with her forefingers. Sniffing hard, she looked away, blinking furiously. "I know I shouldn't have, but… I get to be happy too, right? I mean, I don't have to live my life alone just because he's not interested, do I?"

Tom thought about marriage vows, respecting the sanctity of the union, but at the same time people needed to feel loved, to feel wanted and it was often the case that if one partner felt routinely ignored or was emotionally or physically absent from the relationship, then one or both straying was quite possible. In fact, amongst his own peer group, it was common. Not that he could personally relate to it. He'd always been one to remain committed, and should a relationship be failing, then it was on both people to seek a resolution. Once one, or both, moved beyond the relationship in search of solace, comfort or a solution, then trust was lost and the relationship was often doomed to failure. It may take a month, a year or longer, but things changed and could never be the same.

"Like I said, I'm not here to judge."

The response was not one Natasha cared for and she glared at him.

"I couldn't stay married to a robot! Not without…"

"Not without?" Tom asked.

She sighed. "Not without…" she hesitated, searching for the right words "… something more."

Tom nodded. "And who is this man?"

Natasha hesitated, chewing her lower lip. Tom forced her to make eye contact.

"Who is he, Natasha?"

"Mark. Mark Stannard," she whispered, taking a deep breath as if she hadn't been able to breathe until she'd spoken his name. "He works at Henry's golf club."

Tom glanced at Eric who was making notes. The detective constable confirmed he'd noted it. Tom looked at Kerry and she left the kitchen, reaching for her mobile phone in her pocket. He turned back to Natasha just as she wiped a tear from her eye.

"What does Mark do at the golf club?"

She sniffed hard. She was agitated, her hands and legs moving with nervous energy as she met his eye.

"He's a professional golfer, but offers coaching to members

on a one-to-one basis, when he's not on the circuit."

"How did you meet?"

She shrugged. "One night, at some do or another."

"At the golf club?" Tom asked and she nodded. "I see. And how long have you been seeing one another?"

She was staring at her feet now.

"Natasha, how long?"

"Four, maybe five months..." she shook her head, lifting her eyes to meet Tom's. "On and off."

Tom thought about his next question. They would look into Stannard and see if he was known to the police already. That was what Kerry stepped out to do. Stannard could be looking to benefit from his lover's relationship with a wealthy man, perhaps he'd even been able to scope their house out during one of their trysts and broke in to rob it, finding Henry there. *Could Natasha have set her husband up, ensuring she was out of the house overnight with Olivia when it happened?* Natasha must have read his mind as she fixed him with a purposeful stare.

"If you think Mark had anything to do with this, then you're wrong."

"Is that right?"

"Yes, it is." She was stern, almost aggressive. "He's not the type."

"What type is he then?"

She shifted in her seat, looking awkward and uncomfortable all of a sudden.

"Mark is... caring. He's a decent man."

Tom found the thought of a decent man having a long-running extramarital affair with a woman to be quite the opposite of what he would regard as *decent,* but he really didn't like to judge. It wouldn't be something he would do, but then again, he'd been on the flip side of that experience himself. Could he always have said the same?

"And how did Mark view your relationship with your husband?"

Again, Natasha eyed Tom warily, seemingly gauging the intimation behind the question. Following a moment of silence, Tom pressed the question further.

"Did he object to you staying with your husband? Has he ever asked you to leave—"

"No!"

Her reaction surprised him. She seemed genuinely offended at the suggestion.

"Nothing like that, at all. I am married – was married – to Henry and he is Olivia's father. The notion that I would separate from him was never on the table, not with Mark, not with anyone."

"I see. Forgive me if this question seems inappropriate, but was your husband aware of your relationship with Mark Stannard?"

She shook her head, averting her eyes from his. "I was always careful. I would see Mark sporadically, when he was around and maybe if Henry was away. Sometimes I would see him a lot and then we'd go weeks without anything more than an exchange of text messages."

"Must have been hard to get together, particularly with a young child around."

Natasha nodded but didn't reply.

"That must have been very frustrating for you... and for Mark."

She laughed then, biting her lower lip and shaking her head.

"Is something amusing?" Tom asked.

"No, not really," she said as the accompanying smile faded. "If you knew Henry, then you would have a deeper understanding of what frustration is and what impact it has." She rolled her shoulders, and Tom realised how tense she must have been. "I know you'll find this hard to believe, bearing in mind my relationship with Mark, but I loved Henry very much for all that he was. Not the material things," she waved a hand around in the air to indicate the house and everything inside it, "although they are wonderful to have, but Henry was worth more than money and… things… to me. He was stable, strong and offered the security to me and my family that I had never had before." She looked to Tom's right, staring at nothing in particular. "He could also be incredibly warm, charming, loving… and passionate…" her gaze drifted back to Tom, her expression adopting a sadness in her eyes he hadn't seen before "… only not with me."

"Is it fair for me to read between those lines and ask you if you think Henry was also having an affair, either now or in the past?"

She wrinkled her nose before shaking her head almost imperceptibly. "I don't know. Maybe. I wouldn't be surprised; he's a man after all. Although, he's never been a particularly sexual man, if you know what I mean? For a girl like me, that was something of a blessing when we first met."

Tom tilted his head in query. She smiled – a warm smile – one that recognised the innocence in his expression.

"For a man to love me for something other than my body…" she said quietly, "was a new experience to me. It made me fall even harder for him." She sighed. "I've often wondered…"

"Wondered what?"

Taking a deep breath, she waved the question away. Her expression shifted, becoming guarded and shuttered.

"If you're looking for someone shady who might know something about all of this, why not ask Alex who the man was that Henry met in his office last week?"

"Alex Tilson, your husband's assistant?" Tom asked. She nodded. "Did Henry not meet people, clients, often in his office?"

"Yes, of course, but this one was different," she said, her eyes narrowing. "And he wasn't a client. I've seen people coming and going many times from Henry's office, but this guy, he was... he was confident, brash... different to the others. You get to see these people all the time and sometimes, you just have a sense that someone is... I don't know how else to describe it. I'm sorry."

"And what makes you think he might know what happened to your husband?"

"After he left, Henry was rattled." Natasha sat forward. "The way Henry looked at me... the way he walked into the house... it was as if he'd forgotten how to make his legs work. He was all over the place. I don't know what that man said to him, but Henry was thrown, and he was so rarely upset by his work. Not like that."

"Can you describe him to me, this man?"

She shrugged. "White... brown hair, forty-something, I'd guess. Average looking. But there was something about him; the way he strutted about. He had an edge to him. Believe me, I've known some characters over the years and this guy was one."

"Alex will know him, you think?" Tom said, glancing at Eric to ensure he was taking it all down. He was.

"Alex was there that day. Come to think about it, he looked just as rattled when this guy left too. I'm surprised he hasn't mentioned it." Natasha looked at Tom and Eric in turn. Reading their expressions, she half-smiled, rolling her tongue across the inside of her cheek. "And it doesn't look like he has mentioned it."

"What makes you say that?"

"Because Alex and Henry were as thick as thieves, always have been since Henry struck out on his own. If Alex hasn't mentioned it, then you can be sure there's a reason behind it, but don't expect a good one."

"And what of Alex himself? Do you get on with him?"

"Not really. Officious little shit, if you ask me."

Although taken aback, Tom didn't let it show. If this was Natasha's first response when asked about the man, then he figured her feelings were most likely even less complimentary.

"I take it the two of you don't get on particularly well then?"

She scoffed. "Yeah, you could say that. Sometimes I wonder if he thinks he's Henry's wife!" Tom encouraged her to say more with a nod. "He's always sticking his oar in on matters that are nothing to do with the office. I know he and Henry are close, they work together day in, day out, and I'm sure Henry probably told him a lot more than he ever told me – probably moaned about me no end – but even so... the man should know his place. Wouldn't you say?"

Tom didn't comment, but glanced towards Eric, who met Tom's eye whilst scribbling in his notebook.

"Can we just go back to this man who you said rattled your husband last week? Is there anything else you can tell us about him?"

Natasha's forehead creased as she thought hard. "Not about him, no, not really. He drove a van though. If that helps?"

"What type of van?"

"A black one... not a Transit or works-van sort of thing, but more like a camper. It had roof rails on it, blacked out windows. It was exceptionally clean, all glossy... as if he was out there every weekend cleaning and polishing it; you know, staying out of the wife's way type of thing? I watched him get in and drive off."

"Did you catch the number plate by any chance?"

She shook her head. "No, sorry. But it looked like new, as if he'd just driven it off the forecourt. Are you going to speak to Mark?"

"You can count on it," Tom said. "When did you last speak to him, in person or through messaging?"

Natasha was hesitant. After a moment, she took a deep breath, exhaling hard. "Saturday. After the party at our second home."

"The day of your husband's death. Where was this?"

"A hotel on the coast. I left Olivia with my mum and went to meet Mark."

"And how long did you stay with him?"

"A few hours."

"Can you be more specific?"

She sighed. "I met him around six o'clock... and we were together until eight-thirty... nine o'clock, maybe. No later than nine anyway. I had to get back to my mum's place to put Olivia to bed."

"Where did your mum think you were?"

She shrugged. "Just out. I had things to do. She's not the most observant at the best of times."

"One last question, Natasha, and forgive me if it sounds a little odd, but when were you and Henry last intimate with one another?"

If she was surprised by the question, she didn't show it. Her expression remained unchanged. She shook her head. "I really couldn't say... more likely months than weeks. Why do you ask?"

Tom smiled gently. "We're just forming a picture. It all helps, believe me."

CHAPTER FOURTEEN

TOM AND ERIC met Kerry outside, the constable was just putting her mobile away as they left the barn conversion. Natasha Crowe quickly closed the door on them, keen to end their visit as soon as possible. Kerry looked past them towards the front door, nodding in Natasha's direction.

"Did I miss anything?" she asked.

Tom and Eric exchanged a glance and Tom smiled. "Quite a bit, actually. What stood out for you, Eric?"

"For what it's worth, I think she was genuine... or at least credible with what she said. She didn't try to deflect the affair she was having, even admitted to seeing him on the night her husband was murdered."

It was a reasonable assessment, but Tom was a little more cynical. Perhaps his thoughts were clouded, no, not clouded, but maybe influenced by his experience. Natasha Crowe admitted to what was both impossible to deny, because of the photographic evidence, and easy to catch her lying about once they spoke to her lover which she knew they were sure to do. How genuine she was would be determined by whether they later found out something she'd intentionally neglected to tell them.

"And their relationship, the married couple, what do you make of that?"

Eric frowned. "It makes me wonder what her life was like prior to meeting Henry Crowe, that's for certain. I said they struck me as an odd couple before, and now... even more so." His expression softened momentarily.

"What is it, Eric?" Tom asked.

Eric looked back at the house. "Daft as it sounds, I really think she loved him."

"Even though she was cheating on him?" Kerry asked.

"Some marriages work in all manner of ways that many of us would think are strange," Tom said. "And it remains to be seen, but there's also the possibility that Henry was playing away himself. Henry and Natasha haven't been intimate for a while, so she wasn't having sex with him the night he died. So, if she's telling the truth, then he was involved with someone else, maybe in a relationship or just as a one-off."

Kerry made an O shape with her mouth.

Tom shrugged. "Although she didn't suspect him, Natasha did say she wouldn't be surprised—"

"Ah..." Kerry said. "Now that would alter the landscape. Any suggestion as to who with?"

"By all accounts," Eric said, "it's likely Alex Tilson will be the one to tell us, if Henry was playing away. They spent the most time together."

"I stepped out at the wrong time, didn't I?" Kerry said, disappointed.

"Speaking of which. Have you found Mark Stannard?"

"Yes, I have. Well, sort of," Kerry said, knitting her eyebrows. "The only address we have on file for him locally is in Heacham, on North Beach. That can't be his main residence though, can it?"

"The beach houses?" Tom asked. Kerry nodded. "They're not supposed to be occupied all year round... but that's only enforced if someone makes a complaint. I know a lot of people do it regardless of the rules."

"Maybe he counts non-occupational time while he's playing away," Eric said.

Kerry grinned. Eric looked at her and then belatedly realised the non-intentional double entendre.

"I meant while he's playing away at *golf tournaments*."

Tom shrugged. "Either, or. Whatever works for him, I guess." He glanced at his watch. "Tuesday daytime. What are the odds he'll be at home?"

"Worth a knock, isn't it?" Eric said.

"Kerry, has he come on our radar before?"

She shook her head. "Nope. There's nothing on the database related to him. I checked out his professional status while you were talking to Natasha. He seems pretty talented, I have to say. Not elite by any measure, but I reckon he's making a decent living on the circuit."

"Do you know golf?" Tom asked. "Personally, I haven't a clue from one end of the bat to the other."

Kerry smiled. "I have been known to spend time on the fairway. My father was a keen golfer and he never had sons, and so he had me practising my swing from the age of five."

"I never knew that, Kerry," Eric said.

"There's so much you don't know, Eric," she said. "*So* much."

NORTH AND SOUTH BEACH ran along the coast from Heacham to Hunstanton; a line of holiday homes set just behind the sea defences, protecting them from the worst ravages of flooding brought by coastal storm surges. The properties ranged from modern, brick-built chalet style houses down to static caravans; bolt holes for owners to head to for a weekend away when the weather was clement.

As Tom understood it, occupancy restrictions varied depending on when planning submissions were made, but none of the homes were supposed to be occupied all year round as a primary residence. The road itself petered out from tarmac to mud as they passed the holiday park, rows and rows of caravans that teemed with tourists every summer. From here on the patchwork constructions continued until they would eventually reach Hunstanton and yet another holiday park.

They didn't get that far; Kerry pointing to a building, or collection of buildings, with quite a ramshackle appearance.

"This is the one, I think."

The property was timber clad, painted black, although the colour had faded to a shade of charcoal, and the salty sea air had also ravaged it over time, the windows were wooden with peeling paint and, even viewing from this distance, in places the frames looked as if they were rotting away. Most of the residences nearby were raised on brick piers; an attempt to help them survive the worst-case scenario. Not this one. How it had remained intact after so many years, Tom could only guess. However, that could explain the incoherent appearance if some parts of the building had needed to be replaced or rebuilt over the years, which seemed likely.

A Volkswagen Golf was parked at the rear of the house. It was a couple of years old, clean and polished, in stark contrast to the property beyond it. Tom noted the stencilling on the driver's door highlighting Stannard's name along with a website address for golf coaching.

"We've definitely come to the right place," Tom said.

They approached the only door visible, its condition comparable to the rotting window frames. The interior was shrouded from view by thick net curtains hanging across every window as well as the glass of the door. They were stained yellow, faded by exposure to sunlight or cigarette smoke, it was impossible to say. The windows themselves were single glazed. This place was old. The thought struck Tom, once again, how anyone could live here all year round, permissions or not? It was doubtful that this place was particularly warm in the winter, and the winters in these parts could be brutal.

He raised his hand and knocked on the door frame. Eric stepped away to their right and looked down the side of the house. The waves were breaking against the concrete sea wall barely a stone's throw away. There was a stiff breeze coming in off the water, but the temperature was still clement. He knocked again, harder this time.

"Mark Stannard!" he called. Still, there was no answer.

"He's in," Eric said, standing ten feet away. "I just saw a curtain twitch."

Tom wagged a pointed finger, gesturing for Eric to walk around the building. Eric nodded and set off. Without needing instruction, Kerry Palmer moved around and down the left side while Tom hammered his fist on the door.

"Police, Mr Stannard!"

"He's running!" Eric shouted, his tone indicating he was already giving chase. Tom set off, rounding the corner and breaking into a run as he saw Eric scrambling up the steep earth bank of the sea defences in pursuit of a man in a navy tracksuit, presumably Mark Stannard. Eric angled his ascent towards the right, moving up with speed, whereas his target went straight up, giving Eric the advantage of cutting off his run should he choose that direction once he crested the slope and dropped onto the promenade beyond.

Tom reached the foot of the bank just as Stannard leaped to the path, heading to his right but he hesitated, spying Eric moving to intercept him. He stopped, spun on his heel, sea spray passing over him, and made off to Tom's left only to find Kerry Palmer in front of him issuing a command to stop. He glanced furtively at Tom and then over his shoulder at Eric, anxiously shifting his weight between his feet as he calculated his options, before deciding that Kerry was his best bet. He put his head down and ran at her; Tom was halfway up the slope with Eric closing in fast.

Kerry took a half-step backwards, turning side on to the advancing man, and for a moment Tom thought she was going to allow him to pass, but as Stannard ran past her she grasped his left arm, spun her body and used his momentum to flip him over her outstretched right leg. Stannard's surprised expression was fleeting as he hit the ground hard, a burst of air escaping his lungs along with a gasp of pain. By the time both Tom and Eric reached them, Kerry had him pinned to the ground and unable to move, an arm drawn up behind his back.

Tom dropped to his haunches, smiling at the stricken man. "Mr Stannard?" He took out his warrant card, breathing heavily from the exertion of the brief sprint. "DI Janssen, Norfolk Police. We'd like a word, unless you have somewhere quite pressing you need to be, what with rushing off like that in such a hurry?" He smiled at Kerry. "And even if you do, we'd still like a word. Going anywhere nice?"

Stannard grunted, meeting Tom's eye but his cheek was pressed into the concrete, Kerry's knee in the middle of his back. Tom indicated for her to relieve the pressure a little and she slowly stood off him, allowing him to breathe. Eric stepped forward and placed a firm hand on Stannard's shoulder as he got to his feet. Eric was red-faced and breathing hard. Stannard glared at Tom.

"What's all this about?"

"Now that's a question you could have asked by opening the door, isn't it?" Tom said, pointing at the dwarf wall behind them running the length of the bank.

Stannard sat down, grumbling as he did so. "I didn't know you were the police," he muttered.

"Of course, you didn't. A good citizen like you. Tell me, if you didn't know who I was, what were you running from?"

Stannard shrugged.

"I wasn't expecting anyone."

He was a slightly-built man, clearly agile by the way he'd made it up the bank along with his running style. He looked familiar but Tom was almost certain they'd never crossed paths before.

"And you always peg it when someone knocks on your door?"

Another shrug.

"I saw your silhouette… looked like a big guy, to be fair."

"Ah, I see. You thought I was someone's husband, right?"

"Yeah, something like that," Stannard said, turning his eye to the sea as a couple walking their dogs passed by, giving them an interested glance but trying not to appear as if they were eavesdropping. Tom waited until they were out of earshot.

"Presumably, you've heard about the death of Henry Crowe?"

Stannard looked at Tom, nodding. "Yeah. So what?"

Tom leaned in towards him, lowering his voice. "Because you know his wife, Natasha, don't you?"

Stannard leaned away from Tom, sucking air through his teeth.

"What if I do? No law against having friends, is there?" he said sarcastically.

Tom looked at Eric who reached into his jacket pocket and produced the copies of the photographs in a sealed plastic bag, handing them over to him. Tom tossed them into Stannard's lap. He looked down at them, momentarily hesitating before picking them up. The photo visible on the top was the one of Stannard and Natasha embracing as he left her.

Stannard sighed, closing his eyes.

"Friends?" Tom asked. "I have a lot of friends, but there's only one person in my life who I could say treats me like that, and we are more than friends."

Stannard handed the photos back without opening the bag. He put his palms against his face, dragging them down across his cheeks before placing them on his legs as he sat up straight.

"All right, yes. I've been involved with Natasha. Big deal. We're adults. What's it got to do with you?"

The question was asked with less hostility. The photographs made denial a ridiculous waste of time.

"You're in a relationship with Natasha—"

"Oh, come on!" Stannard said, throwing his head back and dismissively waving a hand in the air. "Relationship! What the hell has she been saying?"

"Well, put it in your own words, if you prefer?"

Stannard shook his head, nervously looking between the three detectives. "I've been sleeping with her. That's it. Fun times... no strings, you know?"

This was not strictly against Natasha's description of their relationship for she, too, made it clear she never had any intention of leaving her husband.

"A fling?" Kerry asked.

Stannard looked at her, anger in his eyes, although that was arguably more due to dented pride of her take down rather than from the question. "Of sorts, yes."

"How long have the two of you been involved?" Tom asked.

He shrugged. "Not sure. Here and there, you know how it is."

"A month, three... six... what?"

Stannard blew out his cheeks, then shook his head. "Six months, maybe a bit more but you lose track, don't you? Nice woman, Natasha. Fun to be with."

"And what about Henry Crowe? How did you get on with him?"

He screwed his face up. "Henry was all right. A bit wet, if you ask me."

"You knew him from the golf club?"

"Yes. Not that Henry spent much time on the course. I always had the impression he was there for the social climbing; being part of the club – the contacts – because that was what he was *supposed* to do, rather than having an interest in the golf itself."

"Did you cross paths with him?"

He shook his head. "Only at the occasional function, if I was invited but I'm pretty much considered as staff, so that didn't happen all that often."

"I was under the impression you were a professional player. Doesn't that grant you a level of kudos in the social hierarchy?"

Stannard chuckled. "Up to a point, yes. Certainly, amongst the wives, it has to be said."

Something about the cockiness of that particular answer irked Tom.

"Are you *friends* with many of the members' spouses, Mr

Stannard?"

His expression changed to a knowing half-smile, and he averted his eyes from Tom's scrutiny, sucking in a deep breath. "This is a small town, Inspector. A quiet one most of the year. There's not a lot to do to keep yourself occupied; social functions at the golf club, village fetes... charity fundraisers... it can all get a little dull, wouldn't you say?" He looked up at Tom, the smile creeping ever wider. He was proud of himself. "It's unsurprising really, that folks look to liven up their days with a bit of entertainment."

"Is that what you describe yourself as, entertainment?" Kerry asked.

Stannard looked at her, grinning now. "You should be so lucky," he said with a wink.

Kerry remained stoic, unflinching.

"So, are we likely to find any other angry husbands on the warpath seeking you out, Mr Stannard?"

He looked confused. "Who says Henry was angry with me?"

Tom cocked his head at the question. After all, Natasha stated clearly Henry was unaware of the affair. "What do you mean by that?"

Stannard shook his head. "Only that Henry didn't have an issue with me, that's all. I'm not convinced that he would, even if he realised I was sleeping with his wife, to be fair."

Tom fixed his eye on him, encouraging him to continue.

"Look... after all the times I saw them together at the club – which is how I met Natasha in the first place – I never got the impression he was all that into her. After all, if he was, why would she come to me?"

"Because you're so entertaining?" Kerry asked.

Stannard didn't appreciate her dry wit.

"Where do you see your relationship with Natasha heading?" Tom asked.

Stannard rolled his eyes. "There you go again with the whole *relationship* thing." He splayed his hands wide, raising his voice. "There isn't a relationship—"

"How about now?" Tom asked. "She's going to be a wealthy woman now that her husband is dead." Tom glanced towards Stannard's home, nodding at it. "Their barn conversion would be quite a step up from this place."

He was irritated, it was clear. "Yeah, maybe you're right. She'll be pretty lonely now, even more vulnerable. I should get stuck in before someone else does, right?"

"That take will certainly put you in the frame for his murder—"

"Hey! Hold on a minute, you never said anything about a murder!" He made to stand but Eric stepped forward and placed a firm hand on his shoulder, keeping him rooted to the wall. Stannard looked at Tom, open mouthed. "I wouldn't kill anyone, I swear. I mean... seriously... I wouldn't last in prison, not for a day, let alone years." He shook his head, fearful. "I've got nothing to do with all this. Nothing at all. I just banged his wife, that's all."

"That's all," Tom repeated.

"Yeah," Stannard said, glaring at him. "That's all."

"Where were you last Saturday night?"

He laughed. "With Natasha, which I'm sure you already know, otherwise you wouldn't be here."

"The whole night?"

"No, not the *whole night* but most of it. We ate, drank... played around, showered and left. Is that all right with the police? I mean, having fun isn't a crime yet, is it?"

"No, not yet," Tom said. "Murdering your lover's husband is frowned upon though—"

"I bloody told you," he said, raising a pointed finger at him, "I didn't—"

"What time did you leave Natasha on Saturday?"

He thought about it, shaking his head after a few seconds. "Eleven-thirty... maybe closer to midnight. Something like that."

"Between eleven and midnight?" Tom clarified.

"Yeah, I would say so."

"Did anyone see the two of you together?"

"No," he said, exaggerating the sound and shooting Tom a sarcastic look. "That's kind of the point of a clandestine fling, you know, that no one sees you together."

Tom nodded. "Of course. Well, I think that covers it for now."

"Great! So, I can go?"

"Yes, of course you can."

Stannard smiled.

"Apart from giving us a DNA sample, your fingerprints and documenting, on record, every word you just said, yes! And I do hope you are consistent, because the three of us have been paying attention. But that will be easy, I'm sure. After all, the truth is easy to remember, it's the lies we struggle to recall."

"Ah, man, come on," Stannard said exhaling hard.

"You can provide all of this voluntarily, of course," Tom said, "or we can arrest you and do it all anyway... and I'm sure the national media will have a field day with the golf pro bedding the murdered barrister's wife..." he glanced at Kerry and Eric "... and I'm sure the golf club will love to hear about it too—"

Stannard raised his hands. "I get it... resist and my life is ripped to shreds. Comply... and my life won't be ripped to shreds just yet, and hopefully you catch the killer before anyone finds out about me. Is that it? Did I sum it up well?"

"Come on." Tom placed a hand on his arm, forcibly helping him up whilst smiling. "You know, if and when the golf career fizzles out, you could have a bright future as an astrologer with the strength of those predictions."

CHAPTER FIFTEEN

TAMARA WAS WAITING for them as they entered the ops room. Tom said hello and Kerry crossed the room to her desk. Cassie was making notes on a white board, occasionally glancing down at her notebook, diligently writing up the details. She smiled at Tom but didn't speak.

"Where's Eric?" Tamara asked.

Just as she spoke, Eric hurried into the room, his mobile firmly pressed against his ear. He was on the phone with Becca, she could tell. Eric always lowered his voice when he was speaking to her, seemingly burying the mobile into his face almost as if he was trying not to be seen. Whereas, when he was on police business everyone could hear his voice carry throughout the room.

"I know, I know," Eric said, his eyes nervously glancing at her as he walked to his desk, each step taking longer as he slowed down. "I have to g—" he looked pained. "I... I have to go."

He hung up and hurriedly put the phone in his pocket, apologising to Tamara with a weak smile.

She smiled back. "Is everything okay, Eric?"

"Yeah, yeah… no problem," he said, slumping into his chair and spinning it to face the front of the room. She wasn't convinced, but she didn't press the issue.

Tamara looked around the room. Everyone was waiting expectantly for the afternoon briefing, all apart from Cassie who was still writing. Tamara drew a deep breath. "Right, Cassie's all but finished, so we'll make a start in the meantime." She looked at Tom. "How did it go with Natasha Crowe?"

"Very well," Tom said. "She was pretty candid around her extramarital relationship – with Mark Stannard – a local golfer who works freelance as a coach alongside playing professional tournaments. We had the evidence, so it was undeniable, but in my opinion, she didn't withhold or try to minimise it. In her view it was a convenience relationship; he satisfied the needs that Henry wasn't interested in doing."

"Sexual?"

"Looks that way. She was emphatic that being married to Henry wasn't an issue for her and she wasn't entertaining the notion of leaving him, for Stannard or anyone else."

"You believe her?" Tamara asked.

He shrugged. "Until she gives me reason not to, yes."

Cassie had finished up transcribing her notes onto the board and took her seat. "Why would she have need to kill him? I told you, she just has to wait it out. Bumping him off is a risky option, high reward but massive downside if she gets caught. Far simpler to play the long con."

Tamara raised her eyebrows. Cassie had a point. "But not everyone is as patient as you, Cassie. Some people want it all, and they want it now."

"Oh, I don't disagree. If it was me, I'd have done him in already."

"Good to know where your head's at, DS Knight," Tom

said. Cassie winked at him. "She pointed us to where we could find her lover. He made for an interesting chat." Tamara inclined her head, keen to hear more. "When we called at his house, he took off like a hare out the back." Tom gestured to Kerry. "Not that he got very far." Kerry blushed, twiddling nervously with the pen in her hand.

"Why did he run?" Tamara asked.

Tom shook his head. "He didn't give a satisfactory answer. He reckons we spooked him, but I identified myself as I was knocking. He bolted straightaway."

"He'd heard about Henry's death," Kerry said. "I mean, who hasn't? It is possible he thought we'd point the finger at him and panicked."

"Certainly, makes me question his innocence by legging it," Tom said. "After that, he was a little more open. He admitted to being with Natasha Crowe the night of Henry's death but there's a window of two to three hours where they disagree with each other. Stannard claims Natasha left him between eleven and twelve, whereas she said she was home around nine to read with her daughter, Olivia."

Tamara folded her arms across her chest. "Two to three hours is more than enough time to see to Henry Crowe. Does he have form, Stannard?"

Tom agreed. "Kerry ran the basics while we were with Natasha and didn't get a hit. It would be a big step to take, doing what was done to Henry as a first crime—"

"That we know of," Cassie said. Almost all eyes turned towards her, all apart from Eric's, who appeared lost in thought. "Just because we have no file on him, doesn't mean he's clean. He could have been at it all his life but just very proficient. Let's face it, we usually catch all the dumb ones." She raised a hand in apology to all those present. "Not that I'm casting aspersions on anyone in this room or their ability, but the thick ones do get caught, don't they? The professionals are a lot harder to catch."

Tamara had to concede that it was a fair point. "Okay, what have you done with Stannard?"

"He's downstairs," Tom said, "sitting in an interview room, ruminating on the questions we're going to ask him again in a little while, I should imagine. Let's take Cassie's point – very well made, by the way – on board and dig deeper into Stannard's background and make sure he's not hiding something from us." He looked at Kerry, silently delegating the task to her. She nodded, making a note. "Although he was open with us, I still have the feeling he was holding something back."

"What was it? Any idea?" Tamara asked.

"Call me crazy, if you like, but Stannard almost intimated that Henry knew about the affair. At least, that was how I read it. What did the two of you think?" Tom asked Kerry and Eric.

Tamara looked at Kerry and she nodded along, agreeing with Tom's assessment. Eric's head was down, his pen drifting across the page in his open notebook, more of a doodle than making notes.

"Eric?" Tamara asked. He didn't look up. "Eric!"

His head snapped up and he saw everyone looking at him. His lips parted slightly. "Sorry, what did you say?"

"Tom's assessment of Stannard, do you agree or disagree?"

"Um… I agree," Eric said, frowning as he looked at Tom. "I think."

Tamara was irritated but didn't show it. Eric was under a bit of personal pressure; it'd been obvious for a few weeks now. It was, perhaps, to be expected with their first child in the home. She could sympathise, even though she had none of her own.

"I pressed him on what he was saying and he offered up some guff about Henry never being bothered by him… no, irritated by his presence, as if that explained what he meant. I'm not buying it. There was another thing, though," Tom said, cupping his chin with one hand, looking thoughtful. "He never asked about the photographs, not once. Not who took them, how did we come by them… nothing at all. More than that, he didn't seem all that surprised to me when we put them in front of him."

"You think he was already aware of their existence?" she asked.

Tom agreed. "I wouldn't be surprised. It's quite possible. Natasha, on the other hand, was pole-axed when she saw them."

"Do you think she could have called Stannard in the time between you leaving hers and arriving at his place?"

"Possibly," Tom said. "But then, why run? He had time to prepare himself for the knock on the door."

"Maybe he wasn't lying," Tamara said, "and you did spook him."

"Maybe he's not very bright?" Kerry said, glancing at Cassie and smiling.

"Shouldn't be too hard to nail him then," Cassie said without looking up.

Tamara took a moment to gather her thoughts, casting an eye over the information boards.

"Dr Paxton sent over his pathology report this afternoon," she said. "Copies of it are on your desks, so please make sure you all familiarise yourself with his findings. He followed up with a courtesy call, and said you were going to speak with Henry's GP?"

Tom nodded. "Yes, Paxton goes way back with Henry's GP and he said we should speak to him."

Cassie chuckled. "Dr Death has a friend that isn't a cadaver? Wonders will never cease."

"He was very complimentary about you, too, Detective Sergeant—"

Cassie scoffed.

"No, genuinely," Tom said. "I think he quite likes you, but I'm not supposed to tell you."

"Ugh... as if my day couldn't get any worse!"

"Back to the GP, Tom, if you don't mind," Tamara said.

"Yes, of course. Henry's medical condition was deemed manageable; the doses of drugs he was prescribed were considered low, so nothing abnormal there. However, he did say Henry had confided in him that he was concerned by his sexual performance."

"In what way?"

"Dr Jenkins thought he was concerned about keeping up with his younger partner, stamina-wise, which was odd."

"There was quite an age gap between them—"

"Yes, but that's not what I meant," Tom said. "Natasha was looking outside of the marriage due to a lack of sexual contact, not because of poor stimulation. She actually stated she was happy in the marriage because Henry didn't seem to value her for her body. She went with Stannard to fulfil those needs of the relationship that Henry didn't want to."

Tamara found herself frowning. "So... what was the marriage like, do you think?"

Tom raised his eyebrows. "If I had to say, at this point, they appear to be more like very close friends, intimately involved in every way besides physical."

"Which is fine... if both parties are happy with that arrangement," Tamara said, thinking aloud. "And if they were, then it rules out a motive for Natasha to have killed her husband."

"Not the boyfriend though," Tom said.

"No," Eric said, looking up, "and, potentially, he had a lot to gain. Natasha would be vulnerable."

"True," Kerry said. "It's such a shame though, isn't it? Henry was looking for medical help to make his wife happier and she wasn't bothered by it. It's so sad."

Tamara noticed Cassie shaking her head, gently chewing on the end of her pen. "What is it, Cass?"

"Well…" she said, meeting Tamara's eye and then glancing around at the others, "has anyone actually considered what is probably really going on here?"

Tamara spread her hands wide. "Do enlighten us, Cassandra, please."

Cassie raised her eyebrows, lowering the pen away from her face, all but whispering, "Henry Crowe was gay."

Silence followed as the others exchanged glances.

"Think about it," Cassie said, "he's worried about his stamina, but the wife pretty much says they never have sex. She didn't say he was rubbish and that drove her to another man, did she?"

Tom shook his head.

"He's gay. That's the logical answer."

"Really?" Tamara asked. "I mean, we haven't heard anyone suggest it… and why would he keep it a secret in this day and age. There's much more freedom to be yourself these days—"

"Well," Cassie said, looking around the room, "speaking for *my people* as the only gay in this particular room, I have to say not everyone is as liberal-minded as you guys. People still live in secret, spend years hiding who and what they are and, often, that's a decision taken for good reason. The real question, if I'm right of course, becomes who was he trying to keep up with if it wasn't his wife?"

"And that might explain why he was so coy on the subject with his doctor," Tom said, frowning. "And it sheds a new light on Henry Crowe having had sexual intercourse on the night of his death."

Tamara exhaled, tilting her head thoughtfully to one side.

"Well, it's a theory." She had to acknowledge the possibility. "And one that would give us another suspect to be on the lookout for. Cassie, see if you can put some substance behind it."

"Will do, Boss."

"Tom, you were due to speak to Henry's former employers today. How did you get on?"

Tom shook his head. "Postponed until tomorrow. Speaking to Natasha and then her lover was more of a priority."

"Right. First thing?"

"Yes, absolutely. I'm meeting the senior partner at nine o'clock in the morning."

"Good," Tamara said, looking at Cassie. "Can you fill us all in on Henry Crowe's current case load, please?"

Cassie sat forward, notebook in hand. "Crowe was working on two cases at the time of his death. One was related to plans for a waste incinerator that the local planning committee initially rejected, but that decision was overturned on appeal by a ministerial ruling. An action group, represented by Crowe, brought a case against the government on environmental grounds. It was contentious, certainly," she shrugged, "but worth a man's life? I don't see how."

"And the other case?"

"Another action group looking into the allocation of lucrative government contracts," Cassie said, scanning her notes. "Crowe was seeking a judicial review over multiple contracts worth in excess of one hundred and forty million pounds over the last two years. The allegation is that these contracts were issued without following due process, without making them available to tender and, furthermore, outside the scrutiny of civil service procurement officials."

"And who benefited from those contracts?"

"Several companies, but I'm yet to understand how they are related to one another. Apparently, they are though. I need to speak to Alex Tilson to get a better understanding of them. There is a pattern though. It seems Crowe was looking into community issues, and going up against the big guns."

"A rebel *with* a cause," Tamara said. "All worthy of deeper investigation. Keep us posted. Kerry, what about former cases?"

"I've had a conversation with an archivist at the Crown Prosecution Service and they're putting together documentation going back four years. I'll be focussing on the most recent and working back as you asked though. Files should be here at some point tomorrow. I'll chase them if I haven't heard by midday."

"Good, don't let them stall you... feel free to be a pain in the arse, Kerry," Tamara said, spotting someone standing at the door into ops. It was Ken Abbott, arguably the most senior constable at the station. He leaned against the door jamb with one hand, supporting his ample frame, waiting patiently for a break in the briefing. Tamara acknowledged his arrival and several faces turned to look at him.

"Sorry to interrupt, Ma'am, but young Eric there," he said, pointing to him, "was asking about a report of a suspicious vehicle; a black camper van."

Eric's ears pricked up and he shifted in his seat.

"We've just had someone call in a report of an abandoned vehicle down at the Hunstanton Sailing Club. The index matches." He shrugged. "I thought you might want to know. A patrol car is going to swing by and take a look, but I thought you might be interested."

"Thanks, Ken." Tamara looked at Eric. "Do you want to swing by and take a look?"

Eric looked horrified, his mouth falling open, and his eyes darted to the clock on the wall. "I–I…"

His expression, as well as his lack of focus on the briefing, belied his thoughts. She chose to put him out of his misery.

"That's okay, Eric. I know you have a lot on. Maybe someone else can take a look."

"I'll go," Kerry said.

"And I'll come with you," Tom said, glancing at his watch. "The report of this camper van has me all curious."

"Great," Tamara said, looking across the room to Ken. "Can you ask the uniform patrol to hold off until Tom and Kerry get there?"

"Will do, Ma'am," Abbott said, smiling and retreating from view.

"Okay, that's it for now everyone. Lots to crack on with, but let's tie things off for today and start afresh first thing."

The group rose from their chairs, Kerry gathering her things together, seemingly keen to continue working. Tamara loved her enthusiasm but did wonder why she never seemed bothered about going home. The job could quite easily burn these personality types out fairly quickly if they weren't too careful. Mind you, that was her task to manage.

"Kerry," she called, and the constable hurried over to her. Tamara lowered her voice. "Don't try and take on too much, okay?"

Kerry Palmer grinned. "I won't."

Tamara wasn't reassured but gave the younger woman an encouraging wink. Eric was hovering nearby, stepping into the breach as soon as Kerry walked away. She smiled at Eric as she passed before quickly averting her eyes. Tamara noticed.

"What's on your mind, Eric?"

"I–I just wanted to apologise…"

"About what?"

Eric glanced around nervously, as if fearful of being overheard. "The briefing… the abandoned vehicle… it's just that Becca wants me home. George hasn't been sleeping well, and… Becca, well… she's not sleeping well. I need to—"

Tamara reached out and put a gentle hand on his shoulder.

"Eric, go home and see your family. There's nothing going on here tonight that can't wait until the morning."

Eric pursed his lips, nodded and walked away. Tom came to stand with Tamara, coat in hand.

"He's got a lot on his plate."

"Yes, but he'll manage," she said. "Keep—"

"An eye on him," Tom said. "Of course."

CHAPTER SIXTEEN

TOM JANSSEN TURNED off Cliff Parade onto the short stretch of road that weaved down to the North Promenade car park where the Hunstanton Sailing Club was located, right on the sea front. The car park was still half-full, despite the time of day. In the off season, the spaces were rarely taken up apart from on the weekends, but as the pop-up food vendors set themselves up for the tourist season, spending time on the promenade became far more popular.

The sailing club, more aimed towards paddle boards and kayaks than yachts, was set back from the car park at the base of the hill sloping up behind it. The hill that became the renowned Hunstanton Cliffs with their almost unique two-tone, red and white-striped rock layers.

Along the front of the sailing club were designated parking spaces for club members, a definite perk of membership, prime parking on the sea front. Outside the club were half a dozen small recreational boats that were covered in tarpaulins and looked as if they hadn't moved in months. Further along was a small wooden storage unit, racks of paddle boards and kayaks were stored inside for renting out to locals and tourists alike, when the weather permitted. Today, the sea was rough.

Low tide saw the beach uncovered but only the hardiest of windsurfers would have been out today in these conditions. There were days when the sea looked almost like a polished surface, calm and serene. On these occasions the club would have people milling around but as it was, Tom looked up at the clubhouse to see three or four people looking on from the raised deck of the first floor.

The liveried patrol car was parked alongside the black camper van and the constables got out as Tom pulled up alongside. They greeted him and smiled at Kerry, usually one of their uniformed colleagues, and pointed to the van.

"We've had a look, but it's all locked up," PC Hutchison said. He indicated the onlookers in the clubhouse. "Apparently, it's been parked here all day, but no one's come or gone."

Tom noted the parking ticket stuck to the windscreen. Vehicles without a valid permit were quickly fined in such a prominent location. He walked over to the van, Kerry a half-step behind. It was less than two years old, judging by the number plate. The windows were all blacked out, aside from the windscreen and front seat door windows. A curtain was drawn across behind the front seats, obscuring a better view of the interior. A few people walked by them on the promenade, a jogger running past at the same time. Everyone was curious as to what the police were up to.

"Is it locked?" Tom asked. Both constables indicated they didn't know, and Tom tried the handle of the driver's door. It was locked. Something along the body of the van caught his eye and he stepped back; the reflected light from the sun, slowly dropping in the sky, was distorted by something on the paintwork around the handle of the side door. Tom leaned in to inspect it, pointing it out to Kerry. It was a smear, dark, and therefore difficult to see against the backdrop of ebony paint-work. Had it not been for the sheen of the polished surface, he probably would have missed it.

"Is that what I think it is?" Kerry asked.

Tom nodded. "I think so." It looked like dried blood in and around the handle of the door. He looked at PC Hutchison. "May I borrow your ASP?"

The constable took the weapon from his utility belt, passing it to him. The driver's door was probably the most used, so Tom moved to the nearside of the vehicle and extended the metal baton. With one hand shielding his face he struck the pane of glass. It didn't break at the first attempt, but the second saw it shatter. He then used the end of the baton to clear the glass away. Collapsing the ASP, he handed it back to the constable and donned a pair of nitrile gloves before reaching in to unlock the door.

A whiff of stale, putrid air drifted across him as the opening of the door sucked air out of the vehicle. He covered his nose and mouth.

"Oh God… what is that smell?" Kerry asked, standing off to Tom's right, covering her own mouth and nose.

Tom knew what it was.

He was thankful that they weren't already in peak summer and that the high point of the day saw a temperature no higher than twenty degrees, otherwise the smell would be a lot worse. Checking the interior for signs of blood or other evidence that he might inadvertently contaminate, he found none. A key fob lay in a cubby hole above the glove box and Tom picked it up. He tentatively reached to his left and drew back the curtain screening the main body of the camper. His heart sank. The scene stirred something within him, and he recoiled from it, hurriedly getting out of the van.

Stepping away he put the back of his hand up against his

mouth as he paced in a small circle a few steps away from the camper.

"Sir... w–what is it?" Kerry asked, watching him, concerned.

He closed his eyes, taking a deep breath to steady himself. He didn't answer her, slowly shaking his head, he examined the fob in his hand. He unlocked the rest of the van, the indicators flashing. Gesturing towards the side door, he had Kerry join him. He carefully opened the door, the panel sliding back effortlessly.

Shafts of sunlight illuminated both the interior of the converted van and the body of a man slumped on a bench seat, his head hanging forward. His clothes were wet-through with blood, a pale shirt, once sky blue, now stained a deep shade of spreading crimson which also marked the trousers and had run through to the carpeted floor. The handle of a knife protruded from the chest, left of centre, and Tom guessed it must have either pierced the heart or come awfully close to it. Death would have been a nailed-on certainty within minutes, if not seconds, of it penetrating the body.

"Better put in a call to forensics," Tom said quietly. "Have them come down here as quickly as they can." He looked at the two waiting uniformed constables. "Can the two of you set up a perimeter? No one comes within fifty feet of this van."

"I'll request the FME comes down as well," Kerry said, taking out her mobile.

Tom nodded, turning his attention back to the interior. He closed his eyes momentarily, whispering a silent curse, before re-examining the scene. He was struck once again, as he always was in cases like this, at how the expression on the faces of the dead portrays the emotions felt in the final moments of life. This man died contorted in agony. He stared into the face, wondering what could possibly have brought him to such a brutal end.

Pete Chard's lifeless eyes stared back at him.

FIONA WILLIAMS, the on-call forensic medical examiner, backed out of the van. Sheeting had been erected around the vehicle so that no one could oversee the police operation and the members of the sailing club gathered on the raised decking, having swollen in numbers following the discovery of the body, had also been ushered inside. Holding up the thermometer, used to pierce the victim's liver, to the light, she squinted as she read it, calculating the likely time of death from the body temperature.

"Well, it was warm today and he's been baking inside that oven which throws the scale off a little," she said, looking up at Tom. She must have read the emotion in his expression, shielded though it was as best as he could, because she appeared apologetic. "I would estimate time of death was sometime last night, no later than midnight I should imagine."

Tom pursed his lips, nodding his thanks.

"Cause of death will likely be quite obvious, too, I should imagine. I think the blade will have pierced the heart and, even if it hasn't, it will certainly have severed blood flow. Death would have been within a few minutes."

Tom put thumb and forefinger to his eyes, turning away from the scene behind the doctor. "Thanks for coming out so quickly, Fiona."

She smiled, cast a quick glance Kerry's way, almost as if she knew something was wrong but she didn't say anything further. She looked at both of them in turn, said goodbye, and departed. Tamara Greave came over to join them, clutching her mobile phone in her hand.

"I've just briefed the chief super," she said, putting the mobile in her pocket. "He's concerned about our lack of progress."

"Well, tell him to feel free to come down here and show us how it's done, if he thinks he can do better," Tom said, staring at the van. Kerry looked awkwardly at Tamara who silently gestured at her with a slight flick of her head and Kerry gratefully accepted the instruction, stepping away from them. Tom held a hand up in apology. "I'm sorry—"

"It's okay, Tom. You were friends. Were you close?"

He took a deep breath. "Very close... once." He shook his head. "But that seems like a long time ago." He didn't take his eyes off the forensics technicians who were now busying themselves processing the murder scene. "You know, he was at our place last night. We all had dinner together. He was quite the hit with Saffy... and now..." he met Tamara's eye, "... I've no idea who was in my home anymore, no idea at all."

"Did he say why he was here?"

"Up with the family, staying with his mother-in-law who's been ill recently." Tom shrugged. "At least, that's what he said."

"You're not so sure?"

"How does he get himself killed if he's here for that? And if he is working an operation, where's his back-up? He's experienced enough to know if he's getting himself into a sticky situation and you'd never go in alone. It's just not done. As far as I know, Cara's mum lives over towards Cromer." He shook his head. "Pete had no business being an hour away on this part of the coast. It doesn't make any sense."

"What time did he leave yours last night?"

"Half past nine… a quarter to ten, maybe. Time was flying —" a thought flashed into his head.

Tamara noticed. "What is it, Tom?"

"I'm such an idiot," he said. "I didn't pick up on it at the time."

"On what?"

"Last night, I offered Pete a lift home, but he said he'd pre-booked a taxi. I pressed it, you know, thinking it would give us more time to catch up. I didn't mind the drive, but he said he'd already arranged the pick-up with the same driver who'd dropped him off before I got home."

"Yes, so what?"

"That's just it, he said Cara dropped him off at ours… he probably had his bloody van parked around the corner… and didn't want me to see it."

"You think he knew we would be looking for it… maybe even for him?"

Tom shrugged.

"Presuming it was Pete, then he was spoken to by uniform a few days back and he gave them a fake name or a carefully curated identification that would likely pass a basic check. He'd be more than capable of fashioning one of those. Either way, he would know he was on our radar after that visit."

"*Could* he have been working undercover?" Tamara asked. "It might explain a lot."

He shook his head, anger displacing the sadness. "I guess it's possible, but I can't shake the thought that he was playing me somehow… he *had* to be playing me."

"Regarding the Crowe case or something else?"

"There isn't anything else… not at our end, and he did ask—"

"What did you say?"

Tom could hear the nervousness in her tone.

"Nothing at all. He's an old friend, but I'm not daft. Besides, he only asked once, and it was casual. Earlier in the day he said he'd seen me on the TV, so the interest could have been innocent."

"What could his interest be, do you think?" Tamara asked. "As far as I know there isn't a Met operation going on around here."

"Not that they'd tell us if they were working this way, I can assure you. We're backward, rural folk remember?"

"Right, I'm going to make some calls... and if I don't get a satisfactory answer then I'll take it higher. If someone's running a covert op on my patch, I'm going to bloody well find out about it," Tamara said. She looked at the van, camera flashes illuminating the area as darkness rapidly approached. "Do you want me to notify the next of kin?"

Tom drew breath, bringing himself upright and nodding. "I'll be waiting for Cara – Pete's wife – when she gets here. I'd appreciate it if you can pass that along."

"If you're sure you're not too close to it?"

He smiled weakly. "She'll need to see a friendly face... I'll be all right."

"Okay, if you're sure."

Tamara reached out and touched his hand. Tom silently thanked her before she moved away. The waves were thundering against the sea wall again now, spray cast into the air and carrying on the breeze.

Walking back to the van, Tom was careful not to obstruct the technicians diligently going about their tasks. He hovered in the background, watching. The shock of the discovery was slowly subsiding, and he was now looking at details he'd not seen earlier. The interior was largely undisturbed. That is to say there didn't appear to have been a fight in such a confined space. Whoever had driven the knife into Pete, they had been able to get close enough to do so without a scuffle. He looked at Pete's hands, hanging by his sides, noticing the lack of defensive wounds on them, the lack of abrasions on the knuckles. Pete was a big man, powerful and easily capable of handling himself in a scrap. Had Pete come here for a prearranged meeting and, therefore, did he know his assailant? Did he feel comfortable enough to drop his guard, perceiving the lack of threat to his personal safety?

Dropping to his haunches, he examined the sole of Pete's right boot. It looked like there was sand in the treads. Stepping back, Tom looked past the van through a gap in the entrance flaps to the tent, eyeing the sea wall beyond. Water was breaching the top of the wall as well as the sealed flood barriers, depositing saltwater and sand on the promenade. The sand in the treads of his shoes meant it unlikely Pete had been in his van the whole time he was here. It would be worth pulling the CCTV footage from any nearby cameras to see if they picked up him walking along the promenade and, with a bit of luck, who he was meeting.

They were in a secluded part of the sea front though. Once past the sailing club there were steep steps up to Cliff Parade and a bowling green, the path continuing along the cliff top from there. Most pedestrian traffic was found further along the promenade, around the old pier and the route past the leisure centre towards the funfair. It was still worth a shot though.

A technician eased Tom aside, walking past him with a folded body bag and it was at this point Tom turned away, removing himself from the tent and taking in a lungful of fresh sea air. The lights strung along the promenade, rocking back and forth on the breeze, lit up the path wrapping around the sea front. The lights of the town above illuminated the clouds in stark contrast with the inky blackness out at sea. Odd flashes of light punctured the gloom on the horizon as passing ships headed north along the coast.

He looked back at the tent; the image of his friend fresh in the forefront of his mind.

"How did it come to this, Pete?" he asked himself quietly.

CHAPTER SEVENTEEN

THE HALLWAY LIGHT WAS ON, and Russell trotted out to greet Tom as he closed the front door as quietly as he could. He needn't have worried because Alice was waiting in the kitchen for him. She threw her arms around him, and only then did he realise how tense he was as she hugged him tightly. Withdrawing a fraction, she kept one hand around his waist, leaning back to view his face, cupping his cheek with her right hand.

"Are you okay?"

She was concerned, her expression a mixture of worry and compassion. He smiled weakly.

"It's not been the best of days," he said, gently placing his hand over hers as she lowered it from his face.

"Have you eaten? I could make you something—"

"No, no. Thank you," he said, leaving her grip and crossing to the dining table.

"I'm so sorry, Tom. Do you know what happened yet?"

Tom pulled out a chair for Alice and seated himself on the next. They sat down and Tom rested his elbows on the table, putting his hands together, one fist balled, the other encompassing it and touching them to his mouth as he slowly shook his head.

"Somebody stabbed him…"

"Dear God!"

He looked sideways at her, biting his bottom lip. "He was into something, but right now I don't know what."

"Did he say anything to you about it, last night, when he was here?"

"As far as I know, he was here with the family." He rubbed at tired eyes with thumb and forefinger. Alice reached out and gripped his forearm. "I don't even know if that was true."

His mobile rang. Glancing at the clock, it was midnight, but he took it out of his pocket. It was Tamara.

"Hey, Tom, how are you doing?"

"Yeah, all good." He dispensed with the pleasantries. "What did you find out?"

"Well," Tamara sounded hesitant, "I think you'd better brace yourself."

He took a breath, his eyes moving to Alice beside him. She was waiting patiently, obviously unable to hear the conversation.

"Detective Sergeant Peter Chard left the Metropolitan Police Service over a year ago—"

"What?"

"I finished up speaking with his former chief superintendent a few minutes ago. He confirmed it. Pete quit the Met in the middle of an internal investigation into the misuse of police information."

"What kind of information?"

"I don't know, Tom." Tamara was evidently pained delivering such news. "The general consensus is that he jumped before he was pushed… or worse."

Tom took a moment to let the information sink in, his worst

fears confirmed. Was anything Pete told him true, or was it all a charade to manipulate him for some reason? He lowered his head, running his free hand through his hair. Alice must have sensed how bad it was because she placed a gentle hand on his lower back, stroking him slowly.

"Okay. So, what was he doing now? Do we know?"

"I asked... but no one knows—"

"No one knows or is unwilling to say?" Tom asked, reacting to her hesitancy.

"That was my thinking, too. He knew more than he was letting on, but there was no way he was going to tell me. I'll have the chief super call him tomorrow. Perhaps he'll be more open with an equivalent rank."

"I wouldn't bet on it," Tom mumbled.

"Did forensics give you anything useful to work with from inside the van?"

"Maybe," Tom said, sitting upright. Alice removed her hand, placing both hands before her on the table. Tom met her eye and forced a smile. She returned it. "It looks as if someone has been living out of the camper van... which, to me, points to a surveillance op. For now, I'll assume it was Pete and that he offered up a false ID to uniform when they spoke to him. It would be a good idea to find out who had the word with him and see if they were paying enough attention to recognise him again after the fact. I should have run the number plate as well, see if it matches the VIN number, just in case."

"You can have Eric or Kerry check that in the morning," Tamara said.

"I will. Scenes of crime didn't find a laptop or mobile phone before I left. The camper was set up with enough tech to run a mobile office. The cabling is all there but no hardware."

"The killer probably stripped it."

"But left the murder weapon… looks amateurish to me. Thinking fast, operating in haste."

"Good. Then they will have made a mistake," Tamara said. "Speaking of the weapon. Is the knife anything exotic?"

"No. Looks like a standard carving knife, judging from the handle and the depth of the blade at the hilt. My guess it's been brought with them, straight out of someone's kitchen. Like I said, amateur. We really need to know what he was doing up here."

"Yes, I was getting to that," Tamara said, pausing and seemingly choosing her words carefully. "Pete's next of kin has been informed… His wife is travelling up from London as we speak."

"What, tonight?"

"Yes, and she knows you are investigating, as you asked me to convey to her, and… she wants to meet you when she arrives."

"And you want me to find out from her what he was doing here… if she knows?"

"Yes. If she knows. This is a difficult one for you, I appreciate that—"

"I can do that."

"Are you sure, because I can always—"

"I'll handle it!" His response was rather too curt, he realised almost immediately and softened his tone. "I'm sorry. I can manage it."

"If you're sure."

"I'm sure."

They agreed to meet before everyone else arrived the next morning, Tamara reluctantly ending the call at Tom's insistence. She was looking out for him. She cared. He got that, but he was already growing increasingly irritated with people worrying about him. He *could* handle this situation.

He tossed the mobile onto the table, Russell, lying in his bed beside the French doors, dropped his head between his paws. He looked up at Alice. She was nervous too. Maybe he wasn't coping with it as well as he thought.

"I'm fine," he said. She cocked her head slightly. He smiled. "All right, I'm not fine, but I'll—"

"Manage! Yes, I got that... and I'm fairly sure Tamara did too."

He sighed, smiling and shaking his head. "I need to work on my delivery, don't I?"

She patted the back of his hand. "It's only because we care so much about you, Tom." She rose from her seat. "Can I gather from your conversation that you'll be heading out again tonight?"

He sighed. "Yes, I'm afraid so. I'm sorry."

She smiled, opening the fridge and peering inside. "In which case I'm making you a sandwich." He made to protest but she cut him off. "No arguments. You have to eat, and I know you won't unless I make you. Feel free to take it with you, but I insist you eat it, and I will check later."

His brow creased and he smiled. "How will you know that I don't throw it away once I'm at the station?"

With one hand holding the fridge door open, she shot him a withering look. "You forgot the bundle of trouble currently sleeping upstairs. I can read a face that has disposed of a nutritious lunch, subsequently claiming to have eaten it, just by looking at one. I *will* know, Tom Janssen."

He laughed. It was the lightest moment he'd had all day.

CHAPTER EIGHTEEN

TOM WALKED out of the police station, scanning the small car park. Only a handful of unmarked cars were present; those officers working the night shift. He heard a car door open and looked to his left, seeing Cara Chard getting out of a red Audi hatchback. She closed the door, then stood still, looking at him across the short distance between them.

He waited, feeling awkward. She did, too, he could tell. Drawing her coat about her, night time was still cool despite summer's rapid approach. They set off at the same time, meeting in the middle. No words were necessary, Cara falling into the comfort of his embrace. She started to cry, a slow release that grew into a sob as she pressed into him. He held her tightly. There was little else he could do.

The moment passed and she withdrew but remained holding onto the lapels of his jacket.

"How have you been, Tom?" Her eyes were red, sore. How she'd made the drive out from London in this state, he could only imagine.

"I'm well," he said, forcing a smile and tilting his head. "Under the circumstances."

She tugged gently on his lapels, smiling at him. "You look well! You really do."

She released her grip on his jacket, flattening the fabric with the palm of her hand. Her make-up had run, and she sniffed hard, touching the back of her right hand to her eyes.

"I must look a mess."

He smiled reassuringly. "You look great..." He grimaced internally. *That was a stupid thing to say.* The thing was it was true. Aside from being visibly upset, she looked very well. Cara had always been the one to dress with style, almost without ever trying; akin to a fashion icon who always seemed to hit the right mark, no matter the occasion. She was also one of the kindest souls he'd ever known.

She laughed, recognising his discomfort. "I know what you mean. Thank you," she said, stepping back and casting an eye up and down him. "Norfolk clearly suits you, Detective Inspector... much better than London."

He nodded. "Yes, I think it does. It was a good move for me."

Her smile faded. There was an elephant present in the room and both were skirting around it.

"You didn't need to come up tonight, Cara. This could have waited until the morning."

She shook her head. "No. I wouldn't have got any sleep anyway... and then I'd have had to negotiate London traffic."

"Fair enough," he said, looking towards the station. "Come inside. I'll sort you out with a cup of tea or something."

"Something stronger would be nice," she said, turning to walk with him back to the entrance.

"Tea is the best I can do, although the milk in the staff room is probably off, so you might get a kick from that!"

"You always did know how to show the ladies a fun time."

He laughed. "Now, I'd say you've already been on the sauce if you think that."

Once inside the station, the two of them sat down in the staff canteen. Apart from the custody sergeant stopping by to raid the vending machine for a coffee and a packet of crisps, they were undisturbed. They were on the first floor, they could see the sea through the window, or the all-encompassing darkness at any rate. Cara cupped her mug with both hands, holding it as if it was her salvation, sitting hunched forward, knees pressed together.

"Do you know what Pete was doing in Norfolk?" Tom asked.

She stared straight ahead, a vacant expression on her face. Then she shook her head.

"I had no idea he was up here." She sipped at her brew. "We haven't spoken in weeks."

He was surprised by that. Not that he should be. After all, he couldn't trust anything his friend had said to him.

"How's your mum?"

She looked at him, clearly surprised. "Good days and bad. How did you know she was unwell?"

"I saw Pete… this past Monday. He came over to mine for dinner. He mentioned it."

She nodded knowingly. "Did he say how utterly hopeless he was in helping me deal with it all, too?"

Tom looked away but didn't comment, sipping at his own tea.

"Yeah, thought not," she said, shaking her head.

"Yes, Pete was never the most empathic person, was he?"

"You can say that again."

"How was the relationship between the two of you, if you don't mind me asking?"

"No, not at all." She put her cup down, interlocking her

fingers. "There wasn't a relationship anymore, not really. Not since we split."

"When was this?"

She fixed him with a stare. "And I can see by the look on your face that he didn't mention that either."

Tom shook his head.

"What did the two of you talk about?"

Tom chuckled, feeling a tad embarrassed by how easily Pete had managed to pass off the facade of his life in their company. "We talked but looking back he was quite evasive."

She smiled. "He wouldn't want you to look down on him—"

"I would never—"

She reached out a hand and placed it on his knee, apologetically. "No, that's not what I meant. Pete looked up to you like no one else. He thought you were the best detective he'd ever worked with or for." Tom flushed. "I mean it. He said it often enough." She shook her head. "Things in the unit turned sour after you left."

Tom felt suddenly self-conscious. She clearly noticed.

"I'm sorry. I didn't mean to bring up bad memories."

"That's okay. I don't think about those times much, not anymore. I probably should, to process it properly, but I've moved on… and there's little point."

He saw her look to his left hand, and he followed her gaze.

"I see you're not wearing a wedding ring, so you've not rebounded into another relationship."

He smiled, Alice coming to mind. "Oh, I have but we're not there yet."

"Good for you," she said, smiling. "Don't wait too long. Not if you want to have children. You don't want to be one of those parents who barely lives to see their children graduate high school."

"Hey! I'm not that old."

She waved away his defiant response. "Look at me, been here five seconds and telling you how to live your life when mine is largely a skip fire."

"Is it that bad?" he asked, feeling for her.

"No, I'm exaggerating… probably," she said, leaning in towards him. The lightness of their conversation had masked her frailties and now, small talk completed, a veil of sadness passed over her expression. Absently tapping her fingertips together, she took a deep breath. "So… what happened to him? What happened to Pete?"

"I was hoping you could help me with that?"

She scoffed, bewildered. "I don't see how." She sat upright. "We separated eighteen months ago, a few months before he was kicked off the force. Pete has become more and more distant ever since."

"I thought he quit?"

"For fear of being summarily dismissed, if not prosecuted."

"Why? What did he do?"

"Hah! And you think Pete was ever going to give me a straight answer? Not that I didn't push, I did, frequently. And I got several answers, all of them contradictory and all of them a tissue of lies."

Tom shook his head. "Pete would sail close to the wind sometimes, but he was a decent copper—"

"When he was managed by someone with capable hands, Tom. Someone like you, but when left to his own devices, he became a menace. That man has so many self-destructive patterns, you wouldn't believe."

She ran a hand through her hair, then drew both palms across her face. Tiredness was seeping in.

"During the investigation, Pete's behaviour started to slip. He became aggressive – not violent with me or the kids – but openly belligerent. It didn't make him friends at work and those he did have started to withdraw from him." She shook her head. "It was as if they could all see what was coming and didn't want to be burned as he went up in flames."

Tom rubbed at his chin, listening to every word and trying to tie it in to the man he knew.

"In the end, it all got too much and for all our sakes, not least Jack and Summer, I had to make a break."

"How did he take it?"

She angled her head to one side. "Not well. His drinking increased. He started turning up at the house, half-cut most of the time, at all hours of the day and night demanding to see me, the kids... the damn cat one time." She laughed but without genuine humour. "Obviously, things got more stressful as he wasn't working, but he did start up on his own."

"Doing what?"

If an experienced police officer set up on their own, there was usually only one use for their particular set of skills, but he didn't want to lead her.

"Training... to begin with."

That wasn't the answer he'd been expecting. "What sort?"

"He told me it was management coaching, team building workshops... that sort of thing. But then I spoke to Kim one evening. You remember Kim?"

Tom nodded that he did.

"Well, I bumped into her at the supermarket of all places, and we got chatting. There was a bit of angst and controversy around Pete's new enterprise."

"Really, why?"

"Word had got back to some of them in the unit that what he was doing wasn't quite as clean as he'd told me," she said, taking a deep breath. "He'd been running training workshops, but Kim said they were counter-surveillance courses."

"Ah... bloody hell, Pete," Tom said, putting his head in his hands, not quite believing what he was hearing and yet, at the same time, he realised it was entirely plausible.

"Yes," she said, nodding furiously. "That's exactly what Kim thought, too."

Counter-surveillance techniques were seldom required by anyone who was operating within the law. Police, the intelligence services or the military carried out such training in house without the need for external contractors. The only people outside of these services who might benefit from such training would be celebrities and their bodyguards, who needed to be aware of malicious stalkers or hostage-takers, and criminals. There were no shortages of the latter in and around London.

"I spoke to Pete about what Kim had said. He was angry... and I mean *really* angry." She sighed. "But I never heard word of those courses again. The support money started to dry up around the same time too. That's not a shock, right?"

"Did you hear any more from Kim or from anyone else in the unit after that?"

She shook her head. "No. I remember thinking it was weird that I bumped into her when I did. I remember she lived over in Waltham Cross at the time, so it was some way off her patch." She shrugged. "I guess she could have moved. I lost touch with the others after we split and then Pete left the job anyway, so I didn't really know what anyone was up to after that."

Tom thought the chance meeting was almost certainly engineered; an opportunity to advise a former colleague – a friend – that their activities were under scrutiny without exposing the fact you'd done so.

"And what did he do after that? You said you'd spoken a few weeks ago."

"Yes, we did. We'd gone months without contact, speaking through solicitors. I'd wanted to try counselling, you know, try to find a way out of the mess we'd got ourselves into. I still cared for him, even if he was driving me nuts. But Pete wouldn't have it at the time. He was never one for *head doctors*. Not that I was suggesting any such thing."

"And recently?"

"The last we spoke, he was different. He sounded different, upbeat. He called out of the blue, apologised and said he'd cleaned up his act. He was back working, sorting himself out. He had a favour to do and then he was coming back. He wanted to meet, to discuss our future, if we still had one."

"A favour? Doing what?"

She shook her head. "I don't know, but he was earning and said he had something big on the go and that it would solve everything. I'd heard it all before, of course, but he sounded credible, as if he really meant it this time." She smiled, locking eyes with Tom. "He said he had a few weeks of work to do and then he'd be back. He wanted to try the counselling, make a fist of it, and he said he'd sort out the money he owed me and the children. I thought he must be drunk, but he wasn't. For the first time in months, I was positive about the future. I really felt he wanted to make a change."

"And he didn't say what he was working on?"

"No, I'm sorry. Do you think… that it might be why all of this has happened?"

Tom raised his eyebrows. "I'll be honest with you, right now I've no idea." He leaned into her and took both her hands in his, staring into her eyes. "But I'll tell you this, I'm going to find out. One way or another, I will get to the bottom of it."

CHAPTER NINETEEN

TAMARA GREAVE RAPPED her knuckles on the door to Tom's office. He looked up, bleary-eyed but still alert. She frowned at him.

"You look dreadful," she said, entering.

"Good morning to you too!"

"Here, I brought you coffee." She set down a takeaway cup on his desk.

He recognised the logo; it was from his favourite haunt.

"Thanks."

"How did it go last night with Chard's wife?"

He picked up the cup, removing the lid and testing the heat of the drink. It was hot but drinkable.

"She arrived late," he said, sipping the brew. "We talked for a while, here at the station, before I found her some digs."

"Where is she staying?"

"One of Alice's colleagues, a doctor on the ward has a holiday let in Old Hunstanton. She knew it was free, someone dropped out last minute, and so she sorted it for me."

"Could she shed any light on what her husband was up to?"

He rocked his head from side to side. "Not exactly. It seems as if he set himself up as a consultant of sorts, running training courses..." He hesitated "... possibly for the other team. Until he was warned off doing it."

Tom decided to leave out Kim Streeting's name for the time being. He wanted to call her first to see just what she was doing warning him off through Cara. Glancing at the clock, he figured he'd try her on the mobile number he had for her from his time working alongside her. In the main, people tended to keep the same number even if they switched phones.

"Well," Tamara said, "it looks like he's branched out into private investigative work."

"Yes, seems so."

Suddenly, Tom felt dog-tired, the lack of meaningful sleep catching up on him. He'd made it home in the early hours only to find Saffy asleep in his bed alongside Alice. The spare bed in the guest room wasn't made up and he didn't want to risk waking either of them by rummaging through the linen cupboard, instead choosing to crash out in Saffy's room. He managed a couple of hours of fitful sleep, but the sky had been lightening as he slid under the duvet, his mind ruminating on the events of the previous day.

"I think it's a priority to find out who he has been working for and how long he's been in and around our patch."

"Agreed. I'll put Eric on it this morning."

"Good. Was... Cara, is it?" Tom nodded. "Was she helpful at all?"

"Oh yes, of course... speaking to Pete's state of mind if nothing else. They split around the time of his leaving the force and he lost himself for a time, by all accounts. But recently, she said he'd picked up his game and was sounding more positive and looking to reconcile." He shrugged. "I don't know what brought that about, but he was earning again and confident about the future."

"Preliminary report from the scenes of crime team?"

"Yes, but I'm not sure how helpful it is. Any usable finger-prints appear to belong to Pete and, as I noticed yesterday, there's no sign of a struggle inside the van. Trace DNA will likely be hard to come by, but I'm still hopeful we'll catch a break there."

"Right. All the tech was stripped from the van?"

"Yes, whoever took it only left the cabling... and no prints were found on the connection points. The killer may have been wearing gloves or put them on for the clear up. They haven't left us much to go on, besides the murder weapon."

"A nondescript carving knife," Tamara said, raising her eyebrows. "Part of a set?"

"Most likely. If we can find a suspect, perhaps they'll be missing one from the block." He exhaled heavily. "That's a long shot though."

"And we need to find a suspect first—"

Kerry Palmer had approached the office, loitering outside, evidently unsure of whether to interrupt. Tom beckoned her in.

"I've been looking into Henry Crowe's case files and found something interesting."

Tamara glanced between them. "I have to brief the chief super, so I'll leave you to it. Fill me in later?"

"Will do." Tom offered Kerry a seat opposite him, and she took it, leafing through her notebook as she sat down.

"Now, it's not a recent case and I know I was to start now and work backwards, but I came across this from early last year and it got me thinking."

"Go on," Tom said, picking up his drink.

"A Freedom of Information request was made to the CPS

archives related to a case from a decade ago. It was a robbery case, in north London, that escalated into a murder trial, four men eventually being sent down. The home owner was severely beaten during the incident."

Tom thought about it. "Okay... and how does Henry Crowe fit into this? Was he prosecuting or defending?"

"He wasn't the lead barrister, but his practice was assigned the case for the prosecution, securing four convictions. The defendants were given sentences totalling forty-two years. The defence team moved to have the charges reduced to aggravated assault, arguing on the grounds that the three men who robbed the premises did not intend to kill the occupant and his death was purely related to his own prior health condition and did not occur as a result of the assault."

"I take it the person didn't die at the time?"

Kerry nodded. "That's right. He died two weeks later in hospital of a cardiac event, whilst undergoing treatment for the beating he received on the night of the robbery. The defence team argued that his death was not their clients' fault. As it turned out, the jury accepted there was no intention to kill, but agreed with the prosecution's case that they were culpable. They were all convicted."

"You said four but only three men carried out the attack."

"Convictions of all four were made under 'joint enterprise', so the driver of the car – who was waiting for them outside – was also convicted."

"I see, and what was the reason behind the FOI request? A miscarriage of justice?"

Kerry shook her head. "No, all four were bang to rights. There was no hint of impropriety there. No, a request was made for all documentation related to the prosecution team: communication records, prison visits, investigative services... everything."

"Aren't they all a matter of public record and disclosed to the defence at the time?"

"Yes, that's how it's supposed to work but this is the issue. It wasn't the defence team who made the request, it was submitted by a solicitor in Holt. As far as I can see, they were not involved in the case at all, either now or back then when it was at trial."

"And their interest was what?"

"I'm afraid I don't know, not yet. I didn't know whether it was something to explore." Kerry looked disappointed. "Should I have gone straight to—"

"No, no, you did right by bringing it to me first."

"What made you zero in on that case, Kerry?"

She flushed. "Sorry, I can't take credit for that. It was the clerk gathering the material for me who mentioned it. She said Henry Crowe was proving popular because I was the second person asking about cases relating to him; hence the solicitors in Holt.

"And they were asking specifically about Henry Crowe and not this particular case?"

"Yes, absolutely."

"Who was the lead in the prosecution team in that case?"

She checked her notes. "Cormac Daley... QC," she added quickly. "He is a—"

"Senior partner at Quercus. The very man I am meeting with later this morning." He put his coffee down, pointing casually at her. "And you're coming with me."

"It's a terrible business, isn't it? I couldn't believe the news when I heard." Cormac Daley QC leaned forward over his large, ornate hardwood desk, resting his elbows on the surface and forming a steeple with his fingers. His Northern Irish accent was lighter than Tom often found with others he'd met from the country, and he wondered if this was a result of softening it for the role of an orator in crown court. "Just awful. What was the motivation for doing such a thing? I'll never understand."

Tom nodded, aware that the full details of the murder scene were not public, and he had no intention of changing that. "Yes. The investigation is ongoing."

Daley met Tom's eye and he had the feeling the barrister was gauging him, but for what purpose, he didn't know.

"Terrible," Daley repeated, laying his hands flat. "Now, what can I do to help, Inspector? I'm afraid we don't work with Henry anymore, not since he left the practice."

"Yes, regarding that," Tom said, "how did that come about?"

"Henry was working with us here for many years and, much as you find in the great partnerships over the years – Lennon and McCartney, the Gallagher brothers and indeed, Tom and Jerry – you exhaust your commitment to one another and need to move on." He shrugged, smiling. "However, I considered Henry a long-term personal friend, and indeed a close confidant. That didn't change after he left."

"So, you would describe his departure as amicable?"

"Of course, yes. Why would it be any other way?"

"As I understand it, successful barristers usually remain where they are, particularly if they have a certain level of status within the profession."

Daley sat back, inclining his head. "There is that, yes. But you have to understand, Inspector, as much as we have a passion for the law, after all that is why we are drawn to the profession in the first place, we are also a commercial enterprise. I know money is cited as the root of most, if not all, evil but it is the nature of the beast. Henry adopted a more *holistic* ideology in recent years and that didn't quite... fit with our ethos."

"We have been looking into his current work," Tom said, glancing sideways at Kerry who was making notes. "Are you saying he was less about the money than you are?"

Daley laughed but it was at best artificial and, at worst, forced.

"That's a brutal way of phrasing it, Inspector. I'd prefer *less commercially viable*. You see, the way the legal framework has been hollowed out in the last decade – since the onset of austerity – it has become increasingly difficult to make a decent living."

Tom glanced around the office, failing to see the effects of austerity in this room or in the building they'd just walked through.

"To erode that further by accepting cases the likes of which Henry was keen to take on... well, it would be professional suicide." He held up his hands in supplication. "Forgive me, Inspector Janssen, but I, Cormac Daley, am in business to make money. I don't seek fame, personal or professional kudos... but I do want to live well."

"Henry didn't seem to be doing too badly."

He laughed. "No, certainly not. You see, if you ask most people, they would tell you that to be successful in this field you need to chase the big clients, pull the media spotlight onto you but, and here's the thing, if you want to make money, you do less of that. You have a medium-sized business, pick up the work that pays the best which I can assure you will not be the big cases. Rates you can charge for court appearances, expenses and what you can bill the taxpayer are so low now that you don't want the lengthy cases that run for months and months! They cost you a fortune." He shook his head. "No, in and out. Those are the ones you want. A good analogy would be developing property; will you make more from working on one or two projects a year or turning over half a dozen?"

"Henry disagreed?"

"That he did, yes. Henry Crowe was a man so rare on this earth."

"In what regard"

"In the regard that he had *enough*." Daley drummed his fingers on the desk. "He was willing to dedicate his time and energy to other things. I applaud him, I really do."

It didn't sound like it to Tom. He found himself wondering if Daley was more convincing when he was at The Old Bailey. He'd have to be.

"Henry's assistant went with him from here, did he not? Alex Tilson?"

Daley looked thoughtfully up at the ceiling momentarily, his lips parting.

"Ah, yes... Alex. I must admit I'd forgotten that, but then again, Henry was rather absent-minded at times. He would always need someone to pick up after him."

"Tell me, I'd like to pick your brains about a case you worked on with Henry some time ago..." he said, looking at Kerry.

She nodded, looking at her notes.

"The press nicknamed it the trial of *The Hampstead Four?*" she said calmly.

There was a flicker of surprise in Daley's expression, and then he nodded casually. Too casually in Tom's mind.

"Yes, of course I do. That was one of those big cases I was telling you about. Back before our earnings were so well constrained," he said, aiming the comment at Tom. "What would you like to know?"

"What are your recollections of it?" Tom asked.

He drew breath, his brow furrowing. "I would refer to it as the classic open and shut case, Inspector. Four young men cruising an upmarket area in search of somewhere to burgle. They chose a particular address and broke in. The occupant was inclined to fight back and, unfortunately, suffered injuries leading to his death."

"But you went for a murder conviction?"

"Oh yes. We had to set an example, otherwise it would be open season on the upmarket areas of London. In the end, the jury plumped for a manslaughter conviction, but we made our case. There isn't much more to say. The intruders were really quite inept; leaving fingerprints and DNA all over the place. It was amateur hour. It must have been one of the easiest cases for your colleagues, Inspector Janssen."

"Was there any controversy surrounding your legal team?" Tom asked. "Either at the time or subsequently?"

"Why ever would you ask?"

"If you could answer the question, please."

Daley exhaled through his nose, looking a little irritated. "No. Not that I am aware of, but I'm sure the defence team would argue differently." He grinned, lifting his entire expression. "After all, if you lose a high-profile case, it's always on someone else. I dare say it is the same with you, isn't it?"

Tom smiled. "For some it is, yes."

"But not for you, Inspector?"

There was a gleam in Daley's eyes, as if there was more behind the question.

"I always make my cases stick, Mr Daley," he said, as measured a response as he could deliver.

Daley nodded slowly, pursing his lips. "Then you are a credit to your profession!" he said, slapping a hand on the desk.

"One more question, before we leave, Mr Daley," Tom said.

"Presumably you often have the need to employ investigative services?"

"In most cases, yes. Certainly, in trial cases where we represent the defendant or when bringing a civil case against a company or organisation."

"And do you have a preferred person, or business, to go to?" Tom asked.

Daley nodded. "I do, yes."

"And who might that be?"

Daley fixed Tom with his gaze, then he smiled. "We use several different service providers, Inspector, depending on the requirements of the case. I should imagine it is a lot like your own investigations. Should you require surveillance it can require the use of multiple people, perhaps several teams. In those cases, the investigators will band together, perhaps subcontracted under one business. If I need to serve papers, then it will be different. Only one person will be needed. Is there anyone in particular you have in mind and, if so, why?"

Now it was Tom who smiled. Daley had neatly skirted answering the questions. Barristers were so good with words.

"Thank you for your time, Mr Daley."

"No trouble at all, Inspector. Any time."

They left his office and were escorted from the building by Daley's personal assistant, a lady who said very little beyond basic pleasantries. Tom felt distinctly unfulfilled by the meeting. Once out in the street, among the throng of midday traffic buzzing around Norwich city centre, and heading back to the car, Tom glanced sideways at Kerry.

"I want to know what the solicitors in Holt were looking for with that Freedom of Information request."

"They might not tell us," she countered. "They're under no obligation to."

"That's as maybe, but he flinched when you said the name. Whatever it is, he was thrown."

"I agree, but he shook it off quickly enough."

Tom laughed. "Barristers have to be prepared, have their schtick ready to go, but at the same time they have to be able to think on their feet. He can blow it off as much as he likes, but there's something there. I can almost smell it."

CHAPTER TWENTY

THEY WERE APPROACHING Brancaster Staithe and Tom knew they were getting close, slowing the car as he scanned the upcoming buildings. The report filed by the uniformed officers cited an address in *The Close*; a small road this side of the village just off the A149 with a mix of semi-detached and terraced houses built in the 1960s.

"There!" Eric said, pointing at an upcoming junction on their right.

Tom turned off the main road and straight into a small parking area, coming to a stop.

"Which house was the call made from?"

Eric checked his notes before looking up. "That one, over there." He pointed to an end of terrace. They climbed out and Eric looked across the road. On the opposite side was another small road servicing what appeared to be a selection of properties converted from a barn. The end building had a set of steps up to the entrance, wooden, with white painted handrails. "And I think... yes, I'm sure, the camper van was parked over there underneath that oak tree."

Tom followed Eric's gaze and saw the mature tree overhanging the parking area, or turning circle, it wasn't clear which. The transmitter tower, the one sparking the terrorism protocols was sited just beyond the tree in a small compound. He looked back at the house. He was quite sure he saw a curtain twitch. This was confirmed as soon as they walked towards the house, some fifty feet away, the front door opened, and a lady stood there waiting to greet them. There were no driveways to any of the houses, just long concrete paths leading to the front doors; a sign of when the houses were constructed, at a time when most residents didn't have cars.

Tom had called ahead, and she was expecting their visit. They were earlier than he'd anticipated, getting through with Henry Crowe's previous employers much sooner than expected, and weren't due here for another hour.

She'd been waiting. It was not a surprise that she'd been the one to call the police regarding a suspicious-looking vehicle.

"Mrs Sampher?" Tom asked as they approached.

"Yes," she nodded, smiling warmly. "Please call me June."

Tom greeted her with a smile of his own. "Thank you for agreeing to see us. I'm Detective Inspector Janssen," he indicated Eric, "and this is DC Collet."

"A detective inspector, how exciting," she said, beaming as she examined both of them.

He took her measure. She was in her early eighties, he guessed, fastidiously presented but in a measured and perhaps understated way. She wore a warm smile on her face, one that looked suited to her, as if this was her default manner.

"Is this about that dodgy character I called you about last week?"

"Yes, it is," Tom said, looking past her into the house. "May we speak inside?"

"Of course. I'll make a pot of tea and I have some home-made coffee and walnut cake, if you'd like?"

Eric's eyes lit up and Tom wondered if he'd been banned from cake as well in this recent health drive Becca was pushing on him. The front door to the neighbouring house in the terrace opened just as June was turning back to lead them into the house. She stopped and leaned out, waiting for the occupant to show themselves. He duly did, glancing sideways at the three of them standing on the front path.

"This is the police, Les!" June called and the man stopped, offering the two of them a curious glance. He shot her an inquisitive look and she grinned. "You remember that black van that was parked up, here and there, every day for a week. They're here about it." She nodded excitedly and he tried his best to seem interested but evidently, he wanted to get on with his day. He was quite scruffy, wearing paint-spattered work trousers and an old shirt. Tom guessed he was a painter and decorator.

"Ah right," he managed to say, smiling at his neighbour. "They'll get to the bottom of it."

He nodded to Tom, trying to keep his momentum going, as if to stop would see him stuck there for ages and he wasn't bothered. Tom pictured the scene indoors, teacups and saucers ready on a tray, freshly-baked cake on a serving plate; she was someone who liked the company of others and paid a great deal of attention to what was going on around her. For the police, people like her were welcome because they saw things that might otherwise go unnoticed.

Everyone has neighbours like June Sampher at some point in their lives, pleasant, helpful and by all accounts wonderful in many ways, but he wouldn't be surprised to find she lived alone, was potentially divorced or widowed with grown-up children who'd long since moved away. The day-to-day feeling of being necessary replaced by looking out of the window. These days, he wondered if she found herself a little lonely. If Tom was right, then to be collared by her for a chat, you'd struggle to get away.

June Sampher ushered them inside. The house had a sweet smell hanging in the air and it took a moment or two for him to figure out what it was: furniture polish. The inside of the little house was as well presented as their host. There was no clutter to see, and every surface was clean and clear. She took considerable pride in her home, it was obvious. She led them into the front sitting room and Tom saw the view she had across the road to where the camper van had been seen.

Looking around, there were a number of family photographs on the walls. Some of them were portrait shots, the ones arranged at a studio with a husband standing behind his wife, hands on her shoulders with young children either sitting on their mother's lap or on the floor by their feet. The colours were faded and the clothing they wore must have been fashionable in the late seventies, lots of pastel, browns and beige. June, returning from the adjoining kitchen having turned on the kettle, noticed Tom's eye lingering on one picture in particular.

"That's my late husband, Derek," she said wistfully. "With the children as well." She nodded at the picture. "We were quite a dishy couple back in the day, I'll have you know."

Tom smiled. "When did you lose him, if you don't mind my asking?"

"No, not at all." She dismissed his question with a flick of her hand. "Eighteen years ago, now. Heart attack." She sighed. "He worked too hard. I always said that." She wagged a pointed finger at them both. "Learn from his mistakes, both of you. Make time to live because life is gone in a flash."

Eric exchanged a glance with Tom and looked past their

host towards the kitchen. June touched him on the arm. "Perhaps you could carry the tea in here for me, young man? My old arthritic fingers struggle with the weight these days."

"Er… yes, I can do," Eric said.

"Good boy. Just fill the pot when the kettle boils and everything else is already set out on the tray."

"You needn't have gone to any trouble," Tom said.

"Oh, now you're starting to sound like young Les, next door!" She rolled her eyes, pretending to swipe her hand across his face from distance. "Be off with you, *trouble* indeed."

Tom smiled. *Young Les* was pushing sixty, if he hadn't already crossed that particular threshold.

"Now, do sit down, Inspector," she said, steering him to one of the armchairs.

He wondered if they would ever be allowed to leave. She took a seat opposite him on the other side of what looked like the original four-panel radiant gas fire, with metal bars across the front and heating controls mounted on top of the wooden surround. It still looked like new. Eric shuffled gingerly into the room bearing a tray with cups, plates and a teapot, slowly placing it down on a coffee table. As soon as he set it down, June was out of her seat assembling the cups and saucers.

Tom thought they'd better get on with it or they'd be there for the remainder of the day.

"Mrs Sampher—"

"June!" she corrected.

"June. What can you tell us about the day you called us regarding the black van?"

"Oooh… let me think," she said, her brow creasing as she thought about it. "I'd seen it the previous day as well, only in a different place, so it had definitely moved."

Tom glanced out of the window from his seated position

and he could still see the spot beneath the oak tree. She raised her eyebrows, fixing Tom with a stare.

"People come and go around here, pass through, but you don't see the same vehicle parked up day after day. Not unless it's one of us who lives here."

"You said it was parked here for a couple of days. Is that suspicious?"

"Four days," she said pointedly, "and only two were consecutive."

"That's one heck of a memory you have there," Tom said, accepting a cup and saucer, the spoon rattling as he took it in hand.

"I made a note," she said, hurriedly pouring a cup for Eric and handing it to him. "Do help yourself to sugar."

Tom declined but Eric, who must have been starved of anything sweet, shovelled two large helpings into his cup. June got up and crossed the room to a sideboard in the dining area at the rear of the house. She took a pad out of the top drawer and returned, leafing through the pages. Tom could see there was handwriting on each page.

"Now, where were we... last week," she said quietly as she found the right page. "Here... it arrived on the Sunday, sometime before eleven in the morning and stayed in place until after I went to bed." She frowned, flipping to the next page. "Then it was back on Monday evening – but parked in a new place – and didn't budge again until mid-morning on Tuesday."

"You... make a note of everyone who comes and goes?" Tom asked, trying hard not to convey how weird a hobby he found that to be. Glancing at Eric, the detective constable had an odd look on his face, staring into his tea, perhaps considering what might be in it. Evidently, Eric thought the woman a little strange as well.

"Of course. You can't be too careful these days, can you? I know how stretched you boys are and you can't be everywhere, can you? The community has to do their bit, don't we?"

He tilted his head in polite agreement.

"Oh," she said, looking between them. "I forgot the cake!"

"No need," Eric said hurriedly, placing a hand on his stomach. "I'm on a diet anyway."

Tom declined as well and June looked disappointed, casting an eye over Eric.

"Dieting at your age. You're a growing boy."

"You sound like my mum," Eric said, smiling. Then he flushed red and looked away. Tom smiled internally at Eric's mild embarrassment.

"June," Tom said, garnering her attention, "do you keep track of everything that moves around here?"

"If I'm home… and up and about, then yes. Is that bad?" She sounded nervous.

Tom shook his head. "No, not at all. We could certainly use the information you have recorded. What do you write down, may I see?"

She passed him her pad. It was a printed *To do* notepad, but one turned over to document vehicles, number plates, antisocial behaviour and he even found a couple of notes made against dog walkers who failed to pick up after their animals' mess, and an excessive hedge encroaching on the public footpath, asterisked for reporting to the local council. He couldn't find any reference to the driver of the van though.

He raised his gaze from the pad. "Did you by any chance see who was driving the van or did anyone approach it at any point?"

"No, not at all. I saw it arrive and park under the oak tree. It must have been late Wednesday or maybe Thursday – it will be in my pad – but no one got out. I watched and waited. I even had the lights out so they wouldn't see, but no one appeared." She raised a finger, wagging at Tom. "And that was when I stopped being suspicious and got a little scared."

"Scared?" Eric asked. "Why?"

"Well," she said, absently fingering her low-hanging necklace, "you hear about people stalking all the time, don't you? Or maybe it was a burglar waiting for nightfall to break in. You just don't know these days."

"Fair enough," Tom said. "And so, you called us?"

"That's right. Not that you took it seriously." She held up a hand in apology. "Well, not you, but your colleagues. They didn't come for hours, and the van left before they got here. They missed it by a matter of minutes."

Tom and Eric exchanged a glance. "That was fortunate for the driver, wasn't it?" Tom said.

"Yes, if they'd only come ten minutes earlier, then they would have found him."

"Yes, unlucky for us, lucky for him," Tom said, holding up her pad. "May I borrow this for a few days? I'll make sure you get it back."

"Erm…" She looked momentarily concerned, but reluctantly acquiesced. "I–I suppose that would be all right, yes."

"Thank you," Tom said, smiling warmly.

They made their way outside, their host lingering on the doorstep and asking Eric if he wanted to take a slice of cake with him. He declined and fell into step alongside Tom.

"She's a bit… off the wall, isn't she?" Eric said, looking over his shoulder.

"It takes all sorts, my mum used to say."

"Mine says people like that are *mad as a brush*."

Tom laughed. "Yes, that too."

"I dread to think what might have been in that cake!"

"She's just a lonely woman who needs a bit of company, that's all. I'm sure there was nothing wrong with the cake."

"But you didn't eat it either, did you?" Eric said, raising his eyebrows.

"No, no I didn't."

Tom looked past Eric to see June Sampher's neighbour loading kit into a Transit van. He tapped Eric on the shoulder, changing their course to speak to him. He spied them coming but carried on loading his things as they approached.

"If I was you," he said, without looking at them, "I'd take whatever she says with a pinch of salt. She's nice enough—" He lifted an old wooden trestle into the back of his unmarked van with a grunt of effort before turning to face them, "—but she's also a mad old bat!"

"She pays attention though."

"Aye, she does that," he said. "She pays too much attention sometimes, sticking her oar in where it's neither wanted nor needed much of the time." He sat down on the tailgate of his van. It was old, dented and looked to be on its last legs. Tom guessed he was a handy man now, doing all sorts judging by the variety of equipment in the back of the van behind him. "Don't get me wrong, she's all right. She never used to be this bad, but after her old man died—"

"Derek," Tom said.

"Yep, Derek, she went a bit loopy after that. Her kids got annoyed by her interference and they ended up moving away. They still visit, mind. It's not like she's all on her own. And I look out for her, if she needs anything like, you know?" He sighed. "I promised my missus I would keep an eye on her, and I do."

"And this black van—"

"The converted VW Transporter?"

"You know your vehicles," Tom said.

He grinned. "Used to have an old VW camper… you know, the proper ones, back in the day? We'd go all over, me, the wife and the little man." He smiled at the memories, then shook his head. "Very different propositions now though, aren't they? That one had solar panels on the roof. What on earth do you need those for?"

"Keeps you connected," Tom said. "You can't be too detached from the world these days."

Les scoffed. "I thought that was the whole point of camping, getting away from it all and being one with nature. Nah! Not for me."

"You weren't suspicious of the van?"

He shrugged. "Why would I be?" He looked around them. "That van alone would cost more than anything you could steal from around here. June… bless her… can make a mountain out of a molehill. You know she complained about my Christmas decorations one year; too gaudy. I mean, it's Christmas… decorations are supposed to be over the top! No, people can get on with their lives and it's none of my business. Or hers, come to think of it." He fixed Tom with a curious look. "Why, what's going on?"

"Just routine."

"*Just routine.* Is that right?" He shook his head. "Nothing is ever routine when you lot get involved." He eyed Tom and then Eric. "You're plain clothes. That means CID. You must be at least a sergeant," he said, looking at Tom. "And you… a detective constable," he said to Eric. "Routine, my arse." He hoisted himself up and off the tailgate of his Transit, bracing himself with one hand on the door. "If CID are investigating, then it's not routine. Do I have to worry about something? Does June?"

Tom read the concern in his expression and shook his head.

"No, there's nothing for you to worry about. It's an active inquiry, but this visit was routine, I assure you."

He fixed Tom with a shuttered look, then smiled and nodded, resuming the reorganisation of his tools. "Happy days then. In which case, I'll crack on then. I'm refitting the cafe overlooking the slipway in Sheringham and the owner's giving me stick to get it done. If you don't mind?"

"No, not at all. Thank you for your time, Les…"

He met Tom's eye, smiling. "Bassham, Les Bassham." He gestured to Eric. "That's a *double S*, son."

Eric smiled awkwardly, revealing the pocketbook in his hand that he'd been subtly holding as they talked. He made a note of the spelling.

"Have a good day, Mr Bassham," Tom said, leading them back to the car.

Once out of earshot, Tom glanced at Eric. "I want you to dig into every address within sight of where Pete was parked up: names, records, backgrounds… employment status. Everything you can find."

Eric casually surveyed the area as they approached the car.

"That's probably fifteen or so properties… unless he was watching the main through-road for someone passing on the 149."

"Unlikely," Tom said. "Not if he was sitting there for the better part of several days." He also looked around, standing beside the driver's door now. "I'll bet some of these cottages are holiday lets; being this close to the coastal path. It'd be worth checking bookings and seeing if anyone interesting crops up." He looked across the car roof at Eric. "Pete was watching or waiting for someone."

"Yeah," Eric said, nodding. "Only maybe they saw him."

CHAPTER TWENTY-ONE

THE HIGH STREET in Holt was as busy as ever. The little Georgian market town, with its narrow streets and independent shops, was thriving. Tom pulled into a parking space in front of a butcher's shop and carefully got out, making sure not to catch his door on the car parked alongside. Kerry pointed a small building out to him on the other side of the road.

"That'll be the solicitors there," she said. Tom followed her indication and eyed a blue door, set between a small ladies clothing store and a flower shop. The solicitor's name and logo were mounted on the wall of the first floor.

"Great. You pop over and make them aware we want to speak to them. I just have to make a quick call first."

She nodded and crossed the road in between passing vehicles, hurrying to the narrow pavement opposite. There was a queue tailing out from the butcher and Tom headed further into Market Place, seeking a bit of space from prying ears. The sun broke through the white clouds casting a ray of light on the cenotaph as Tom dialled the number. The call connected but wasn't answered and he began to wonder if he should leave a voicemail or not, but then a familiar voice answered, all official and dead pan.

"Hello, DI Streeting."

"Hey Kim, it's Tom." He tried to keep his tone light. "It's been a while."

"Tom…

"Janssen—"

"Yes, I know," she said, sounding flustered. "You just… threw me there for a second." There were voices nearby in the background. "This is a surprise! I mean… welcome, but still a surprise."

"I know, it's been too long. Congratulations on the promotion. How's…where are you now?"

"Machynlleth," she said chuckling. "Less of the bright lights and the big city, but the same old, same old. How have you been Tom?"

"I'm well, Kim, really well. Listen, I'd love to have a proper catch-up, but—"

"Ah, here it is," she said, chiding him ever so slightly. "I knew it would be too much to expect a call from an old friend out of the blue without a catch."

Tom laughed. "Yeah, I'm still not one for small talk, but I'm working something and… there's no easy way to tell you this, so I'll be blunt… Pete's been killed."

"Pete?" she asked. He confirmed it. "How?"

Tom waited until a couple walked by him. They were elderly and taking great care on the narrow pavement and Tom stepped into the road to make room for them both. They thanked him and he acknowledged their gratitude with a quick smile.

"He was found stabbed to death yesterday… out here on the coast."

"My God! What in the hell happened?"

"That's what I'm working on now. I saw Cara last night—"

"Oh... how's she doing?"

"Been better, but she told me about the warning you gave Pete through her—"

"Hang on a second, Tom," Kim said.

He could hear her standing up from her desk and the voices in the background grew louder as she walked past them. Soon, the sounds in the background drifted away and he heard the hinges of a door squeak, followed by a couple of thuds, all accompanied by Kim's breathing growing more laboured. And then she was back, her voice sounding hollow and distant.

"I know the occasion you're talking about," she said. "I'm not going to lie to you, Tom, I could get into a lot of trouble—"

"I'm not looking to cause trouble, Kim, but I need to understand what Pete may have been up to."

He guessed she'd retreated either into a stairwell or to the toilets where she'd checked to make sure she was alone before speaking.

He heard her sigh.

"Kim, it's important. Pete's dead and I need to find answers."

"Okay," she said. He could hear the stress in her voice. "After Pete split with Cara, or she kicked him out... whichever... he went off the rails a bit; started drinking, showing up late or not at all... really started to take the piss, you know? To cut a long story short, he crossed the line once too often and he was under investigation—"

"Yes, so I gathered, and he jumped before the investigation was completed."

"That's right, he was in real trouble, Tom. I don't know the full extent, but he was using the PNC to gather intel... personal intel and..." she exhaled heavily, "...the rumour was he was moonlighting, selling restricted data and such. To whom or why, I really don't know, but that was the talk amongst the team. And then strange things began happening around that time. We started to find some of our cases unravelling, nothing major at first, just incrementally, bit by bit... things we'd been carefully laying the groundworks on for months started to go awry; raids turning up empty when we knew a couple of days before that they were fully loaded, that sort of thing. Fingers were being pointed and they started to take aim at Pete. That was the internal investigation's direction of travel anyway. It looked like he was in trouble, real trouble."

"So, he got out before they could finish it?"

"Yeah, although they were still looking at him even after he left. It wasn't common knowledge, but they were. I heard things, you know?"

"Are you telling me Pete was bent?"

"No! I'm not saying that, but he was in a state and when someone gets that low, they can be vulnerable to certain characters. It's never cut and dried, but you know how it plays out; it's a bit of intel for you here and then you do them a favour there. It can quickly grow arms and legs and, if you're not careful, you can wind up in trouble without quite understanding how you got there."

"So, you warned him?"

There was silence. He knew she was still on the call; he could hear her breathing.

"Yes, yes I did. I couldn't see Pete as being on the take. I can imagine him being manipulated, even getting desperate and maybe pushing the line a little, but on the take? No, not for me."

"Did the problems with the cases subside?"

"Yes, they did," she said, and he recognised the shift in her tone. "I knew he'd set up in private business, but he was really cagey about what he was doing. All I know is a number of our targets were managing to drop their surveillance with consummate ease, finding ever more clever ways of meeting outside of our view, that type of thing. They were getting help. And it was *our* targets. I mean, it was too much of a coincidence, right? I had to reach out to him, not just for his sake but for all of ours as well."

"And did that change your view of Pete and what he may have been up to?"

More silence.

"I don't know what you expect me to say to that, Tom."

"How about the truth."

She laughed; it was strained. "It took me a while. I–I just couldn't believe... I mean, it's Pete, you know?"

"Yeah, I know," Tom said. He'd been drawn in over dinner the other night, remembering the man he knew – thought he knew – and now that memory was becoming ever more distant by the day.

"Do you think that this is all related to his death?" Kim asked.

"I don't know, Kim. I really don't."

Glancing at the clock, mounted on the roof of a brick-built and pan-tiled bus shelter, Tom knew he had to go.

"Listen, I'll need to speak to you about this again, Kim. If this isn't related, then I'll do my best for you, you know I will, but..."

"Right." Her response was curt, but he was only being honest. "Look, I know I screwed up, but you know how it works; if one person falls under suspicion of... then the shadow is cast across the entire team and many of us had put a lot of work in over the past couple of years. You know we did."

"Yeah," Tom said, disappointed. "And some people had careers to think about—"

"That's not fair, Tom!"

A door opened beside her, he recognised the sound of a self-closing mechanism operating and, after a moment passed, DI Kim Streeting lowered her voice.

"Besides, all of this was a year ago… why would it resurface now?"

"I don't know. Maybe it's not related, but it's early days this end. Tell me, on a side note, do you remember a burglary in Hampstead a while back? It all went wrong, and the homeowner died. Apparently, it was a pretty big case."

"The Hampstead Four? Yes, doesn't everyone remember that one?"

"I don't but it was before I transferred to London and it does seem like I'm the only one who's in the dark," he said. "Do you know if Pete was involved in that case at all? Did he ever mention it to you? He would have been a DC or maybe even in uniform back then."

"I'm sorry. I don't recall him saying anything about it. Not to me, at least. Why do you ask?"

"Oh, it's probably nothing, just one of those random links that come up. I'm probably seeing patterns in the clouds where there isn't anything, that's all. Forget I mentioned it. I have to go, Kim, but we'll speak again."

Whoever had been in the toilets with her left, Kim waiting until they were alone again before speaking.

"Okay. I–I hope… well, you know?"

"Yes," Tom said quietly. "I know."

"You were always straight down the line, Tom. It's one of your strengths."

He picked up the regret in her tone and he hoped she

wasn't about to ask him to bury any inconvenient truths. He needn't have worried.

"Don't ever compromise on that..." she said, "...not even for an old friend."

The line went dead before he could reply. Putting his mobile away, he saw a break in the traffic and crossed the road, heading for the solicitor's office.

CHAPTER TWENTY-TWO

Tom was ushered into an office as soon as he arrived by a pleasant lady who must have been waiting for him. Kerry made to stand as he entered the room, as did a rotund, rosy-cheeked balding man who smiled warmly as he came from behind his desk and offered Tom his hand.

"DI Janssen, I presume," he said as they shook hands. "Barry Lewis, senior partner here at Paterson's." He gestured to an empty chair alongside the one occupied by Kerry. "I'm afraid DC Palmer has been a little evasive as to the nature of your visit today."

There was no hint of irritation attached to the comment, he seemed curious.

"Yes, please accept my apologies. I had to make a phone call and it took longer than anticipated."

"That's quite all right, Inspector. I have a rare window in my schedule today, in any event. What is it I can do for you?"

Tom settled into his chair, the conversation with Kim still present in his mind. He tried to push it aside for now.

"You submitted a Freedom of Information request to the CPS regarding the trial of The Hampstead Four."

Whatever Lewis was expecting to hear, it wasn't that.

"Um…" he mumbled and a moment later he threw his hands wide before him. "Yes, I did."

"I'd like to know why and on whose behalf."

Lewis cocked his head, glancing between the two detectives. Blowing out his cheeks, he shook his head.

"I'm not entirely sure how much I can say…" he said, glumly. "Mind you, I suppose it doesn't really matter much now." Drawing breath, he fixed Tom with his gaze. "It was an unusual request… one I wouldn't normally take on; we are a small practice, Inspector. We deal with family matters, divorce… property conveyancing, that sort of business. But, on this occasion, the client was… compelling."

"Who was it?"

He raised his eyebrows. "A local woman: Margaret Aldren."

Tom looked sideways at Kerry to see if the name registered, and she dipped her head in answer to the unasked question.

"Aldren was the surname of one of the four men convicted in the Hampstead case," Kerry said.

"That's right," Lewis said. "Margaret was his mother."

"Was?" Tom asked.

Lewis nodded. "Yes, she passed away earlier this year…" he looked up and to his right, searching his memory. "Or maybe it was late last year, around Christmas perhaps. A stroke… she lingered for a while in hospital but never recovered and passed away. It was a shame."

"I see. And the case you were working on, what did it entail?"

"Margaret was under the impression that something untoward was going on during that case between the defence and prosecution teams, and that her son had become not only an unwitting accomplice to a murder, but also a pawn in a larger game."

"She wouldn't be the first mother to wholeheartedly, and blindly, believe in her child's innocence—"

"Oh, I can assure you, Inspector, I felt very much the same way during our initial consultation. I was all set to politely decline her request, but... something about her passion and spirit struck a chord with me. Had I passed on the case, I am certain she already had a list of others to work through until she found someone willing to take it on. She was formidable."

"But he..." Tom glanced at Kerry, the name escaping him. "The son?"

"Chris," Kerry said.

"Aldren never denied he was there, did he?" Tom asked.

"No, absolutely not." Lewis sat forward in his chair. "But he did contest the motivation for his being there."

"Please explain."

"The prosecution always alleged the crime was a robbery that went wrong, however, Chris claimed he was unaware of the robbery. As far as he understood it, they were going to the address to pick something up. It was only after the event that he realised what he'd been a party to. Seemingly, two of the other three – those whom Chris barely knew – were subsequently identified as gang members tied to drug dealers. He believed that the others knew the owner of the house and that the *robbery* was no such thing."

"Forgive me," Tom said, frowning, "but I have heard many tales of woe given over by suspects, and indeed convicted criminals after the event, in order to minimise their involvement, to excuse their participation—"

"I don't doubt that Inspector," Lewis said, holding up a hand. "As have I. On this occasion though, had you met Chris and his mother, I think you might take a different view."

"Okay, let's go with your premise. What were they looking for, to overturn the conviction?"

"No, no, certainly not. Joint enterprise leaves little in the way of flexibility... Chris was present. What he knew or did not know was considered by the jury at the time and had he known at the time, what he later understood, then he may have raised a different defence. He was a naive young man, but no, there was not enough there to mount an appeal in regard to the safety of the conviction. That wasn't our task."

"In that case, what were they looking for?"

"Due to the nature of the assault on the victim, the convicted men – although Chris was barely of age – were considered a substantial risk to members of the public and placed in Category A prisons to serve their sentences. Well... things happen behind the walls of a prison, Inspector. Dark things, as I'm sure you know." He shook his head. "Chris Aldren should never have found himself in a maximum-security facility. He'd barely been in trouble in his life. He moved to London to attend university; he was a bright young man. Not that he was a saint, by any means, but I fear that he was judged alongside the company he kept that fateful night."

"And the case they wanted to bring, Chris and his mother?"

"The prosecution never brought the argument that the attack was in fact related to the drug scene, preferring a direct approach from the robbery angle—"

"Because they couldn't prove it," Tom said.

"That's my thinking, yes. Now, had they done so, then it would have caused issue with painting Chris as a hardened criminal. They kept their rhetoric simple. The defence team, on the other hand, I suspect didn't want to bring up the activities of their clients in greater detail for obvious reasons, and so Chris was... lost somewhere in the middle. Following the convictions, however, approaches were made to Chris; attempts to recruit him to help the prosecution in widening their scope."

Tom glanced at Kerry. This implied they saw Chris Aldren as an asset, possibly recognising the lack of involvement he'd played in the case after all. They would never have brought that up themselves at trial for risk of harming their chances of a result.

"And there is evidence of this?"

Lewis appeared reticent. "That is what I had been working on. You see, Chris was a frightened young man, more so once he found himself moved from being remanded in a Cat B prison, terrifying enough for most, to a Category A facility. He was willing to help, comforted by a promised reduction in his sentence for doing so."

"I sense that it didn't turn out that way."

"No, Inspector. It most certainly did not. Somewhere along the line word got out about Chris's willingness to cooperate." He sighed. "This was not a positive turn of events."

"Retribution?"

Lewis nodded. "Of which I find quite unimaginable… and I have always prided myself on my creativity."

"And the case you were looking to bring…"

"To find out who exposed my client, because that is what I believe happened in this case. Someone deliberately fed Chris to the wolves, and we wanted to know who and why?"

Tom's curiosity was piqued.

"What have you found out?"

Lewis averted his eyes from Tom, exhaling slowly. "The case was in its infancy, Inspector. I'm afraid Margaret's passing effectively took all of the wind out of our sails."

"But Chris?"

"Is a broken individual, Inspector Janssen, highly

damaged. His mother was the driving force and I'm afraid his interest dissipated soon after her passing, if it was ever there in the first place."

"Where is he now, do you know?"

Lewis shook his head. "I only met him once or twice and, as I said, in his state of mind he was difficult to work with… to manage. I would struggle to provide credibility inside a court of law with a man so troubled."

"I should imagine what you were working on would also be costly—"

"Never came into it, not really."

Tom was sceptical and it must have shown. Lewis bridled.

"Not all of us are seeking a payday, Inspector. Margaret had a little money at the outset, but that was swiftly exhausted, believe me. I can assure you that the only way I would have recouped my costs in this endeavour would have been through an award of costs or some form of compensation for my client. Either way, in my opinion that was very unlikely under the circumstances. Had Chris been willing to continue the fight, then I would have continued my representation of him. Some things go beyond financial return."

Tom felt embarrassed. His conversation with Kim may well have triggered his cynicism and he'd projected it onto the man opposite. He felt suitably admonished.

"Can I ask you if you use any private investigation firms?"

"Yes, of course. I have several on my books, one-man operations in the main. I use them primarily for serving documents or to find people who don't wish to be found."

"Did you hire one in this investigation?"

Lewis met Tom's eye. "No, not in this case." He shrugged. "Perhaps I may have done further down the road, but no. We hadn't got that far."

CHAPTER TWENTY-THREE

Tom was standing in front of the whiteboards in the ops room when his mobile rang. He answered without looking at the screen, keeping his eyes focussed on the information before him.

"Tom Janssen."

"Hi, Tom."

His attention immediately switched to the call, and he headed for his office.

"Hi love, what's up?"

"Does something need to be up for me to call you?" she asked.

"No, no, of course not." He realised his tone was more brusque than normal, so caught up was he in trying to sift through what was important and what wasn't. "But is everything okay?"

"Yes... no, well, I think so."

He waited, careful not to snap. He closed the door to his office and crossed to the desk, perching himself on the edge.

"It's this whole thing with Olivia's father."

"Henry Crowe?"

"Yes. Saffy came home from school today," Alice said, concern edging into her voice. "Obviously Olivia hasn't come back in yet, but Saffy... she asked whether she should hang out with Olivia because... because she knows what Olivia's going through."

"Ah... damn. You know, I didn't even think about that."

"Don't be too hard on yourself, Tom. I didn't either. What kind of a mother forgets that sort of thing?"

"One who is busy running a home, a job and looking after her own mother as well, that's who," Tom said, spotting Tamara entering ops. She looked around, made eye contact with him, recognising he was on a call and instead of coming to him, she made a beeline for Cassie, hunched over her desk. "What did you say to her, to Saffy, I mean?"

"Not the right thing..." she said, glumly. "I was so proud of her for thinking of someone else but, at the same time, all that emotion came flooding back and I didn't want her... or me, I guess, to have a setback. I didn't even think about how this might affect her. She's barely over Adrian's death herself..." she audibly sighed with frustration. "Oh, Tom, I was too dismissive of her."

"You're trying to keep her safe."

"Yes... but by doing so, I upset her."

"How is she now?"

"Shut herself in her room. She hates me!"

"She loves you," Tom said. "And sometimes it's a good thing to give her a bit of space to vent. She'll come round and maybe you can talk to her about it again. She caught you by surprise. Maybe we should have seen it coming."

"*Definitely* should have seen it coming," Alice said.

"Probably. Listen," he said, looking out into ops as Tamara looked at him again, "I need to go."

"Okay, thanks for listening," she said. "Will you be late home tonight? Not a problem if you will be."

"I don't know. Things are a bit manic here trying to make heads or tails of all this, but I'll let you know."

They said goodbye and Tom put his mobile on his desk and walked out into ops. He joined Tamara at the information boards. She smiled as he approached.

"Everything all right? You looked very serious in there."

"Life with a young child is always serious!" he said, grinning. "It'll be fine."

"Where are we at?" she asked, turning her gaze to the collage of pictures, short snippets of information handwritten beside or below each one.

He shook his head. "It's like trying to piece together a jigsaw with bits from two different pictures! Bloody frustrating is what it is." He folded his arms across his chest. "We have two dead bodies and multiple lines of inquiry... even several potential suspects but nothing concrete when it comes to motive."

Tamara took a deep breath. "What about Natasha's lover? He stands to gain from her husband's death, and he not only has a potential motive but there's a discrepancy in his version of the time line not backed by Natasha. He has several hours on that Saturday night that are unaccounted for and he did a runner when you knocked on his door. Why aren't you pressing him more?"

"It's not a matter of..." he shook his head. "Neither he nor Natasha seem remotely interested in being anything more than casual lovers," Tom said. "Yes, you're right, Stannard ticks a lot of boxes but the manner of Henry's death, the torture... it strikes me as way too personal for a casual lover to have committed. We are always going to suspect a lover. If he, or both of them for that matter, are being clever then they would have arranged better alibis. They'd certainly not use one another as their alibi. It makes no sense."

"Remember, criminals can be thick as well, Tom."

He smiled. "I know. And I'm not discounting Stannard, but I feel we need more before I'm ready to pin my investigation on him alone." He looked at the board, pointing a finger at Pete Chard's photo. "And I still don't have a link between Pete and Henry Crowe. What motive does Stannard have against him? A woman, Margaret Aldren, hired a local solicitor to look into the circumstances around her son's conviction in a manslaughter trial—"

"The Hampstead Four case. Yes, Cassie just filled me in. Henry Crowe's former practice were prosecuting the case, right?"

"Yes, but there is still no link to Pete in there. The local law firm in Holt deny hiring him and I haven't been able to find any reference to Pete having an involvement with the case either when it was tried or subsequently." He could feel his shoulders tensing as he spoke. "I have Eric looking into anyone in the area where Pete was carrying out his surveillance. I'm hoping to get a bite there, but so far, no joy."

"Could Pete have been working for Henry Crowe in some capacity?"

Tom thought about it. That would make sense. "I'll pay Alex Tilson a visit. It's about time he started being useful. Cassie!"

She finished typing something before turning to look at him. "Yes, Boss?"

"Alex Tilson. You were speaking with him, weren't you? Why hasn't the board been updated?"

"Ah, not had the conversation yet, sorry," she said, grimacing. "I arranged to meet him on Tuesday, but he called to postpone and asked to reschedule. He was a bit emotional... about

Henry's murder and processing it all. What with the Chard murder as well, I haven't managed to speak to him yet. If it's urgent, I'll call him now."

"I want to know if Pete was working in some capacity for Henry," Tom said. "Tamara's right, it would make sense. Unless everyone else is fibbing, it's the only plausible explanation. If so, what was he doing for them? Double check his background as well. If he's likely to try and palm us off with some nonsense, I want to be able to see it coming." He bit his lower lip, looking at the photo of Tilson on the board. "And yes, I'm irritated, so consider it as urgent."

"I'm on it," she said, spinning her chair back to face her desk.

Tom looked back at Tamara. "So far, no one claims to know what is going on and yet I have this nagging sense that we're being kept in the dark. Don't you?"

Tamara didn't get a chance to answer.

"Sir?"

Tom looked past Tamara to see Ken Abbott striding across ops towards him clutching an envelope in his hand. He handed it to him. "This just came for you."

Tom looked at the front. It was addressed to him at the station, but there was no stamp.

PC Abbott pointed casually to the letter. "You'll see it's not been franked, so it was hand delivered."

"Did you see by whom, Ken?"

Abbott shook his head. "No, sorry. It must have been posted through the door at some point today though... after the postie made his daily drop."

Tom flipped the envelope over in his hand, seeing no return address on the rear and then he noticed it was addressed in a similar handwriting style as the package containing the photographs of Natasha Crowe and Mark Stannard.

"Do me a favour, Ken, pull up the CCTV from the front of the station and see if you can spot who delivered this, would you?"

"Sure, I'll do it now."

Tom exchanged a glance with Tamara, feeling a rectangular lump inside the envelope. He gently prised the flap apart, teasing it open. There was no written letter inside, the envelope containing a thumb drive. He angled the envelope so Tamara could see.

"I wonder what they've sent you this time?" she asked.

Tom put on a pair of forensic gloves and carefully took the drive out of the envelope. It would need to be dusted for fingerprints but, as they had found with the photographs of Natasha and her lover, he expected it to be wiped clean. Eric brought a laptop over to them and Tom connected the drive. No one spoke, all keen to see what was on it.

Opening the drive, there was only one MP4 video file available. He double clicked on the icon and the footage started to play. The camera was placed at an odd angle, looking up and past a leg, bent at the knee and wearing blue jeans.

"I think that must be set up in the footwell... is it Chard's van?" Tamara asked.

Tom slowly nodded, looking at the interior lining of the roof where it met the passenger side door. It was night time; the area near to the car lit only by artificial light. Nothing was said, but the sound of rainfall drumming gently on the roof and windows could be heard. They didn't have to wait too long before the passenger door opened and a woman got in, shaking the rain from her head as she put her shoulder bag in her lap and threw back her hood. It was Natasha Crowe.

Tom tried to remember the last time they'd had any persistent rainfall to get an idea of when this meeting may have taken place. Even now, he didn't know if this was Pete Chard because the driver was off camera. That particular question was answered as the familiar voice spoke first.

"You're late."

It was dead pan, accusatory.

"Yeah, well… Henry had the idea something suss was going on."

Pete scoffed.

"Really? He doesn't strike me as the intuitive type."

"You don't know him," Natasha said, looking straight ahead.

"Well?"

She looked sideways towards Pete, clearly annoyed.

"I'm waiting, love," he said. "And I've been waiting long enough."

She sighed, righting the bag in her lap, looking down and reaching into it. She produced a large brown envelope, folded into a packet the thickness of a clenched fist and twice as long. Pete took the package from her, unfurling it.

"It's all there," she said, her tone hostile.

"I think I'll be the judge of that."

He made a show of opening the envelope, angling the opening towards the camera and removing some of the contents; cash, in what looked like ten and twenty-pound denominations. They were wrapped with a teller's band. She must have withdrawn it from the bank recently.

"Happy?" she sneered.

"Yep, that'll do," Pete said, ensuring once more that the exchange of money was caught on camera. "For now."

She shot daggers at him. "What do you mean *for now*?"

Pete chuckled. "Don't be daft. You know how this works."

"You said—"

"I said what I needed to get you to play ball."

She stared at him. He held a wedge of money up in front of her.

"You didn't honestly think you could buy my silence for a measly five grand, did you?"

She looked away, her anger morphing into resentment and then fear. He laughed.

"You did, didn't you?"

"I took you at your word—"

"Yes, well… that was a mistake, but not quite as big a mistake as dropping your knickers for anyone who came calling—"

She lashed out at him, but he easily deflected her hand away and when she attempted a second with her other hand, Pete deftly caught her wrist, twisting her arm and forcing her down and away from him. She squealed in pain.

"Now," Pete said firmly, "let's not have any more of that." He released her and she lurched away from him, pressing herself against the passenger door. If she'd got any further into the door, she'd have become one with it. "We're both grown-ups, Natasha," he said quietly, the sound of the envelope being repackaged could be heard off camera. "And as long as you keep doing your bit, then Henry need never know that you can't keep your legs closed… or that his precious little girl isn't his—"

"You wouldn't!" she said, glaring at him.

"Oh, I bloody well would," he said, with distinct glee. "And that one's just a bonus. Once I got to know the type of woman you are, it was only common sense to arrange a DNA test. It's so easy these days, you know? Order a test kit… a little swab, a bit of hair from a brush… easy."

"You're a proper bastard—"

"Language… disgraceful, you being a mum and all. What

example are you setting to little Olivia? I wonder," Pete said, changing tone, "where would you find yourself if Henry got wind that he wasn't her father?" he said, sucking air through his teeth. Natasha looked across at him, scared. "Move back to your mum's maybe? You'd be back doing hair and nails, I expect. It'd be a shame, Olivia leaving the school… all her friends. Sad."

"Y–You don't have to say anything." Natasha's voice was all but a whisper. The fight was gone. "Henry doesn't need to know any of this."

"And he won't," Pete said, slapping his hand against the package of wrapped money, "as long as you keep up your end."

She shook her head. "You've no idea how hard it was for me to get that money, no idea at all. Henry keeps an eye on everything—"

"And yet, here it is!"

Pete sounded gleeful. It made Tom feel sick to his stomach.

"I don't know if I'll be able to—"

"Oh, yes you will. You're a very resourceful woman, Natasha. Otherwise, you'd not have Henry eating out of your hand for as long as you have. Although, things can change… quicker than you might think."

She stared at him. It was unclear what counter argument, if any, she was formulating.

"You can go now," Pete said. She didn't move. "Don't worry. I'll be in touch."

She glared at him once more and then reluctantly opened the door, slowly getting out. She closed it firmly, but without aggression and disappeared from view.

"And that is how it's done," Pete said to himself.

The footage abruptly ended.

Tamara looked at Tom. He held her gaze for a brief moment

before averting his eyes and looking at the floor. No one spoke. Cassie put a hand on Tamara's forearm. She looked at her and Cassie spoke, exaggerating a wide-eyed expression and raising her eyebrows knowingly. "I told you. It's always the spouse."

Tamara stroked her cheek with her right hand, looking directly at Tom. "I want Natasha brought in."

He agreed. "And Stannard too. Pete was blackmailing her… it's logical she'd turn to her lover to help relieve herself of the problem."

"And what about Henry?" Tamara asked. "Half an hour ago, you didn't see what was in it for them."

"Yes, that's true." Tom sighed. "And half an hour ago, I didn't know about this," he said, pointing at the screen. "We've no idea when this was filmed… and it could have been weeks or even months ago. Maybe she didn't come through with the money… and Pete threatened to tell Henry. It could have forced her hand."

"That's cold," Cassie said, "if you're right, of course."

"Yeah," Tom said, "but I've been wrong about everything so far, so… I–I need a moment," he said, stepping away and turning towards his office.

"Take it," Tamara said. He thanked her with a curt nod over his shoulder and walked away.

"That's going to hurt," Cassie said, watching him go.

"There's nothing quite like it when it comes to betrayal… a betrayal of your own judgement," Tamara said. She pointed at the white boards. "Get the two of them in here, now! It wouldn't hurt for them to see one another going into different interview rooms as well, if you get what I mean?"

"Let them think they'll be grassed up by the other?" Cassie asked, smiling. "I like your thinking."

Tamara crossed the office and gently knocked on Tom's door. It was open. He beckoned her in.

"How are you doing?" she asked.

"How do you think?"

She entered, folding her arms across her chest. "That bad, huh?"

"That obvious?" he replied. "That man... the one in the recording... is not the man I worked with."

"Are you sure?"

"He was a decent copper. He was my DS... I'd know if he was bent!"

Tamara pursed her lips, leaning her back against a filing cabinet.

"Are you sure?"

"You doubt my judgement?"

She scoffed, lowering her arms to her side and putting her hands in her pockets. "No, of course I don't! It's just, sometimes, we miss the signs and, sometimes, we choose to."

He sank into the chair behind his desk, bringing his hands up and rubbing at his cheeks.

"How could I have got so much wrong in the space of a week?"

"Well, that remains to be seen," Tamara said. "We don't know the circumstances of what that transaction we just witnessed was all about—"

"I think it was pretty damn clear, don't you?"

She shook her head. "Not really, no. What if that was Pete's way of getting her infidelity and the question of Olivia's parentage on the record?"

Tom sat back, thinking hard. "And what... Pete tells Henry... and so Natasha has him killed before she's turfed out in the street with a child in tow?"

"Maybe."

"In which case, why then go and kill Pete?"

"Because he would be able to offer a motive for her killing

her husband. Stands to reason," Tamara said, shrugging. "And maybe she approached Pete to try and cut a deal, only for him to get a little more than he bargained for. Maybe Pete was asking for a lot more this time to keep quiet seeing as we were involved. She could have sent Stannard to make the drop this time."

"It would explain how the killer was able to get so close to him without an apparent struggle. But…" Tom frowned.

"What?"

"That doesn't clear up who's sending us the helpful photographs and home video, does it?"

Tamara angled her head. "There's still work to do."

Eric approached the office, gently rapping his knuckles on the door frame. Tom beckoned him in. "I've just had the forensics report back from Chard's camper van," he said, looking between them. "The van was wiped clean and there is very little there for us to work with apart from one thing."

"Which is?" Tom asked.

"The knife used to stab Chard… it matches the set in the Crowe's kitchen."

Tamara looked at Tom, raising her eyebrows. "Well… that's a gift if ever there was one."

CHAPTER TWENTY-FOUR

"I REALLY DON'T UNDERSTAND why I have to come in here for a chat," Natasha Crowe said, clearly annoyed at making the trip to the station.

"I'm sorry, Mrs Crowe," Tom said, gesturing for her to walk with him along the corridor. "I have to run a couple of things past you, just to clear them up so as we can move on with your late husband's case."

"I know," she said, curtly. "But I still don't see why we couldn't have done it over the phone."

Tom stopped at the entrance to an interview room and as Natasha walked past the adjoining room, the door opened, and Cassie stepped out in front of her.

"Oh, I'm terribly sorry, Mrs Crowe," Cassie said, blocking her path.

She'd left the door to the interview room open, and Natasha couldn't help but glance inside. She made to dismiss Cassie's apology, only to see Mark Stannard sitting behind a table inside the room. Their eyes met in the carefully contrived *chance* meeting and instead she said nothing, looking away from her lover. Her lips parted as she stared blankly at Tom.

"This way, Mrs Crowe," he said, opening the door to another room on the other side of the corridor and ushering her through it. Once they passed her, Cassie winked knowingly at him.

"Target acquired," she whispered quietly.

Tom walked into the room, not letting Natasha see his half-smile.

"Please take a seat," he told her, pointing to the chair on the other side of the table. "Constable Palmer will be joining us shortly and then, with a bit of luck, you'll be on your way."

Natasha reluctantly walked to her chair. Her movements were rigid, and she seemed uneasy as she pulled the chair out and sat down, placing her hands together in her lap. She looked like a child waiting outside the headmaster's office, nervous and vulnerable.

The door opened and Kerry Palmer entered, a laptop and a folder under her arm.

"Sorry, sir," she said, sitting down next to Tom.

"That's okay, Constable Palmer," Tom said, clearing his throat. "I just need to run through your rights, Mrs Crowe."

"M–My rights?"

He reached across and turned the recorder on. Natasha's eyes widened at this point. Tom read aloud her rights, Natasha looking increasingly like a rabbit caught in a car's headlights.

"Do you understand the rights as I have read them to you?" he asked. She stared straight ahead, unflinching. "Mrs Crowe? Do you understand?"

"Yes… yes, I do."

Tom smiled, indicating for Kerry to open the laptop. She duly did so, lifting the screen and unlocking the machine.

"Mrs Crowe…" Tom said.

"What's with all the formality," Natasha said. "I've been Natasha up until now. What's going on?"

"Do you know Peter Chard, Natasha?"

"No, I don't think so. Should I?"

"He's a private investigator… who has been working in this area—"

"Oh yes. He's the one they found dead in Hunstanton. I saw it on the news."

"Murdered, yes," Tom said. "We believe he may have been doing some work for your husband, Henry, recently."

She shrugged. "I wouldn't know. You should speak to Alex about that, he'd be the one to know."

"We are, Natasha," Tom said. He shook his head, fixing his eye on her. "But what about you?"

Kerry passed him the folder and he opened it, taking out a picture of Pete Chard. It was an outdoor shot, one Tom had received from Cara, Pete's wife, and in it he was outside at a family occasion, smiling. Tom put it on the table in front of her. She glanced at it, then shook her head.

"Nope, sorry."

He took out a photograph taken at the scene of his murder, reversed it and slid it across the table beside the first.

"What about now?"

She swallowed hard, recoiling from the image and averting her gaze. Again, she shook her head.

"Are you sure?" Tom asked.

"Yes, I'm sure!"

Tom glanced sideways, giving Kerry a nod, and she turned the laptop so the screen was facing Natasha. Reaching around, Kerry clicked play on the covert recording they'd been sent in the post. Natasha closed her eyes.

"That's okay, Natasha. There's sound on the recording as well, so you can just listen if you prefer."

She muttered some choice words under her breath. No one spoke until the video finished playing. Kerry left the screen facing Natasha, moving the slider back to a point in the recording where she was clearly visible.

Tom took a deep breath. "And... how about now? Do you remember Peter Chard?"

"I didn't know his name!" she hissed.

"But you're not denying this is you in the footage, meeting Peter Chard in his vehicle—"

"Well, there wouldn't be much point in denying it, would there?"

"And paying him five thousand pounds?"

She glared at him, her lips curling into a snarl. "I didn't have a choice." Her hand flashed up and she angrily gesticulated at the screen. "That man was evil! He was blackmailing me. You can see it—"

"Yes, he was. Tell me, when you saw him meeting your husband at your home, had he already approached you? Had this meeting already taken place and you had to pretend never to have seen him before?"

"He approached me weeks before. I knew he was working for Henry by then... the man made my skin crawl."

"And that gives you a perfect motive for wanting him dead, doesn't it?"

Eyes wide, her mouth fell open. "And you think... I... could do something like that?"

"Something like what, Natasha?"

"*Something like wh*—?" she said, shaking her head. "Like *killing* a man!"

"Did you?"

"No, of course I didn't!"

"So, you were content to continue paying him?"

"Don't be so stupid, Inspector Janssen." She was flushed now, her neck and cheeks reddening. "Henry would have found out eventually."

"I'm thinking he already had."

Tom folded his arms across his chest, sitting back and watching her reaction.

"I–I… but Henry didn't know about… Mark and me. He didn't. I'd have known. He would have said."

"Think it through from our point of view, Natasha. Should Henry find out that you are not only having an affair, but that Olivia isn't his child, then you could stand to lose an awful lot. Granted you'd receive a settlement in a divorce, and it would be decent, I'm sure, but nowhere near as much as you are used to living on now. And Henry would likely fight tooth and nail for it, which would take time and he knows the law better than most. In the meantime, where would you go? How would you manage—?"

"Stop it!" she barked.

"Much easier to enlist the help of that chancer you call a lover… only you didn't bank on Chard coming forward and demanding ever more money. How much did he ask for to buy his silence over Henry's murder… fifty grand… a hundred? How much was too much before the two of you concocted the idea of disposing of him too?"

"No," she said, shaking her head and staring at the table before her. "That's not what happened at all."

"You arranged a meeting, either on the pretence of negotiating a sum or to hand over payment, I don't know which, but Pete got more than he was expecting, didn't he? Who delivered the fatal blow; you or Mark?"

"No, no, no."

"You see the thing is, the murder weapon has been identified and it's yours—"

"What?" She shook her head. "I don't understand."

"The knife used to stab Peter Chard to death came from your house, from your kitchen. How is that possible?"

"No... that can't be true... you're lying," she said, desperation in her tone.

"It is true, Natasha. You met Peter Chard one last time and you killed him."

"No!"

"Then you took his laptop, mobile phone, camera and any other piece of tech you thought might have the proof of what the two of you just did... only, you missed something," Tom said, reaching out and pushing the laptop an inch or two towards her. "And we found it."

"Enough already!" Natasha shouted, clamping her palms to the sides of her head and squeezing hard. Tom waited in silence as she clamped her eyes shut, her head sagging forward. "Enough," she repeated quietly, "please." She slowly lifted her eyes to meet his. "I didn't kill my husband, Inspector. And I didn't kill this... this Chard guy either." Her eyes glazed over. "And I don't care what..." she pointed a quivering hand at the screen "... *he* had to say or anyone else for that matter, *Olivia is* Henry's daughter and no *half-arse* DNA test bought on the internet is going to tell me any different."

Tom watched her as she gathered herself, her composure slowly returning.

"Henry hired Pete Chard to spy on you."

She steeled herself, meeting his eye. "He never said anything... the investigator or my husband. I never had the impression Henry was suspicious. I was careful. We were careful."

"Clearly not careful enough. You're aware we are also talking to Mark," he said. "This might be your best chance of getting your version of events on the record." He slowly shook his head. "Because from here on in, it gets ever more difficult, and in murder trials credibility is everything. You don't want to be in the position of playing catch-up."

She sat forward, placing her hands flat on the surface of the table. They were no longer shaking. Her words were measured and delivered calmly.

"Whatever Mark has to say... the truth will be no different to what I've just told you. If he says something else..."

"Then what?"

She pursed her lips. "Then he's lying to you."

"And why would he do that, do you think?"

She shrugged. "For all the fun Mark is to be around, he couldn't lie straight in bed."

"Let us be clear," Tom said, "are you saying you and Mark have had no involvement in the murder of your husband or Peter Chard?"

"No... what *I am* saying is that I have had no involvement. If Mark has done something, then he did so off his own bat, and it has absolutely *nothing* to do with me." She sat back, folding her arms defiantly across her chest. "Is that clear enough for you?"

"YOU'RE MAD!" Mark Stannard threw his arms in the air as if to emphasise his point. "Stark raving mad, if you think I've had anything at all to do with *any of this*. In fact," he said, sitting forward and jabbing a finger towards Tom, "if I had a half-decent amount of cash, I'd sue the hell out of each and every one of you."

"That is your prerogative, of course," Tom said.

"Actually, I'll start with an official complaint. Even I can afford to do that."

"Of course," Tom said. "I'll ensure PC Palmer provides you with the appropriate forms as soon as we are done with this interview."

Stannard offered him a dismissive shake of the head, rolling his eyes.

"Now, let's get back to late on Monday night. Where did you say you were between nine o'clock and midnight?"

Stannard exhaled hard, raising his hands behind his head and interlocking his fingers. He blew out his cheeks. "I told you, I was at home – alone – watching television."

"That's right, you did. All night?"

"All night," Stannard said. "From the time I got home, which was around eight, eight-fifteen. I went out to get a Chinese. Then I sat in front of the telly, eating, having a couple of cold ones—"

"Beer… wine?"

"Beer."

"And what was it you were watching that held your attention?"

"A lot of things…" Stannard said. He didn't appreciate the look Kerry gave him. "I was channel hopping, all right? Who watches one channel all night, especially these days? It's all rubbish anyway."

"Okay, Mark," Tom said. "What was the last thing you remember watching?"

"This is getting ridiculous…" Stannard's shoulders sagged, and he lowered his head into his hands. Moments later, he sat upright, ran his right hand through his hair, scratching at the back of his head. Tom's attention was drawn to his hair, but he couldn't quite understand why. "Okay… the last thing I remember is waking up on the sofa… must have been almost one in the morning. There was some politics chat show on the box. Not my thing, so I turned it off and went to bed. Not exciting," he said, splaying his hands wide, "but it is what it is."

"We have a search warrant for your house, Mark. We are

going to pull it apart piece by piece and I hope for your sake we don't find any of Peter Chard's tech stashed in your house."

"Well, if you do, then you'll be the ones who bloody put it there! Don't you dare try and stitch me up for this."

Kerry fixed him with a stare. "You can always add it to your complaint, if you like."

Stannard sneered at her. "Maybe I will."

"Let's roll it back a bit, Mark. The previous Saturday night, the night your lover's husband was murdered... where were you that night?"

"I told you this already, countless times, *I was with Natasha at my place.*" He was annoyed. "She's in the next room, ask her yourself."

"That's just it, Mark, I have, and she says she left yours between half eight and nine and headed to her mother's house to put Olivia to bed."

Stannard's face dropped. For the first time, the veneer of confidence and aggression slipped. For a second, he looked scared and then he seemed to shake it off, his expression lightening, changing to a broad smile.

"Nice try, Inspector Janssen. You had me going then, you really did."

"Oh, I'm not winding you up, Mark. That's what she's told us repeatedly. She's left you wide open in the time frame of Henry's death. The drive time to their house – where Henry was all alone – is barely half an hour... less so at that time of night, I'd reckon. You had plenty of time—"

"No! I'm not having this," Stannard said. "You're not pinning either of these on me."

"I don't have to, Mark," Tom said. "You're doing it all for me, aren't you?"

Stannard glared at him, raising his hands in the air before him in frustration.

"Do what you want, Janssen, but I didn't bloody do it!" He slammed his hands down on the table.

"So, you say, Mark, but your girlfriend doesn't seem inclined to help you out. I wonder why that might be?"

"She's not my girlfriend, for crying out loud." He shook his head. "Have you any idea how many women I can sleep with, if I want to?"

Kerry snorted. "I'm surprised you found one, to be honest."

Tom would rather she hadn't made the intervention but decided to speak to her about it later. For now, he remained impassive.

"Are you telling us you are in more than one relationship?"

"There you go again with the whole relationship argument..." he leaned forward over the table. "Not everyone wants a *relationship* these days."

"I didn't have you pegged as some old hippy, giving out free love—"

"Yeah, *free love, man,*" Stannard said, smiling. "I'd have been at Woodstock... if I'd been born."

"Right," Tom said. "But you see my problem here; you have a motive – regardless of your denial, you do – and you don't have an alibi—"

There was a knock on the door, breaking Tom's train of thought. The door creaked open, and Cassie peered in.

"Sorry to disturb, sir, but can I have a word?"

He wanted to say no, he was in full flow, but her expression was so focussed he knew it was important. He slowly rose out of his seat and joined her in the corridor. Eric was anxiously standing behind her. He avoided Tom's gaze, shifting his weight between his feet.

"Eric has something you need to know," Cassie said.

"Well, it had better be good, Eric, because I'm a little busy right now…"

Eric looked like he was about to cry. Tom took a breath, holding up a hand in apology.

"What is it, Eric?"

"Well, you remember after we brought Stannard in – the first time – I sat him down in an interview room to take his statement and then he gave us his fingerprints and DNA—"

"Yes, of course. So?"

"Well… what with everything going on, I–I… once I'd taken his prints, I forgot to run them against the crime scene. I mean, we had the sets found at the Crowe house that we attributed to the cleaners… and then the others for…"

"Richard Carver," Tom said. "Yes, I remember."

Eric hesitated, looking at Cassie for support.

"Well, that's just it, Tom," she said. "Eric ran Stannard's fingerprints through the system… and he *is* Richard Carver."

"Stannard is Carver?" Tom asked.

"Changed his name when he was twenty-two," Eric said.

"And why am I only hearing about this now?" Tom asked, looking between the two of them. "For crying out loud."

He turned away from them, opening the door and entering the interview room. Kerry read the look on his face, watching him intently as he sat down. Sitting forward, he rested his elbows on the table and put his hands together.

"So, Mark… or should I call you Richard?"

Stannard met his eye, visibly shrinking under the intensity of Tom's gaze.

CHAPTER TWENTY-FIVE

Tom stared at Stannard, watching him squirm in his seat. It was the first time he'd actually looked seriously rattled. He'd been angry, detached and decidedly reticent at times, especially on their first meeting, but now he was exhibiting something else altogether: fear.

"Why the name change, Mark?" Tom asked.

He held Tom's gaze, then looked at his hands, absently wringing them in his lap. He shook his head.

"You see, to me, it looks like you're trying to hide something."

"No, it's not like that, Inspector," he said quietly. "Sort of… but not really."

"Try me."

Stannard took a deep breath, exhaling slowly. "Have you ever done things you regret, Inspector Janssen? Done things you wished you could take back?"

"On occasion, yes."

"Well, magnify whatever you've done by a hundred and you'll find me!"

Stannard put his head in his hands, speaking quietly to the

table in front of him. Tom realised what had caught his attention before; Stannard dyed his hair a deep shade of brown, but the ginger roots were showing close to the scalp.

"I was such a little shite when I was a boy... I mean, most of us are, aren't we? But I was a proper little scrote. I drove my mum mad." He lifted his head. "You see, my old man took off when I was seven or eight. I barely remember him. What I do remember was that he was a proper waster. Then it was just Mum and the four of us; me being the youngest to my three sisters. Imagine that; one lad up against four women." He looked at Kerry. "Your lot don't make life easy, you know?"

"Okay, times were tough, I get it—"

"Oh, do you, Inspector? You get it, right. Well, Mum was out working two jobs, if not three, and us kids were left to fend for ourselves. It wasn't her fault, she was doing her best, but I found myself drifting around with whoever, doing whatever, much of the time. I wasn't interested in school or bettering myself... I was a mess... looking for trouble to get into."

"You certainly did that..." Tom said, making a show of reading through the arrest record of Richard Carver, "and I think there's one person who can attest to your temper. Tell me, do you get a kick out of beating an old man half to death?"

He shook his head emphatically. "That was a long, long time ago."

"And yet here we are, years later, looking at a robbery where the occupant of the property is beaten to death... and you not only know him, but your fingerprints are all over the house—"

"Of course, they're all over the house! I was sleeping with his wife," Stannard barked at him. "Do you think we only met in hotels and at my place... or a quick bunk up in the back seat of my car? No, of course I saw her at her place!"

"You didn't mention that before," Kerry said.

He glared at her.

"Like I was going to put myself at the bloody scene... with my background," Stannard growled. "I'm not the sharpest tool in the kit, but I'm not thick. Why don't I dance up and down with a neon sign above my head while I'm at it!"

"Nonetheless," Tom said, holding his hands out wide, "your prints are at the scene."

"But not where the murder was done though."

"You sure of that?" Tom asked. Stannard's lips moved but no sound came out. "I mean, how would you know?"

"Natasha told me," he countered, nervous. "She told me he was killed in his study and I never went in there... looked in once or twice in passing maybe, but never went in. You'll not find my prints in there."

"Maybe you cleaned them up?" Kerry said.

"Either way," he said, "you don't have them at the murder scene, do you?"

"You seem very confident," Tom said.

"Innocence is the armour of the accused, Inspector Janssen."

"Who said that?" Tom asked. "It sounds like someone intelligent."

"Me, I said it," Stannard said. "Just then."

"You are pretty cocky for a man facing a double murder charge—"

"I didn't kill either of them... I didn't and you can't prove it either."

The bravado was a show, a mask to hide his anxiety. He must have been using that since his father left him as a child and he'd been projecting an image ever since.

"So why the name change?" Tom asked.

"Because..." he looked at the ceiling "... because I didn't want to be that kid anymore. I only had one future ahead of me if I walked that road... and it would be more time inside, only it would be in proper prison, not that," he waved his hands in the air, "young offenders borstal place. Do you know," he said, sitting forward, "there wasn't one quiet night in that shit hole – not one – while I was in there. People screaming night after night, smashing their cell up... smashing each other up! It was hell on earth... and you think I want to go back to a place like that? Really?" He sat back again, folding his arms across his chest. "Seriously, the entrance exam for the police force must be *really* easy."

"The deterrent argument only works for politicians," Tom said. "Criminals never think they'll get caught."

"Yeah, well, I know better, don't I?" Stannard said. "I didn't want that. I wanted a future... and I cut myself out of that life, moved on. And I'm not naive enough to think people will give me a second shot... the kid who beat a war hero half to death for the price of a few pints and some scrap metal?" He shook his head. "Nah... I was done. Everyone knew me, knew my past... and they called me out time after time after time. And I took the bait, fell for it... scrapped with anyone who wanted it. Then I'd end up in the company of your lot; the good old boys in blue." He waved his hand casually at Kerry. "And girls, obviously. But your lot had my card marked too. It was *always* my fault. And I knew it always would be."

"So, you made a change?"

"Yes, that's right. I made a change... for the better." He smiled. It was a sarcastic, mocking expression. "And I'm not perfect, far from it. But I'll tell you this, I haven't cleaned up my act just to throw it all away again over a slice of fine-looking woman! And she is fine, but I ain't going to prison for her." He shook his head. "Whatever she's up to, it's not on me."

"She's in line to inherit a fortune," Kerry said. "Your future could be luxurious—"

"My life is all I need right now, Constable," he said calmly. "Do you think I'm poverty stricken? Last year I picked up nearly six figures on the pro circuit in prize money and sponsorship. I can play. I'm not the greatest, not famous by any stretch, but I'm consistent and I put in the time. Do you know how I came to be so good at golf?"

"Please enlighten us," Tom said.

"My mother was many things, Inspector. She worked hard, raised us as best she could, and she was also quite a woman. Even with four kids in tow, and one evil one like me—" Tom didn't buy the self-deprecation at all "—she still managed to get herself out there. She didn't stay single for long; married a decent bloke, to be fair. Boring, but decent. And he didn't have children of his own, no family to spend his money on, and so he happily spent it on us. Golf was the one thing I was good at, even if I couldn't be bothered half the time in my teens."

"How is this relevant?"

"Because my stepfather died a decade ago, leaving everything he had to my mother," Stannard said. "And a mother's love is unconditional, Inspector. It is never lost… tested at times, certainly, but never lost. You talk about Natasha's inheritance? Well, I've got one of my own coming and I don't need to risk my future to benefit hers! So that's why I sound so sure. I have *zero* need of her money." He slammed a flat palm on the table and then raised a pointed finger at Tom. "I did the right thing. I cleaned up my act and made something of myself. Now, I may not be your idea of a picture of morality, but I'm a long way from who I was back then. Charge me or release me, because I am done answering your stupid questions."

KERRY CLOSED the door to the interview room behind them, walking with Tom to meet Tamara who was waiting for them at the end of the corridor. He looked to the constable.

"I want you to find his mother and check out his story. It sounded plausible, but let's make certain this time."

"I'll do it now," she said, nodding to the DCI and heading off.

Tamara leaned against the wall, pursing her lips. "What do you think?"

She had been watching from the adjoining room.

"I'm inclined to believe him. How about you?"

"Same."

"Which leaves us where?" Tom asked. "He wasn't on the video footage we were sent and his logic on the fingerprints at the house is sound. The CPS will never charge him off the back of what we have. It's all circumstantial."

"Could Natasha have done it by herself?"

Tom tilted his head in response. It was possible, but unlikely in his opinion.

"It takes a lot to kill a man, particularly in this way," he said. "And then to kill a second—"

"Brutal as it is, it is still possible," Tamara said, then she mock grimaced, shaking her head. "Not happening, is it?"

"Nope. Not for me, but she does have the strongest motive. Maybe she enlisted someone else, someone we're not aware of yet."

Tamara frowned. "Like who?"

He shrugged. "Like Eric said, she moved in different circles to Henry. Maybe she has contacts from her previous life prior to marrying Henry?"

"That she could get to commit a murder on her behalf?"

Tom had to admit, the theory was thin... wafer thin.

"We'll have to go through all her associates, trawl her social media… pretty much start again."

"What if your instinct is right," Tamara said. Tom looked at her quizzically. "Well, let's say we discount her motive and dismiss her as the murderer or orchestrator of it. Who else do we have to look at?"

"I thought you favoured Stannard and Natasha as the killers?"

"I do, but Stannard was convincing. Humour me, I should trust your instincts more. Let's not be blind to other possibilities. Who else do we have?"

"The Hampstead case was being looked at by one of the defendants or being pushed by his mother at least. That investigation was starting up around the time Henry left the partnership at Quercus. This was also around the time that Henry was receiving those threatening letters as well. Although, we are yet to actually see them."

"Coincidence?" she asked.

"Maybe, maybe not?"

"But the mother passed away, correct?" Tom nodded. "Okay, let's speak to her lad and see if it was all a mother's attempt to make her son as perfect in the eyes of the world as he was in her's or whether the complaint had merit. The solicitor she hired must have seen merit in it. What's his name again, the son's?"

"Chris Aldren."

"Right. Who else could help with that?"

"Alex Tilson should be in the loop, and we need to speak to him anyway. He's supposed to have gone through Henry's files and advised us of anything missing but that hasn't happened."

"Chase him up and let's see where it takes us."

"Something's bothering me," Tom said, his brow creasing.

"Our anonymous contributor has provided us with some wonderful help regarding motive, obviously steering us towards Natasha and her lover. But… it doesn't work. I mean, if Pete was hired by Henry Crowe to find evidence of her affair, then he can't take money on a regular basis from her if he exposes the relationship between them."

"True."

"Therefore, it makes sense that the blackmail was a by-product, a side-line earner for him, and not the main job Henry recruited him for. That follows, right?"

"Yes," Tamara said, concentrating. "In which case, presuming he was working for Henry then he must have been working on something else. Any ideas?"

"The threatening letters perhaps, or maybe investigating something else we're unaware of?"

"Speak to Tilson. Find out."

"And then there's the question of how the footage was obtained from Pete? Did he pass on the recording to someone, other than Henry, or was he working on something else entirely and only stumbled across Natasha's affair by accident?"

"And saw an opportunity to exploit it?" she asked. "Maybe. We are working on the assumption that if Natasha was involved then Pete was killed to stop the footage coming out, but it could be as simple as Pete's killer took it from him, along with the photos, and is using them to deflect the investigation away from the real motivation for both murders. Putting it squarely onto Mark and Natasha."

Tom looked back towards the two closed doors, Natasha Crowe and Mark Stannard sitting in their respective interview rooms, chaperoned by a uniformed constable a piece.

"Speaking of which, what do we do with those two?"

Tamara clicked her tongue on the roof of her mouth.

"Release them pending further inquiries," she said. "We don't have anything on Stannard, not really, not unless something comes up from the search of his home; a matching knife set maybe? Hold him here until confirmation the search is complete, and as for Natasha… motive isn't enough, not in this case. We need more. Send her home."

"We're close," Tom said. "It might not look like it, but I think we're close."

CHAPTER TWENTY-SIX

THE TWO DETECTIVES entered the ops room side by side, Tom beckoning Cassie over to them.

"Have you arranged to speak with Alex Tilson yet?"

"Yes, I've agreed to meet him at Henry's office this afternoon," she said. "He's over there now gathering together the information we are after."

"Good. We'll call in early and not let him settle himself."

Cassie looked confused. "Are we trying to unsettle him?"

"Yes. Eric," Tom walked straight past her and on to where Eric was beavering away at his desk, "where have you got to with that list of people who were potentially targets for Pete Chard's attention?"

"Over at June Sampher's place?" Eric asked. Tom nodded. Eric rooted around on his desk, eventually producing a notebook and leafing through it to the right page. "There isn't a lot there, I have to be honest. None of the neighbours have any criminal records to speak of. I found several with traffic violations – hardly crimes of the century – one disqualification from being a director off the back of a false accounting charge... but that was years back and there's nothing active on it. The company was dissolved twenty years ago. Even by Norfolk standards, it's a sleepy old town full of holidaymakers and families who have been there for generations."

"What about the holiday lets?"

"Five of them listed on different websites for rent... only three had people in that week," Eric said, concentrating hard. "Of those, two have got back to me and the people check out; no criminal records or associates." He shrugged. "Still waiting on the owners getting back to me about the last one, but I've left a voicemail and I'll chase them again later."

Tom sighed. "All right, but Pete was there for a reason, and we need to keep plugging away. How about June Sampher herself... and her neighbour?"

"June is a model citizen, unsurprisingly. As was her late husband. One of her children is a bit of a scally though. He's been done for receiving stolen goods and has a two-year suspended sentence for fraud against his name."

"And has he been around recently?"

Eric shook his head. "Not that I can see. Les Bassham was right, the children have scattered to the four winds. Four children, three girls and a boy. The son, Barry, lives in Newcastle and as far as I can tell he's lived there for years. I did a bit of social media stalking, and he was on holiday in Tenerife with his wife and children the week Pete Chard was sitting outside his mum's house. There are plenty of family pictures and location drop-ins to back that up. I checked with the Border Force to be sure, and they confirmed he was out of the country for ten days." Eric looked forlornly up at Tom. "I guess I could speak to some of our local counterparts in the northeast anyway and see if he's on their radar at all, but I think it unlikely he's Chard's target. Besides, he doesn't seem like he's been up to anything dodgy in years."

"And Les Bassham himself?"

"Clean as a whistle," Eric said. "He's ex-army, served twenty-two years in the infantry, including two tours of Iraq in the first Gulf War. I requested his service record from the MOD and he was decorated twice. Pretty decent on the Army Boxing Team as well, by all accounts. His commanding officers had nothing but praise for him. Since he came back to civvy street, he's not appeared on our radar other than being spoken to relating to a road-rage incident four years ago. No charges were brought, not even a caution. A ticking off was all that was deemed necessary by the visiting officer. According to the Electoral Roll, he lives alone. Odd that, I thought he said he was married."

"He said he promised his partner he'd keep an eye on June."

"Ah right, that was it."

"And what does he do now?"

"Carpentry," Eric said. "He's been a sole trader for years, has a decent star rating on Trust Pilot, too."

Tom patted him on the shoulder. "Keep at it, something will give. I also want you to find Chris Aldren for me. What's he up to now and when was he last in the area? If he felt something iffy went on with the prosecution team during his trial, maybe he decided to take matters into his own hands and mete out some retribution."

"Lost faith in the judicial system, that sort of thing?"

"Yeah, that's my thinking," Tom said. "Have Kerry help if you need it. Come on Cass, time to go."

Cassie gathered up her mobile and car keys, hurrying to catch up with Tom as he strode out of ops.

NATASHA CROWE'S car was parked in front of her barn conversion when they pulled up outside. When she'd been brought in for questioning, her mother had collected Olivia and taken her back to her house. Tom figured she would have gone there prior to coming home. He was surprised. It didn't matter, he wasn't here to see Natasha again anyway.

They walked around to the side of the barn towards the entrance to Henry's office. Another car was parked here, presumably Alex Tilson's.

"Good, he's turned up this time," Cassie said.

The entrance to the office was ajar and, as they got closer, they could hear raised voices; one aggressively shouting and the other was quite the opposite, high-pitched and pleading. Tom and Cassie exchanged glances and hurried to the door. Tom got there first by dint of his massive strides, shoving the door open and peering inside, with Cassie a half-step behind.

"Blimey," she said quietly, and he could tell she was trying not to laugh. "I didn't expect that."

Alex Tilson was on his knees, hands clasped to the top of his head, desperately trying to remove Natasha's hand from an apparently vice-like grip she had on him. If he hadn't begun screaming at that very moment, it might have looked comical. Tom stepped forward just as Natasha saw their approach, spinning to put the kneeling Tilson between her and them. The movement twisted her body and therefore her grip on his hair, Tilson yelping in pain.

"Let go of me, you psychotic bitch!" he screamed.

She swung her free hand down, raking the side of his face with her pristinely-manicured nails. He screamed again.

"Natasha! Release him, now!" Tom shouted but she only glared at him, and the instruction only seemed to further strengthen her resolve. She yanked Tilson closer and snatched up a pair of scissors from a desk nearby. She stuck them against her charge's throat and Tilson cried out.

"Please don't!"

Blood was streaming from a wound to the side of Tilson's face, just to the side of his right eye. His tie was pulled across his chest and his shirt was ripped clear of the top two buttons. Natasha's thigh-length red coat showed a tear at the seam where her left arm met the shoulder, and her hair was dishevelled. These two must have been going at it for some time.

"Natasha, let him go," Tom said, changing his tone.

Cassie moved to Tom's right, attempting to circle Natasha and close in on her from a different angle. She noticed, shifting herself again to place Tilson between the two detectives, furtively looking from one to the other. A sheen of sweat was breaking through her make-up, and her breath came in short, ragged draws. Tilson's chest was heaving, his submissive expression a mixture of fear and exhaustion. The fight had clearly left him.

"Natasha," Tom said, holding his hands up in a non-threatening manner, "think about what you're doing. This solves nothing and only makes matters worse."

"He did this!" she hissed. "Whispering poison into Henry's ear day after day. All of this is his fault!"

"No, no… that's not true," Tilson said quietly, his hands hanging in the air and making him resemble some obscure, macabre art installation. "I swear I didn't."

Tom was certain Tilson would have been shaking his head if not for the point of the scissors nestling against his skin.

"Liar!"

"I only ever wanted the best for Henry," Tilson whispered. "I swear I'd never do anything to hurt him. I loved him."

That particular comment only served to anger his attacker more, her expression darkening further as she looked down at

Tilson, the point of the scissors breaking the skin. Tilson yelped.

"Natasha! Think about your daughter," Tom said. "Olivia's lost one parent... don't make her lose another."

Her head snapped up to look at him, eyes wide and tearful. "But it's his fault, don't you see?"

"And I'll deal with it, Natasha," Tom said. "I promise you, I will deal with it."

She closed her eyes and then released her grip on the scissors which clattered to the wooden floor. She let go of Tilson's hair, a clump of which fell from her recently clenched fist as he sank to the floor before scrabbling away from her on his hands and knees. Cassie stepped forward and took a firm hold of Natasha just in case she changed her mind and went for Tilson again.

She didn't. Head bowed, her shoulders sagged, and she started crying.

Tilson scuttled past Tom, turning and sitting back, resting against the side of a desk in the shadow of the relative safety he provided. Here he inspected his wounds, tentatively touching the side of his face and cursing at the sight of blood on his fingers.

"Crazy bitch!" he muttered, looking up at Tom who was supervising Cassie placing Natasha Crowe in handcuffs. "They'd put down dogs who behave better than—"

"That's enough from you for the time being!" Tom said jabbing a pointed finger at him. Tilson looked away, suitably chastised. "Arrange transport with uniform for her back to the station," he told Cassie. Looking at Natasha, her demeanour had completely changed.

"I'm so sorry," she said quietly.

"You have some explaining to do, Natasha. You really do."

Cassie escorted her out of the office and back to the car to await the arrival of their colleagues. Tom scanned the office. They'd managed to make quite a mess. He turned to face Tilson, still sitting on the floor and cradling his face, dabbing at the blood with a handful of tissues he'd found from somewhere nearby.

"I'm sorry."

"What for?" Tom asked.

He shrugged. "For reacting like that. I–I don't really think she should be put down. I was just... scared."

"I know." Tom cast an eye over the man. Blood had run onto his shirt, a pink shirt with white pin stripes. It would be a devil to get clean, but it was ripped at the collar anyway. "That was quite a ferocious assault."

"Wasn't it just?" Tilson said. "I knew she was a piece of work, but I didn't think she had all of this in her."

"All of what?"

"Well... this," he said, waving a hand in a sweeping arc to indicate the office. "And I'm starting to think she must have had something to do with Henry's death... her and that pathetic bit on the side she's been sleeping with."

"Who is that?"

"The poser from the golf club. You know the one... Stannard."

"You're aware of their affair?"

He scoffed. "Of course, I am. So was Henry... although he swore me to secrecy. For the life of me, I'll never understand why."

Tom perched himself on the edge of a desk. The blood flow appeared to be easing and Tilson scrunched up the tissues into a ball and lay them carefully on the floor beside him. He was a methodical man, neat and precise.

"How long have you known, and Henry for that matter?"

Tilson looked thoughtfully up at the ceiling, then reached up to touch his eye. It was starting to swell.

"Months... two maybe?"

"And how did he find out? Did he tell you?"

Tilson nodded. "Yes, he hired a private investigator a while back."

"Peter Chard?"

"Yes, yes, of course. The chap who... yes."

"Specifically, to follow his wife—"

"Oh no! No, it wasn't like that. Henry hired Chard to find out who was sending the threatening letters, that's all. They were growing increasingly hostile... and Henry was frightened. Not just for himself, but for Olivia and Natasha too. Chard must have looked at all angles, even considering Natasha's lover as a source."

"Is that what Peter Chard reported back?"

"I'm not sure. Henry didn't give me all the details," he said pensively. "Natasha and I... we don't get along well much of the time, as you can see."

"Did Henry find Chard through his work at Quercus?"

"No, no he didn't. We used to hire investigators for cases at Quercus frequently, but Henry didn't want to use those contacts because of how things were between him and Cormac Daley. They were all on retainers you see."

"I gather there was a dispute over the cases Henry wanted to take on."

Tilson hesitated. It was momentary but more than enough for Tom and he seized upon it.

"Care to tell me the real reason Henry left Quercus?"

"Well... i–it was a complex—"

"Henry's dead, Alex. Whatever it is that everyone is skirting around and doesn't want to mention is going to come out. I will make sure of it." Tom folded his arms. "Now it will be far better for you I'm sure, and for Henry's memory, if I don't have to keep kicking over rocks to find it."

Tilson held Tom's gaze for a time. He swallowed hard as if his mouth had run dry.

"I will find out, Alex. With or without you. I'm tenacious like that... I never let anything go. You should ask my partner."

Tilson exhaled, lowering his head and rubbing at his forehead.

"All right... it probably doesn't matter anyway, not anymore." He sighed, leaning his head back against the desk and sniffing hard. "It goes back a few years to a case Henry was working on with Cormac. It was high profile, good for the exposure of the practice."

"You're speaking of The Hampstead Four?"

"Yes, that's right." Tilson's eyes narrowed but he went on, undeterred. "You are obviously already looking at it, so I'll spare you the basic details of the case, but it was prosecuted as a planned burglary that went wrong. We thought – Cormac thought – that the best course to chart to get a result would be that angle and, as it turned out, we had to go that way regardless."

"The homeowner was the target after all?"

Tilson smiled. "Yes, he was. Not that he was an innocent by any stretch of the imagination. I'd have thought you'd know about this stuff already." He rolled his eyes. "Police forces really don't talk to one another, do they? You see, there was already an investigation underway and two of The Hampstead Four were under surveillance. It was a Drug Squad operation... looking into the structure of a supply chain originating in South America and routing shipments into Europe through the port of Rotterdam and on into the UK among other places. They'd been working it for months, mapping out the network of dealers and transport routes. When they brought it down, it would be massive."

"And these two were involved in that how?"

Tilson waved away the question. "They were small fish in what looked like a very big barrel, but we weren't a party to every detail. As I understood it, they were working for a guy who was looking to advance his position in the network. The homeowner either stood in the way or was offering patronage to a rival... something like that, but either way he had to be eliminated."

"They were part of the same network?"

He nodded emphatically. "Oh yes. What's that old saying *keep your friends close, but your enemies even closer?* Well, they were both and, more importantly, close enough to get to him. We think they were trying to make it look like a break-in that went wrong." He chuckled momentarily which Tom found a little odd. "They made a bit of a hash of it, bearing in mind he nearly survived the assault. At least, they got manslaughter charges rather than murder which was what they had in mind when they forced their way in."

Tom frowned. "So why didn't this come up at the trial?"

"Your colleagues, Inspector. If they let it play out as a burglary, then their investigation could continue. A setback, certainly, but the operation wouldn't be a complete bust."

That made sense. If the burglars were convicted of just that, then it would be business as usual, and the team would be able to cultivate other sources of information.

"What about Chris Aldren?"

The light-hearted tone dissipated as Tilson looked away, hesitant.

"His family employed solicitors to look into the trial. What for?" Tom asked. "What did Henry do wrong?"

"Nothing!" Tilson said, but his defence was tinged with something else, a lack of confidence perhaps.

"Then why were they looking at it and how did this lead to Henry's departure from Quercus?"

Tilson put his head in his hands, resting his elbows on his knees that were drawn up by his chest and stared at the floor between his legs.

"Aldren was the weak link. Their weak link. The three who broke in were low-level dealers... and Aldren was just getting started with them." Tilson looked up at Tom, hugging his knees now as he told the story. "He was an addict, you know. Aldren was a drug addict when he drove the car that night and he remained one while he was inside... and I dare say he's one now. Did he know what he was getting into when they went to the house that night?" He shrugged. "I've no idea, none of us did. But he was young, raw... and the police wanted to use him."

"Use him how?"

"He knew people, knew routines... and the others were far too experienced to work with the police. They knew what would happen to them if they did. Aldren...? He didn't. They could get to him. They began negotiations with him while he was on remand, offering possible sweeteners if he helped. He was terrified of the prospect of spending a decade or more behind bars and was open to help. He fed information to the police and them to us. After all, if the prosecution did their job too well, then the overall investigation might be at risk."

"I didn't see a reduced sentence for Aldren in the case file when I read up on it, though."

He shook his head, dismissively. "Because it never came off. The defence team got wind of it and... let's just say Chris Aldren felt the wrath of the people he was looking to sell out.

That poor man... what he went through must have been horrific."

"Who leaked it?"

Tilson stared up at him, fearful.

"Was it Henry?"

Tilson shook his head. "It came from his office... and he was able to cover it up. At least until Margaret Aldren stuck her oar in... and her solicitor stumbled across it."

"Across what?"

"An email..." Tilson said, dejected. "One simple email, within which was a comment about the assistance offered by Chris Aldren – a single one-line reference – and that was enough to condemn him to a sentence of torture."

"Was it intentional?"

Tilson threw his head back and laughed. "No, Inspector. It was an email that went to a handful of people but... an email address was copied in in error... and it was sent directly to the defence team. It wasn't the result of corruption or retribution for a lack of cooperation; it was good old-fashioned incompetence. When it looked like it was in danger of coming out, Cormac Daley went ballistic. Henry stood his ground... and ultimately had to separate himself from the practice with half an eye on the expected fall-out."

"They threw Henry under the bus in order to save their reputation?" Tom asked.

Tilson shook his head, a gesture accompanied by a wistful smile. "No. Henry threw himself under the bus to protect *my* reputation. I sent that email, Inspector Janssen, but I did so from his account. I was rushing to get finished up that day, I had plans with friends and I was running late." He dragged a hand through his sweaty hair, pushing it to one side, away from his forehead. "Henry was a loyal man. He left the practice that he loved rather than expose me."

"Why would he choose to do that?"

Tilson hauled himself onto his feet, using the edge of the desk to brace himself as he levered himself up off the floor, groaning at the effort required. He faced Tom and smiled.

"Because he loved me, Inspector... and had done so for many years. He just couldn't find the strength to be honest about it with everyone else. Not even with his wife."

"And Chard's report – the one he handed over to Henry detailing Natasha's affair – did you have access to the footage?"

"Footage?" He was perplexed. "What footage?"

"The photographs and the video," Tom said. "Chard's attempt at blackmailing Natasha."

"I–I..." he stammered, his eyes narrowing. "What are you talking about?"

Cassie entered the office. Upon reading Tom's expression, she glanced at Alex Tilson.

"Okay, what have I missed?"

Tom looked at her. "Chris Aldren. Find him, now!"

CHAPTER TWENTY-SEVEN

Tom strode purposefully into ops. Cassie garnered his attention as soon as he'd hung his jacket up next to the entrance. Natasha Crowe was downstairs in a cell waiting to be interviewed following her arrest for assaulting Alex Tilson. The attack demonstrated her possession of a quick temper as well as a capacity for violence, one he never knew existed.

"Chris Aldren hasn't been seen or heard from in nine months," she said as Tom came to stand alongside her. "He was reported missing by his mother, Margaret, at that time. She was concerned for his wellbeing." Cassie turned to her computer screen and read through the information in front of her. "During his time in prison, Chris was repeatedly hospitalised due to his mental health."

Tom was surprised. "He must have been in quite a state. As I understand it, half of those in prison are considered to have mental health issues and there are nowhere near enough resources within the system to cope with that."

"Yes, the prisons just have to make do with what they have." Cassie opened another file, scanned documents provided by Her Majesty's Prison Service. "Seemingly he managed quite well whilst on remand but following his conviction things took a turn for the worse. He was placed on suicide watch only two weeks after sentencing and there are multiple references to episodes of self-harming."

Tom's brow furrowed. "Can you skip forward to the incidents that Alex Tilson mentioned; the acts of retribution Aldren experienced for assisting us."

"Sure. The first incident that stands out was an attack in his cell where boiling water and sugar were thrown over his face. The sugar burns hotter than just using the water and it sticks to the skin as well. It's a poor man's napalm; ingredients are readily available and it's quick and easy to concoct." Cassie glanced at the screen again. "Superficial facial injuries on that one. The next time they went for his feet."

"Did they break them?"

Cassie shook her head. "No, they set fire to them. Report says someone sneaked out white spirit from the machine shop... highly flammable, doused his bare feet and set them on fire."

"Turps," Tom said quietly.

"What's that?"

"Turpentine. It's basically white spirit and that was what Henry's killer burned his feet with." Tom sat down on the edge of a desk, folding his arms across his chest. "We've found our link."

"Yeah, that can't be a coincidence," Cassie said.

"What can't?" Tamara asked. They both turned to welcome her as she joined them. "Apparently you have Natasha Crowe in custody?"

"When we went out to her place to meet Alex Tilson, we found her attacking him in Henry's office earlier today. Tilson and Henry were lovers and have been for a long time, their relationship even predating her marriage to Henry."

"Right, so it's a bit rich for Henry to be hiring a private investigator to follow her around, isn't it?"

Tom shook his head. "We don't think that's what he was doing, though. The affair, and the blackmail, was a side-line to the main reason Pete was investigating."

"Which was?"

"The threatening letters he was receiving. According to Tilson they were getting ever more graphic, and Henry was frightened, not only for himself but also for his family, Natasha included." Tom gestured to the screen with a casual flick of the hand. "Chris Aldren was tortured in prison for negotiating with the CPS to provide evidence against drug dealers. That's from what we can gather anyway. Henry Crowe was tortured in a similar manner, remember the state of his feet?"

"Set alight and then put out," Tamara said. "Yes, I do. Nasty. You think it's Aldren retaliating against the people he thinks revealed his actions to the dealers?"

"That's what we're thinking," Tom said. "Aldren went missing nine months ago. It was reported by his late mother—"

"This is interesting!" Eric called and they looked over at him. He was staring at his screen and didn't look up to make sure he had their attention, assuming they were listening. "A member of the public called in a report of a disturbed individual standing at the top of Hunstanton Cliffs two nights before Margaret Aldren reported her son missing. Uniform attended but when they arrived no one was there and despite a search they couldn't find anyone. The caller's description matches that of Chris Aldren; right age and ethnicity."

"Probably matches a quarter of the town, too, though, doesn't it?" Tom said.

"True, but Aldren's bank account wasn't accessed after that date, although a large sum of money was withdrawn three days prior to it. None of his friends or contacts ever reported seeing him again, not that he had many friends on the face of it. It was put to his mother that this was a possible outcome of his disappearance, but she claimed to have seen him loitering near her home late one night three weeks after she reported him missing."

"Maybe that was true or, which I'd find more likely, she was desperately trying to keep the investigation into his disappearance alive," Tamara said. "She may not have realised it, but by claiming to have seen him she was reducing the likelihood of us searching harder. What about mobile phone records?"

Eric shook his head. "He didn't have one after his release. At least that was what his mum said, and the missing person's team couldn't find a record of him owning one." Eric shrugged. "He could have had a pay as you go... it's what he'd have been used to with phonecards in prison."

"Did any unidentified bodies wash up anywhere along the coast in subsequent weeks or months?" Tom asked, well aware that bodies could be given up by the sea many weeks after they entered it. More often though, they were permanently claimed if drawn out far enough.

"Oh yes, several. Let's be honest, that isn't uncommon." Eric's fingers were a blur on the keyboard, his face a picture of concentration. After a minute he looked up. "One of the bodies *could* have been Aldren. The post-mortem recorded accidental death by drowning... and the general description is similar to Aldren, but it was estimated the body spent a month in the water and that changes the appearance quite a bit. They logged a DNA sample on file prior to burial just in case a family member came forward to claim the body later. So far, no one has." Eric's eyebrows knitted. "Could he have faked it? His death, I mean. His solicitor told us he didn't have faith in the system, didn't he? Maybe he took the situation into his own hands."

"That's true," Tom said, glancing at Kerry.

Cassie was sceptical. "This guy was a mess. Do you think he'd have the wherewithal to pull all this together? Where has he been for nine months? How has he been living?"

"Well," Tom said, thinking hard, "he wasn't an innocent in all of this. The judge at trial found him equally culpable and the sentencing reflected that fact. Even a conviction under joint enterprise leaves room for the judge to apply mitigating factors and she chose not to do so. That says a lot."

"Your point?" Tamara asked.

Tom shrugged. "That Aldren knew people who live and earn money outside of regular channels, and he'd just served a lengthy custodial sentence in the greatest training ground a criminal could ever wish for." He looked at Cassie. "He could easily have developed the skills to pull this off." He blew out his cheeks. "It doesn't mean I think he did, mind you. I'd like to find him and ask though. Is there a living relative who could supply a DNA sample to try and match to the unidentified body pulled out of the sea?"

Eric's brow furrowed. "I think Chris was an only child. I don't know. I'll have to look."

"Do it," Tom said. "If he isn't dead, then I want to find him."

Cassie scoffed. "If missing persons drew a blank, what are we supposed to do?"

"Missing persons were searching for an adult who no one had seen," he said, "one who could choose to walk away from his life and has the right to do so. We are looking for a murder suspect. A convicted criminal recently released on licence. I doubt they were busting a gut to find him, do you?"

"Fair enough," she said, tilting her head to one side. "If he's alive, we'll find him."

"Right, I'm going downstairs to have a word with Natasha," Tom said. "Seeing as she's allowed us to see more of her than ever before, I'm planning to see how open she'll be. Maybe there's something she'd like to tell us."

Tamara put a hand on his forearm as he passed her. "Do you still think she had nothing to do with either murder?"

He thought about it for a second and shook his head. "No, I don't but I'm more than happy to be proved wrong."

Tamara withdrew her hand and Tom left. Cassie looked over her shoulder at the DCI.

"He'd rather have us chasing ghosts instead," she whispered.

Tamara placed a hand gently on Cassie's shoulder, leaning into her. "It's not often that he's wrong though, is it? But don't tell him I said so."

CHAPTER TWENTY-EIGHT

Tom opened the cover to the peephole and looked into the cell, glancing sideways at the custody officer and stepping aside so he could unlock the door. The heavy iron door groaned and shrieked on its hinges as it opened. Natasha didn't look up as Tom entered. The cell was twelve feet long and just shy of six wide. To the left of the door was a stainless-steel toilet with no seat and Natasha was sitting on the bed, a raised platform with an inch-thick mattress wrapped in blue plastic. The cell was minimalist in the extreme.

Tom took a couple of steps inside, turning and leaning his back against the wall, hands cupped in front of him. Natasha sat with her knees against her chest, hugging her legs with both arms, gently rocking backwards and forwards and almost imperceptibly humming a tune. He thought it was a familiar lullaby, but he couldn't work out which one.

"How are you, Natasha?"

She didn't acknowledge him, instead, she stayed staring straight ahead, eyes wide with a vacant expression, repeating the same tune. Tom angled his head, leaning directly into her line of sight in an attempt to get her attention.

"It's been quite a week for you, hasn't it?"

Her eyes shifted slightly, glancing up at him before slowly moving away again, the humming ceased.

"I loved him," she whispered. Tom straightened himself up, nodding. "I really did love Henry, regardless of what you all think."

"I don't doubt it, Natasha."

She looked at him then, her focussed expression gauging the authenticity of his statement. Seemingly satisfied, she lifted her head away from her knees and slowly nodded.

"Thank you."

"Why did you attack Alex Tilson?"

She raised her eyebrows, taking a deep breath. "I shouldn't have done that... I was angry." Looking around the cell, she dismissively shook her head. "To think I put so much effort into keeping my time with Mark a secret from Henry and he knew, had done for months... but he didn't say a word."

Tom pursed his lips. "People deal with things differently—"

"Yes, he dealt with it by having sex with his personal assistant." She lifted her left hand fractionally, apologising for snapping. "I'm sorry. All this time... I thought Henry was one of those men who just didn't like sex." She looked at Tom, fixing him with a stern look. "Some men are like that, aren't they? They don't care for sexual relations, they're..." she struggled for the right word.

"Asexual," Tom said.

"That's it. I often wondered if that applied to Henry." She shrugged. "I didn't mind, not really. I could satisfy those urges elsewhere without threatening my marriage. It looks like I needn't have bothered hiding it or paying that sod Chard!"

Tom felt something rise within him. Even though Pete had

proven to be someone he didn't recognise, the memories he had were still strong.

"He didn't do right by you, that's true. My best guess – for what it's worth – is that Chard told Henry about your affair with Mark Stannard, and he wasn't fazed by it. He probably admitted he wasn't likely to confront you and Chard saw an opportunity—"

"To exploit me?"

Tom tilted his head in acknowledgment. "It is pure speculation on my part though, so take it or leave it."

"He couldn't even get angry about me playing away." She lowered her head back to rest on her knees. "How little must he have thought of me?"

"Quite the contrary," Tom countered. "I didn't know him well at all, but I should imagine he found it hard to be who he truly was. No one doubts the love he had for his daughter and his fear of anything happening to either of you was very real. He wanted a child, a family, but he couldn't live a life that was entirely true to himself. His relationship with Alex predates your marriage—"

"So, the deceit started from the very beginning?" she said, sneering.

"That's one way to look at it."

"There's another?" she asked, genuinely interested.

"Maybe he chose his life partner very carefully; someone he considered would be a good wife, a great mother… and someone he could trust to spend his life with."

She met his eye with an inquisitive look. "Do you believe that? I mean, *really* believe that?"

Tom shrugged. "I think it is possible. He created the perfect home life for his family, giving them almost everything he had to offer… apart from a physical relationship with you. And he didn't appear likely to demand that you end it. He'll have known what you were up to – Pete Chard told him – and yet he said nothing." Tom gave it a moment for the words to sink in. "You think he didn't care... I'd argue he cared enough to allow you the freedom to fill that gap in your life that he knew he never could. I think he loved you very much... in his own way."

She sat back against the cell wall, running both her hands up her face and through her hair. She bit her lower lip. "All that paranoia he had... around the letters, his relationship with Cormac and Quercus ..." she laughed. "Even the hissy fits he used to have over the cleaner."

Tom smiled. "The cleaner? She was Portuguese, wasn't she?"

"Estella, yes," she said, smiling. "But I didn't mean her. I was paranoid about her for a while. Henry adored her. After Olivia was born, I felt all mumsy and frumpy... and thought that was why he didn't come near me anymore." Her smile broadened. "I guess we know the real reason now, don't we? He was having his jollies with Alex, and I was, what, an incubator?"

Tom didn't know what to say, so he kept his counsel.

"Besides, I didn't mean her. Estella went home after her mother got sick, to look after her and her father, and we got someone else. I made sure she was older," she pointedly jabbed a finger in the air. "I felt less threatened by her, although she was useless. I mean, as far as cleaners go, she was the worst ever!"

"And Henry didn't like her?"

She grinned, the first such gesture that he felt derived from real humour. "He couldn't stand her! That's what I meant about paranoia; he had it in for her right from the start, said she was nosy and in the end flat out accused her of stealing."

"Wow. She doesn't sound great at all. Was she, stealing I mean?"

Natasha shrugged. "Nothing of mine went missing and she was nice enough to me. I reckon she was too old to do the job. The house was too large or something because I could see her struggling with the workload, but Henry had a real thing about her. He said he'd find her places she shouldn't be... skiving off and not actually working. I wanted to keep her around, despite her being useless."

"Less of a threat?"

She smiled, nodding slowly. "Yes, that's about the size of it. In the end, I had to give in and let her go. It was the only way to shut him up" He'd go on and on... I was tired of it. I told him he'd have to hire a bloke instead." She tilted her head, exaggerating the widening of her eyes. "Little did I know, hey?"

Tom smiled. "Did you ever get to the bottom of it? Was she stealing?"

Natasha shook her head. "No, I don't think so. She was hopeless at her job, that was true, but I couldn't see her being a thief. Like I said, nothing of mine went missing and what on earth could Henry have that was worth taking? When can I go home, Inspector?" Natasha asked. "Olivia will be getting scared. I know I shouldn't have attacked Alex, but you won't keep me here overnight, will you? I really don't know what came over me."

Tom stared straight ahead, thoughts coming to mind quicker than he could process them. *Could it be that simple?* Suddenly doubting his train of thought, he tried to shake the sensation.

"Inspector Janssen?"

He looked at her. "Sorry, w–what did you say?"

"I was just asking when you thought I might be able to go home?"

"Soon," he said, smiling warmly. "Believe it or not, but Alex Tilson doesn't wish for us to press charges and so I expect a caution will suffice, under these particular circumstances. It will need to be agreed with a senior officer, but it shouldn't take too long." She looked relieved. "Tell me, your cleaner – the one you let go – what was her name?"

"Oh…" Natasha said, appearing thoughtful but shaking her head after a moment. "Maggie… something… I'm sorry, I can't remember. She was only with us for a month or two and she wasn't very chatty. Not with me, anyway. Why do you ask?"

He smiled. "No, it doesn't matter. Just a thought."

CHAPTER TWENTY-NINE

TOM PARKED the car at the end of Beach Road at the top of the slipway. A skiff was sitting on a trailer waiting to be collected and Tom glanced past it down to the small section of beach enclosed by the sea wall and strategically placed rocks used to break up the pressure of the tides on the old harbour. The lifeguard flags were in position designating the safe swimming area and he could see two guards at the station above keeping watch on those making use of today's calm sea. The water wouldn't be particularly warm at this time of the year, even with the air temperatures increasing as the onset of summer took hold. The best time to appreciate the waters around the British Isles was in late September or early October as the sea had had months to warm up throughout the summer.

The breeze was gentle, the smell and taste of salt water carried on the air.

"It's that way, isn't it?" Cassie asked.

Tom nodded and the two of them set off along the promenade in the direction of the colourful beach huts that lay at the foot of Sheringham's steep cliffs. The cafe was the last building on the promenade, opposite the lifeguard station and with a line of tables and chairs for patrons to sit out alongside the railings overlooking the beach below.

The distinct sound of a circular saw came from inside as two tradesmen, painters and decorators judging by their spattered dungarees, opened the door and stepped out. Tom held the door open, and the two men sidestepped them, laughing at some passing reference one had made to the amusement of the other.

They entered. The cafe was compact with more seating outside than in. A small counter lay off to the right with a line of raised bar stools to the left beneath the picture window giving views out to sea. Tables and chairs ringed the side and rear walls, although they were all covered in plastic sheeting to keep them clean. Three of the walls were freshly coated and the team were working on prepping the woodwork judging by the wood dust that was hanging in the air.

The joinery was taking place in the adjoining room, the kitchen and food preparation area. Tom stood in the doorway and called out. The intense sound of the spinning blade quietened as his presence was noticed.

"Ah... Inspector Janssen, isn't it?"

"Yes, Mr Bassham," Tom said. "Can I have a word?"

Les Bassham came out of the kitchen wiping his grubby hands on an old rag. He glanced between Tom and Cassie as he came to stand before them.

"Will this take long?" he asked, looking around. "The decorators want to be in there after their break and I'm a bit behind."

"I wanted to ask you about Maggie."

Bassham looked straight at Tom, his eyes narrowing. "Oh... whatever for? I can't see what interest the police have in her."

"You weren't married, were you?" Cassie said.

He shook his head. "Nah, didn't see the need. Go through

all that hassle just for a slip of paper. So what?" He frowned. "What's all this about?"

"She worked, didn't she, Maggie?"

"Aye. She never liked Maggie as a nickname though. Her mother used to call her by it," he said, a half-smile fleetingly crossing her face. "I had to use Margaret. Seriously, what's this about?"

"I think you know, Les," Tom said, fixing him with a stare. "And I think it's time to drop all the smoke and mirrors and just be honest, don't you?"

He laughed nervously. "Now, I *really* want to know what you're talking about."

"I'm talking about your late partner's son, Chris." Bassham's expression changed. "And the job she took cleaning for Henry Crowe at his family home and office."

Bassham took a deep breath, averting his eyes to the rag in his hands. Casually wiping his hands once more, he lifted his head and tossed the rag onto the counter sucking air through his teeth. He nodded. "Right you are. I understand."

He looked pale, glancing around for a seat. Cassie lifted a plastic sheet and took one, sliding it out for him. Bassham accepted it, gingerly sitting himself down. He only had eyes for the floor at his feet.

"Tell me about her," Tom said, leaning against the counter. "Why did she take the job at Henry Crowe's place?"

Bassham laughed. It was a sad sound devoid of genuine humour. "She had to get herself close to him," Bassham said, shaking his head in resignation. "I told her, *leave it to your solicitor,* but she wouldn't have it. She thought she'd be able to make the difference."

"How?"

"Well, I don't bloody know, Inspector." He looked up pensively at Tom. "Find something maybe."

"Find what?"

"The truth! That's all I ever got from her, that she was after *the truth*; whatever the hell that was. She was even worse after Chris... disappeared."

"Where do you think he went?" Tom asked.

"The state he was in?" He scoffed, shaking his head. "I don't see him coming back, let's put it that way. And nor did his mum, not that she'd ever say it." He sat upright, taking a deep breath. "To admit Chris was gone would be to admit the end of her cause," he said smiling ruefully, "and she could never do that, it was all she lived for."

"How did she pass, if you don't mind my asking?"

He looked at Tom glumly. "Massive stroke. Looking back, she'd had multiple warning signs that it was coming but they'd passed quickly enough and neither of us realised what we were dealing with, not really. Stress didn't help..." he cocked his head "and she's had plenty of that over the years. You'll have pulled Chris's file by now, I'm sure."

"Margaret believed her son's experience was a miscarriage of justice?" Tom asked.

"No, not a miscarriage; Chris was guilty as sin. They all were," he said, snorting a laugh. "But he didn't deserve what happened to him. I know that for a fact." The moment of deflation had passed and Bassham's expression lightened ever so slightly. "You know I was in the army once?"

"Yes, we looked you up. Decent soldier according to your commanding officers."

He grinned, showing a tar-stained smile. "I was, but all that's a long time ago. You know, back in the late eighties, when I was stationed in the old West Germany as it was back then, we had a bloke in our company. A real Jack-the-lad character, quick-witted, really fancied himself. I never liked him, and I wasn't alone. He was the type who pushed things too far." He sat up, briefly raising his hands in supplication. "I wasn't perfect, most of us in that unit weren't. Believe me, very few people join up because it's their best career option; more like we're hiding from something, but that's another story."

"The guy, the one you didn't like?" Tom asked. "What about him?"

"Well, we were on downtime one night – it was a Friday, I think – and we're hanging out at the NAAFI having a few beers as you do, and word comes through that there's been a shooting in the town." He shook his head. "Turns out there'd been an armed robbery in the town and the guy had fled. They were looking for a Brit, his German was pretty rubbish and they clocked him as a foreigner. Some taxi driver got shot that night, too, and they reckoned it was the same bloke, right. The description was awful familiar."

"You thought it was him?"

"This guy was out and about that night – no one knew where – and he turned up eventually, late on… proper shifty-looking he was too. As it happens, he'd checked out a firearm from the armoury that morning, taking in some shooting practice or so he said."

"And was it him?" Tom asked, curious.

"Oh yeah, without a doubt. Not that he'd fess up to it. At least, not of his own accord." There was a gleam in his eyes as he looked up at Tom. "You know it took four of us to hold him down while someone put the iron on his back… man did he scream… and in the end he gave us the truth. It was him all right."

Tom was shocked at the casual manner in which he described such an episode.

"I can see you disapprove, Inspector."

"That's not how it works."

"Except in this case, had we not done that he would have got away with it. I often wonder why he killed that taxi driver? Was he excited by the thrill of the robbery and went a step further or did the driver figure out what he'd done and would be able to identify him? Maybe he didn't have a reason and he was just a sick bastard?" Bassham shrugged. "Whatever went on, a dead man deserves justice, wouldn't you say?" he looked first at Cassie and then Tom, where his gaze lingered. "You're a police officer. Wouldn't it be galling to see a guilty man escape justice?"

"It happens all the time though. We make our case but ultimately the system decides and—"

"That's where it's wrong, though, isn't it? The system isn't fit for purpose if the guilty walk freely among us."

"And yet it's the only one we have, and we must accept the rulings and decisions are made in good faith, be them for or against us, because otherwise there would be chaos."

Bassham shook his head. "Not chaos, Inspector Janssen. *Justice.*"

"And what did you achieve by killing Henry Crowe?"

"Achieve?" Bassham hissed. "What that man did cost Chris his life and in losing him, I lost Margaret! She was consumed by it all... wearing her down, dismantling her piece by piece... for years! Why did that happen? Because some rich bloke revealed Chris to be a grass. Do you know what it was like for him after that?"

"I can imagine it was difficult—"

"Difficult!" Bassham bitterly shook his head. "His life wasn't worth living. They tortured the boy almost every day. He tried to kill himself multiple times, even started taking drugs just to get by. Do you know he took more drugs in prison than he ever did on the outside?"

"And that's why you pumped Henry full of methamphetamines, isn't it?"

"Damn right, yes! When Chris came out, he was a wreck... an addict. His mother and I tried to set him straight, but we couldn't. We tried our hardest, even got him drugs to try and wean him off his addiction. It felt weird at first, buying it, but once we understood that it was what Chris needed, then it got easier. We tried everything we could think of for that boy, but nothing worked. I gave Crowe what we had left over. That way, he would know what it felt like."

"A suitable punishment for Chris's suffering?"

"Something like that. In the end, it all got so bad for him, the prison staff had to do something for Chris, and they ghosted him... do you know what that is?"

Tom shook his head.

"No, of course you don't! Why would you care? It's when they *disappear* you... flush someone into the system, move them around so no one knows where or who you are. Prison to prison, at a moment's notice." He shook his head, staring at the floor. "And even that didn't work, because inmates are a curious bunch, Inspector. They want to know who you are and what you're in for; there are hierarchies at work in those places and everyone has a story. If yours isn't known, then they look at you even more. Chris ended up in secure wings, living with the sex offenders; child rapists and paedophiles... and do you think they respected who he was? Those weirdos don't stop offending just because they're locked up, you know. Chris's fifteen years felt like thirty." He looked at Tom, jabbing a pointed finger at him. "People should be punished for what they do. It doesn't get any simpler than that."

"And that was what Margaret was looking for whilst working at Henry Crowe's home?"

"Yeah... anything she could find to prove what he'd done. I

told her she was bonkers. I mean, what would she find? It's not likely he'd have written down his role in some great conspiracy theory for her to find, is it?"

"But her solicitor found it, didn't he?"

"Oh yes, worth his weight in gold that one. Not that we had any money to pay him, mind you."

"What about Peter Chard—?"

"That piece of work?" Bassham said dismissively. "He was pure scum."

Tom felt himself bridle but remained impassive. "Did he deserve to die too?"

"You know, he came to me... after June had spotted him sitting outside in his van for a few days. I hadn't noticed but she did; the woman sees everything!"

"How did he find you?"

Bassham laughed. "The letters. I shouldn't have sent the letters... but I'd just lost Margaret and I was in a bad place. I don't know how he figured it out, but he did. Same way as you, I guess."

"What did he want?"

"Money," Bassham said. "He said he'd been hired by Crowe and that he knew what I'd been up to. He said he could make it all go away," he sneered as he spoke, "for the right price."

"How much?"

"Does it matter?"

Tom inclined his head. "I guess not."

"He would only have come back time and again asking for more," Bassham said. "That's what people like him do. It's what they are, leeches. There's no way I was going to pay him, so I went to Henry first. I wanted to look into his face and see his fear, his regret for what he was responsible for. Margaret had a set of keys to the house. She'd had spares cut while she worked for them, handing their set back after she left their employ."

"You went to his place to kill him. The drugs alone were enough to do it, but that wasn't enough for you."

"No! That's not true!"

"But that's what happened—"

"He told me what happened, that Chris was a criminal and that was how these people treated one another in prisons. He didn't care... he didn't feel responsible at all. Not for Chris, not for Margaret... our life, *nothing!*"

He was speaking through gritted teeth, his fists balled so tight Tom could see the whites of his knuckles.

"And yes," he stared at Tom, "I killed him that night... and he deserved it! I just wish Margaret had been there to see him get what he deserved."

"And Pete Chard? You had no choice but to kill him, right? I mean, he knew who you were and what you'd been up to. One phone call to us and you were done for."

"I met him... on the proviso I'd buy his silence. He wanted more than I could possibly afford." He shook his head, averting his eyes from Tom's gaze. "I had no choice."

"Only that's not quite true, is it?" Tom said. Les Bassham met his eye, gently biting his lower lip. "I think you knew exactly what you were planning to do the very moment you killed Henry."

"Is that a fact?"

"Yes, because you went to Henry's house knowing full well what you intended to do. You tortured him in the same manner as they did to Chris... and you didn't ask him what happened."

"That's a bold statement for someone who wasn't there. What makes you so sure?" Bassham asked.

"Because it wasn't Henry Crowe's fault Chris's intentions

came to light. It was a junior assistant who made an error when sending an email… a tragic, but an honest mistake. Just as we hear alarmingly often how an MOD employee leaves a top-secret file on the top deck of a London bus or loses their briefcase with sensitive information inside in a pub. It's incompetence, certainly, but it's not deliberate."

"I did what needed to be done!" he snarled.

"And you think Margaret would have wanted you to do that?" Tom asked. "To premeditate a double murder—"

"I told you I never planned it!"

"And yet you took a kitchen knife from the Crowe house on the night you killed Henry, and then used that to murder Peter Chard several days later?" Tom said, coming to stand over him. "You went through Henry's office in search of evidence all right, anything that might point us in your direction. But what did you find, Chard's photographs of Natasha and her lover… video footage as well, or did you come by that when you cleaned out the camper van the night you killed him? You took that knife from the house for one reason and one reason alone; to kill Pete Chard with it and then you led us to Natasha Crowe and Mark Stannard."

Bassham glared at him, his face reddening. "Yeah, well… if you lie down with dogs, you get fleas."

Tom felt his anger rising. "You were happy to see two innocent people go to prison, leaving an eight-year-old girl effectively orphaned, to save your own neck! And you have the bare-faced cheek to sit there using words like justice to explain away your actions. You're no better than the people you despise… and probably much, much worse."

Bassham looked away, staring out through the window. He didn't say another word.

CHAPTER THIRTY

SAFFY CAME BOUNDING up to them, throwing herself into Tom's arms on the assumption he'd catch her. He did. The sun was shining and with the tide out, the golden sands of Old Hunstanton beach were the open playground for the families of locals and tourists alike.

"You said we could get ice creams," Saffy said indignantly.

"Yes, that's true," Tom said, "but that was if we went for a walk along Hunstanton promenade. However," he jabbed her playfully in the chest, "you chose to come to Old Hunstanton beach for the sand instead and there is only the one shop here and it's closed right now—"

Saffy waved her hand in the air towards the lighthouse car park above them where an ice cream van had arrived, just as it played the tell-tale music announcing its presence.

"See… ice cream," she said, beaming.

Tom laughed, glancing between Alice and Cara Chard.

Alice smiled. "I'll go. What am I getting?"

"A 99 for me, please," Saffy announced confidently. "And with a double flake—"

"You'll have a single, young lady," Alice replied. Saffy

pouted in that way she did when she wasn't really offended but would let you think she was. Alice turned to Cara. "How about yours, Cara?"

Cara looked across the beach to her children, Saffy running back to join them. Russell, her dog, broke away from the older children and bounded towards the little girl.

"They'll both have the same as Saffy," Cara said. "They're not fussy."

"And you?"

Both Tom and Cara declined. Alice set off, Saffy making a beeline to join her. Russell followed, hesitantly before turning back and running to the others.

"She's a great little girl, Tom," Cara said, hooking her arm through his as they slowly walked.

"I know. We couldn't hope for more." He looked down at his feet. "Perhaps she could be quieter… but aside from that."

Cara laughed.

"How are your two coping?" he asked. Both of them looked at her two children, the dog running back and forth between them.

"They miss their father," she said, "but that's nothing new. He hadn't been around for some time, but we always expected him to come back to us one day. Now he won't… and they haven't processed that yet." She looked at Tom. "I haven't either, to be honest."

"Give it time."

"What else have I got," she said, wistfully.

They walked for a minute without speaking, Tom wary of broaching what he had to say. She noticed.

"What is it, Tom?"

He cocked his head, smiling apologetically. "You're going to hear some things… when this comes to trial."

She was surprised. "I thought he confessed, this Bassham guy?"

"He did," Tom said before sighing. "And subsequently retracted every word as soon as he spoke to a solicitor."

"Can he do that," she stopped, withdrawing her arm and turning to face him, "get away with it I mean?"

"He will certainly try. There's a lack of forensic evidence at either scene directly tying him to the cases, and he did a decent job of making Henry Crowe's wife and her lover look like key suspects."

"But he won't walk away—"

"No chance, not in my opinion. We're working to tie the threatening letters and the evidence he fed us together. We found a printer at his home and forensics are certain they'll be able to tie what he sent us to that machine. That will be a firm link. It won't take long and I'm confident."

She smiled weakly and they started to walk back, spotting Alice heading back down to the beach, Saffy making short work of her ice cream cone. Tom leaned into Cara, gently nudging her with his elbow.

"Don't worry," he said, "contrary to widespread belief some of us coppers are actually pretty clever. He'll not get away with it."

"But if he's pleading not guilty then there will be a trial," she said, sorrowfully. "I'm disappointed – no, bloody angry actually – that my children will have to go through that."

"Me too."

"What things?" she asked. He glanced at her. "What things are going to come out… do you mean about Pete?"

"Yes. I would prepare yourself," he looked at the children, "and the kids too."

She took a deep breath. "That bad, huh?"

"Well, you know Pete… without anyone to rein him in—"

"You were the one who was always able to do that, you know." She reached out and touched his arm. He appreciated the gesture. "When left to his own devices... Oh... never mind."

Alice handed Cara's children their ice creams and headed towards them, Saffy bobbing around her excitedly, playing loose and fast with her cone regardless of Alice's encouragement to be careful.

"So how long are you going to dither?" Cara asked.

"About what?"

Cara casually indicated Alice, sweeping her flowing hair away from her face as she shared a joke with Saffy, both full of smiles.

"Those two."

"I don't know what you mean," he said.

"Really?" She stepped in front of him, barring his way. Alice was only a few metres away now, but Cara had her back to her, and the breeze carried her words away from the approaching pair. "They both adore you, you know? You're their entire world."

"You think?" he said, unsure.

"Yes, I do. To an outsider like me, it's obvious," she said, smiling.

"Besides, I don't see what's wrong with the status quo. We're doing okay."

"Take it from me, Tom, okay is all right for a while but don't leave it too long. If you do, you'll regret it."

"What are the two of you whispering about?" Alice asked coming to join them.

"Oh, nothing... much, really," Tom said, feeling awkward and not understanding why. He'd been thinking about his relationship with Alice for a while now, but things were going so well that he didn't wish to jinx it. Maybe Cara was right, and this was the nudge he needed.

"You're a terrible liar, Tom Janssen," Alice said, slipping her arm around his waist and leaning into him. "It's a good job you're on the side of the good guys or you'd be stuffed."

"Can't argue with that," he said. Saffy came before him, raising a hand aloft and extending a half-eaten, sticky-sided ice cream cone towards him. "What's this?"

"Had enough," Saffy said and as soon as he took the cone from her, she bolted back to join the other children, Russell coming part way to meet her.

"I guess I'm finishing this then?"

"And it's not all you have left to finish, is it, Tom?" Cara asked, winking at him. He felt his face redden.

Alice saw the exchange. "Okay, now I'm really curious!" she said, smiling.

Tom looked between both women. Both were amused by his discomfort.

"Remind me not to invite you back any time soon, Cara."

Cara feigned offence and Alice reached across and touched her hand. "You ignore him. You and the kids are welcome here any time you like."

Tom didn't disagree, turning his attention to Saffy running back and forth, changing direction on a sixpence and outfoxing her dog. He drew Alice in a little closer and she smiled up at him with a curious look. He smiled but said nothing.

FREE BOOK GIVEAWAY

Visit the author's website at **www.jmdalgliesh.com** and sign up to the VIP Club and be the first to receive news and previews of forthcoming works.

Here you can download a FREE eBook novella exclusive to club members;

Life & Death - A Hidden Norfolk novella

Never miss a new release.

No spam, ever, guaranteed. You can unsubscribe at any time.

Enjoy this book? You could make a real difference.

Because reviews are critical to the success of an author's career, if you have enjoyed this novel, please do me a massive favour by entering one onto Amazon.

———

Type the following link into your internet search bar to go to the Amazon page and leave a review;

http://mybook.to/fool-me-twice

———

If you prefer not to follow the link please visit the sales page where you purchased the title in order to leave a review.

Reviews increase visibility. Your help in leaving one would make a massive difference to this author and I would be very grateful.

THE RAVEN SONG - PREVIEW
HIDDEN NORFOLK - BOOK 11

THE WHITE LIGHT on the horizon blinked on and off as the sash window rattled with yet another fierce gust of wind driving against it, followed moments later by a spatter of rain carried in off the sea. Searching the growing gloom for the speck of light, it reappeared momentarily before vanishing a fraction of a second later. Were the crew hunkered down inside, safe against the ravages of nature hammering the ship, or were they battling to keep afloat, to stay alive?

The howling wind dissipated for a second. A moment of quiet calm descending on the room. Had the storm passed? The window shrieked again making her jump, accompanied by a squeak passing from her own lips.

"Come away from the window, darling."

She remained where she was, staring out at the passing ship whose lights were, once again, winking at her from the darkness. In that moment she wanted to be on board that vessel – wherever it was going – rather than here in her bedroom. Would someone be on that ship staring at the lights from her home atop the headland, envious of the safety and security that the mainland had to offer?

It isn't any safer here.

"Are you going to come and read?"

She looked back, smiling at the man lying on top of the duvet, feet crossed with an open book in his hand. With one last glance towards the ship out at sea, she crossed the room and climbed over her father and slipped under the duvet.

"Don't you want to close the curtains?" he asked.

"No." She stared out into the black of night. "I want to see the stars if I wake up during the night."

"I don't think there will be any stars tonight, darling. This storm won't pass until tomorrow morning."

She shrugged. "I don't care."

Nestling into her father, he held the book open with his right hand and put his left arm around her.

"Now, where did we get to last night?"

"There," she said, pointing to a break in the text at the top of the right hand page. Her father paused, rereading the section before.

"Yes, you're right."

"Tim is searching for his brother...* and everyone has heard about him but no one knows where he is."

"Right... I remember," her father said quietly. "I think."

"I can tell you..." She offered, nervous. "If you like?"

"Yes, thank you."

How he could have forgotten, she didn't know. They'd read three chapters the previous night, far more than the one chapter they usually read. That was probably down to today. Neither of them had been looking forward to today, attempting to put it off as long as possible. But as night follows day, it had come. There was no way of avoiding life, or death, as it transpired.

"Tim has died... and now he is looking for his brother in the afterlife." She hesitated.

"What is it darling?"

"Tim... he can walk here... he can run?"

"Yes, that's true. It's a good thing." Her father shifted in the bed so he could look sideways down at her and read her expression. "Isn't it?"

"Yes, of course... but..."

"But what?"

"He isn't in pain any more. He is... normal."

The weight of that last word sounded heavy as she spoke it.

"Yes."

"And... in the afterlife... that's how it is?" He looked at her quizzically. "I mean, if you are ill in real life, you don't carry that across with you?"

"No... it's a fresh start... sort of, but with all the memories, thoughts and feelings of your life carried over with you."

She thought about it for a moment, reluctant to ask the question although she could tell he was preparing himself to hear it.

"And what about Mummy?"

"She is there too."

"And she isn't...* hurt anymore?" She was scared of the answer. Whatever he said, it wouldn't take away the pain she'd felt all day but it might, at the very least, offer a crumb of consolation.

"No," he said quietly, "she isn't in pain. Not anymore."

She teared up, burying her face in the side of her father's chest to hide the tears from him. He had been upset enough already and she didn't want to add to his burden. Yesterday he'd walked in on her as she wept and his smile had rapidly faded and within minutes, as he consoled her, he was in tears again. She couldn't remember the last day that passed without her seeing him cry. She resolved not to be the cause of yet more upset. She couldn't bear it.

"And she can run, like she used to when I was small?"

She didn't look up but she could hear the emotion in her father's voice, cracking as he spoke.

"Yes… she can run as fast as she likes… and for as long as she wants to."

He leaned into her, stroking the back of her hair and kissed the top of her head. She said nothing, images coming to mind of people dressed in black, stern faces and tears… lots of tears.

The organist played a sombre piece while they all filed out of the church. Looking at her hand, she could almost still feel the discomfort in her fingers, her father's grip so tight that she thought she might scream as they left the church. This was her experience today, being led around by the hand, passed between adults, no one really knowing what to say to her. She did get a lot of smiles, affectionate strokes of the hair and gentle touches, but the sense that everyone was keen to move on as soon as possible wouldn't leave her. They were protecting her father, giving him a break.

Where were these people when Mum really needed them, when she really needed them?

Their expressions were all so similar today… pity in their eyes… sorrow in their smiles. Artificial. Forced.

Now she pictured her mother running along the golden sand, the sunset behind her as the waves broke upon the shore. She couldn't quite believe it was her mother… because she had never seen her mother that way. She couldn't run, even if she had wanted to.

"Why couldn't it be different, Papa?"

Her father choked back tears as he drew her closer to him, but he didn't speak.

She looked up at him. "Why do these things happen?"

He took a deep breath before answering. "Things happen in life... things that are beyond our control. And we have to accept them."

The answer was unsatisfactory, but truthful.

"And where Mummy is now, with Tim and his brother, bad things don't happen?"

"I like to think not, no."

"I hope I find her one day," she whispered.

"I'm sure you will darling," her father said, tightening his grip around her. "I'm sure we will."

BOOKS BY J M DALGLIESH

In the Hidden Norfolk Series

One Lost Soul

Bury Your Past

Kill Our Sins

Tell No Tales

Hear No Evil

The Dead Call

Kill Them Cold

A Dark Sin

To Die For

Life and Death *FREE - visit jmdalgliesh.com

In the Dark Yorkshire Series

Divided House

Blacklight

The Dogs in the Street

Blood Money

Fear the Past

The Sixth Precept

Box Sets

Dark Yorkshire Books 1-3

Dark Yorkshire Books 4-6

Audiobooks

In the Hidden Norfolk Series
One Lost Soul
Bury Your Past
Kill Our Sins
Tell No Tales
Hear No Evil
The Dead Call
Kill Them Cold
A Dark Sin
To Die For
Fool Me Twice
The Raven Song

In the Dark Yorkshire Series
Divided House
Blacklight
The Dogs in the Street
Blood Money
Fear the Past
The Sixth Precept

Audiobook Box Sets
Dark Yorkshire Books 1-3
Dark Yorkshire Books 4-6